CONSORTIUM OF ACQUAINTANCES

BY JAMES FARNWORTH

Consortium of Acquaintances

ISBN # 9798486815522

"You can have anything you want if you want
it badly enough. You can be anything you want
to be, do anything you set out to accomplish if you
hold to that desire with singleness of purpose."
~ Abraham Lincoln

"They can have anything but they can take nothing."
~LaVerne C. Farnworth

Consortium of Acquaintances

Acknowledgments

To them that made me,
to them that raised me,
to them that supported me,
to them that kept me going,
without you all, this book would not exist.
I thank you all.

Consortium of Acquaintances

Prologue
Early Evening on November 14th, 1868
East Hartford, Massachusetts

When Francis Bowen and the Enterprise of Boston, as they called themselves at the time, departed New England, it was under the cover of darkness. They traveled light as any grifters would worth their weight under the circumstances. They did so to avoid allegations that were sure to come with the morning sun.

He had many names throughout his long life. He had been known as Francisco Garcia Delarosa from Maine, changing his name as often as some would change their shirt. Everyone that traveled with him this night was more than familiar with the art of becoming someone completely different.

He once had a wife, who had long since left him for a more stable relationship. He had forgotten long ago what name he had used when he was in love with his Southern Bell. "It started with the letter F, or maybe, I'm just confused about the sound," he uttered, looking over the fields lit up by the full moon. He closed his eyes in an attempt to clear his thoughts.

"Cover yourselves. We have riders heading this way," stated Fergus, tapping his driving whip on the dash rail and making a clicking sound with his lips to get everyone's attention as a conductor would of his orchestra pit.

Most of the passengers were already covered; however, several hammers were thrown back on their respective revolvers, including the blunderbuss sitting on the seat next to Fergus. The sight of such a weapon usually kept things civil when it came to highwaymen.

"Whoa, whoa," called out Fergus as he pulled back on the reins and slowed the six-person carryall-carriage in time to avoid a collision. He glanced back at the carriages behind him before turning his attention to the man that seemed to be in charge.

"What brings you into my county so late into the evening?" asked the man who wore a badge declaring him of his right to stop a man in the night. He pulled on his reins and moved the horse's head between the carriage to maximize his protection.

It was an action that didn't go unnoticed. Fergus tapped on the carriage's dash to cover the sound of hammers being pulled on the respective revolvers in the hands of his friends. "Greetings Magistrate, we are heading to New York for an engagement at the Broadway Theatre. You, sir, have stopped a band of entertainers as harmless as church mice," he responded, pausing to gauge the man's demeanor.

"Are the two carriages behind you traveling with you?" asked the man who was now leaning forward in his saddle, resting his hand on his revolver. He believed himself quite handy with the tool of his trade.

A point noted by more than one occupant of the carriage. It was silently decided by several of the occupants that he would be the first target if it escalated to the point of gunplay. It wasn't the first time a man held a badge and decided to regulate who entered their respective counties.

"Yes, we finished a play this evening and headed out of town; we left just as many stagehands back in Boston to pull the sets down as we have here. We just need to get some sleep and be there as soon as possible," answered Fergus as he spoke; he glanced back at his passengers, looking for cues from them. It wasn't long ago he had misjudged a situation and was nearly killed by not acting quickly.

If it came to gunplay, he would disappear behind the carriage dash letting the trouble be worked out by everyone else that cared to chime in. He allowed a smile to bloom on his lips as he turned back to face the sheriff and his men.

"If you want to be in New York as quickly as you suggest, I would stop in Hartford and take the train to New Haven then hop on the train to New York," said the lawman, relaxing his grip on his revolver as he shrunk into his saddle. The action affected the rest of the posse, and they continued their conversations amongst themselves.

"We are grateful for your directions. I will talk it over with everyone and see what they want to do," repeated Fergus, looking back at the passengers, who were nodding and talking amongst themselves. It was a ploy they often used. Their conversations were meaningless, for they still had their weapons at the ready.

"The moon will be over the horizon about the time you hit Hartford, so either way, you will be stopped for the night unless you have oil lamps hiding in the carriage's boot," said the lawman, looking back and motioning for his men to move the wagon from the road.

"We will more than likely take the train as you suggested," said Fergus, adjusting himself at the anticipation of the lawman moving from the roadway. He let a smile form on his face as the wagon began to move.

"Evening folks, you have a nice trip. Maybe I will come to see a show," announced the lawman, tipping his hat while he motioned for his men to clear the road.

"Well, hunky-dory, we are unscathed as I foretold this route is the perfect path to our salvation," declared Fergus rapping the dash rail with his driving whip as they left the lawmen behind them.

The passengers grew quiet until Francis spoke up, breaking the silence. "Yes, I remember it was Phillip, and her name was Danielle. She was pretty and polite, as I recall. It was not her fault, for you see that her gardening was interrupted by a contingent of constables," he answered, stopping to ponder the exact question that was being asked of him before he had taken several tangents.

"It was probably your fault," laughed Fergus. He liked to get a jab in every once in a while on the robust man.

"Fergus, pay attention to your horses, my dear. If we are to meet Albert on time in New York, we need to stay vigilant," admonished Virginia.

"Why did you want to know her name?" asked Francis, looking over at Mortimer, who was holstering his revolver before picking up his notebook.

"You asked me what name you should use in the next town. You should use Phillip Daniels," replied Mortimer, scribbling the name in code into his little notebook.

"How about Frank Daniels? After all, we will be out west in that little town for at least a couple of years. What is the name, Yeahkemo City?" asked the man suddenly named Frank Daniels.

"Yakima City," corrected Virginia, "although, from what I understand, it is more of a water stop than a town."

"Why on God's green earth would we want to hold up there?" asked Fergus.

"We go where we are told, and if we are told to go to Yeakemo City, we will go to Yakeno City," lectured Frank again, making the mistake of looking out into the passing fields feeling sick once again.

"Ya ki ma City," stated Fergus, speaking slowly to correct him like it was his mission in life.

Frank closed his eyes in an attempt to center himself again. He had a darker reason for wanting to stake a claim in the Washington Territory. The only man that knew of his plans was chained under a lumberyard back in Boston.

"I just don't see what is to gain crossing a continent," whispered Fergus.

"Fergus, you sell the other two carriages in Hartford, add it to the money you already have. Remember, the Broadway theatre is owned by a man that I have known for years. He does not have an understanding of how we choose to make our living. He wouldn't be receptive to the idea. Go to him. I am sure he will have work for you if you mention my name," said Frank, adjusting his massive frame in the tiny seat.

"Which name does he know you by?" asked Fergus, not trying to goad his employer into another verbal tussle but because he needed to know.

"I am sure I will remember it by the time we get to Hartford," he answered as the carriage passed a sign stating it was just 3 miles to Hartford.

Fergus had his name and knew what he would have to do by the time they departed for the west.

They rode into Yakima City almost six months after taking a ship to Central America. With a combination of walking, train, and carriage travel, they crossed Nicaragua. Boarding a steamship from there, they traveled north to Portland via San Francisco. Two steamers up the Columbia to a town called The Dalles, from there, they bought horses to travel to Yakima City.

They left Boston with twelve but lost Mortimer to a fever in a nameless town in Nicaragua and a woman named Carina to greed off the Mexican coast. She was bobbing in the Pacific Ocean's cold waters after attempting to steal a strongbox belonging to the consortium.

They were bedraggled by the time they reached their destination in the Washington Territory. The group as a whole was well versed in the plan laid out by Frank Daniels. They would find jobs that most people would overlook. Each grifter would fade into the background hiding from fame and recognition.

"Frank, shouldn't we stop somewhere's in town. You seem to be heading out the other end," said Robert Hinkle, riding a little faster to catch up.

Frank's group of weary travelers hunched over their saddle horns, passing businesses that weren't much more than unpainted store-fronted tents that kept the rain off proprietors with hopeless-looking faces. The town was a shadow of its name.

When Frank finally spoke, he muttered, "Fella's, I've seen outhouses with more appeal than this town." He turned his horse around, waiting for everyone to quiet down.

Consortium of Acquaintances

"We certainly have our work cut out for us, for we will need to change the plan. We will take over this town instead of looking for work. We will need to become pillars of the community. We stay close enough to watch out for one another but stay far apart so we are not hung with the same rope if one of us gets caught. So just like in Boston, we marry and cheat our way until we have a controlling interest in every profitable business in this town," said Frank Daniels, climbing from his horse and into a pile of cow manure. He almost lost his temper for being sent to a small town in the middle of nowhere for a reason he could not share with anyone.

Chapter 1
Noon on April 1st, 1873
Yakima City, Washington Territory

The clouds hung low in the sky, casting a thin shadow upon the sagebrush-covered hills, only broken by a gap in the ridge, making way for the Yakima River to flow through on its way to join the Columbia River. It was surprising to see just how green the countryside is in the spring.

John smiled, looking back at his wife Elizabeth, then pointed at the signs of spring both far away and near their fingertips. She leaned back against the tailgate of the buckboard, smiling as the sun washed over her face and exposed skin.

Mr. Harrison had offered them a ride to Yakima City in his wagon. He pointed out that the green rolling hills and prairie were misleading in the spring. "In the summer, under the unrelenting sun, the grasslands and the hills turn a dull tan. Winters are cold. The temperatures drop so low a man wishes that the sun would come back. By spring, the valley renews itself to give the hills this green hue," he said, sitting up on the seat to observe a coyote running across the dirt trail and disappearing in the brush by the river.

John and Elizabeth Springer had come a long way since St. Louis. They worked their way up the Missouri River on a steam-propelled Mountain boat only to spend the winter at Fort Benton. The hardships they shared on the Mullan Road, not to mention the last 90 miles coming from Fort Walla Walla in the back of a wagon, had made them both beggarly in appearance.

"It sure is pretty in the spring," said Elizabeth, feeling ignored in the back of the wagon. She smiled whenever John would turn and look in her direction, checking to see if she had fallen asleep. Each time the wagon rolled over a rock, everything in the back lifted into the air. After the last bump, she felt the need to check for loose teeth.

What passed for a road in the Yakima Valley wasn't much more than a hunting path, the wagon wheels one moment mired in the bogs of the Yakima River or kicked up dust from the powdery trail that seemed to meander as much as the river.

"You haven't felt fear until you see a tumbleweed as tall as a man roll off the hill engulfed in flames. It will fly through the air, set down just long enough to light a field on fire before it takes flight to repeat the process," he said with a tone in his voice that neither John nor Elizabeth would dare to question. The older man was full of random facts with significant gaps of silence in between. It made the last few days rather interesting for the couple.

They had spent the last few months alone making their way over the Mullan Road. Each night they camped with a small fire to keep the predators away. They welcomed the distraction of his tales the first night, but he seemed to repeat himself by the third day. Most of the time, he changed the endings and occasionally the moral of the story to fit his mood.

On the fourth day, they entered Yakima City through the gap in the hills that united the Upper and the Lower Yakima Valley. Later they would learn the ridge to the east was called the Rattlesnakes, and the rise to the west was called the Ahtanum Ridge.

"Is that the same river we have been following the last three days?" asked John, looking across the river where he spotted a man throwing out a net to catch fish.

"The same river just more defined from here to where it begins somewhere up north," answered Mr. Harrison, waving at the man, who in turn returned the gesture cheerfully.

"Do you know the man?" asked Elizabeth, leaning forward to be heard.

"I don't believe I do," he answered, pulling the horses back onto the road from where they had wandered. His eyes wandered a bit as he thought about his answer. "I suppose I waved to the fisherman so'd he would know he wasn't alone."

John nodded in understanding even though he only caught half the meaning.

At first, they were not sure what to think of the small town. From a distance, it looked like a collection of shacks. The closer they got, the newer it seemed. The business side of the buildings were facades. They whitewashed them like a thin veneer on a rotted bookcase. Towards the center of the town, the fakery was less pronounced, and the buildings were an improvement from the shacks that were torn down only a few years before.

John pointed at a dust devil kicked up by the wind that hung in the sky as if it were placed there by an unseen hand, perhaps warning them from the quiet town. Elizabeth had instilled respect in John for things he used to call superstitions. She changed his mind about her superstitious ways the night they left their lives back in St. Louis.

"Over yonder is Yakima City, the largest settlement from the Columbia to the Cascades. It is not much to gander at right now, but it's growing," said Mr. Harrison, tipping his large-brimmed hat as he shook the reins to send vibrations to the lead set of horses. The wagon, in turn, lurched, speeding up a little.

"What a nice day this turned out to be, it must be in the eighties, and the sun is playing peekaboo with the fluffiest clouds that I ever did see," said Elizabeth. It was hardly noticeable that she was older than her husband by almost nine years. Even covered in dust and grime from the trip from Walla Walla, her beauty would still turn the heads of single men. She looked up from the back of the wagon at her husband, who sat next to Mr. Harrison, wondering if he had heard her.

She was surprised when he turned to respond. "I was hoping it would rain, so we can clean up a little before we head over to the hotel to present ourselves," said John, feeling guilty for making his wife sit in the back of the wagon like livestock. He had told her they would stop in Yakima City for a few days of rest in the hotel. He was sure that he would not hear the end of it once they were alone.

It had been either ride in the back or walk because it was Mr. Harrison's wagon and he had told them it wasn't proper for her to sit next to a married man. His notions of what was proper were not their own, but he was nice enough to give them a ride to Yakima City for free.

They were new to the Washington Territory, and they were of limited means, having talked and bartered their way halfway across North America. They both looked the part of wanderlust homesteaders but worried their troubles would catch up with them from St. Louis.

They still had the money for the land that they gained back in St. Louis. They had planned to purchase a home in Seattle. They only had to take a few dollars out to get them here, near the foothills of the Cascades.

They climbed down from the wagon in front of Jackson's Livery barn just off Main Street, across from what looked like a collection of tents. They couldn't help noticing that the town was a busy hub of trade and traffic heading out in all directions. The settlement was like the Springers. It seemed full of hope for a prosperous future.

They could hear the sounds of hammers being brought down just out of sight. Much like growing pains in a child, the town seemed to call out to both of them. The streets were practically yelling, 'I'm growing.' John imagined the men working on some project just out of view, maybe a house or a new shop, like he dreamed of buying in Seattle one day soon.

He was in his early twenties and two inches shy of being six feet tall. He was lean and showed as a testament to their struggles over the last six months.

Back in St. Louis, most women found him handsome with brown wavy hair, which wasn't any style he wanted, rather a touch of neglect. He wore a brown bowler, all the style back east, but here on the edge of the Scablands, his bowler did little to keep the sun off his neck.

His wife was every bit of average in height, standing 5-foot, 3 inches. Even under the coat of trail dust, she was as lovely as the day he spotted her crossing the floor of the saloon.

She looked at her man both for support and for protection leaning close to give him a quick peck on his cheek. Her messy red hair tangled, ending midway down her back, but under the layers of grime, she was as pretty as a daisy. She pulled at her purple dress that hung on her frame like a hand-me-down of an overweight sibling. She had lost weight and would need a few days to regain her strength.

The Springers honestly looked like they needed a bath before finding a place to fill their bellies. They were passing through on the way to Seattle, but the town of Yakima City had a lure.

"Take care of your youngins' ma'am," yelled Harry Jackson, the proprietor of Jackson's Livery. He was a short man of around fifty, but his looks made him seem much older, cleanly shaven, which appeared to be rather unusual for these parts. He was the kind of man to carry tools in his pockets just because he might need them.

Elizabeth watched as a pretty woman in a yellow dress walked out of the livery. She went about gathering up her children to herd them into the building.

"My apologies," smiled Molly in the direction of John and Elizabeth. Then nodded at Mr. Jackson and headed back into the large door to the livery. "Taylor and Annie, come back inside. If you need sunlight, you can head out the back."

They nodded at the woman as they continued to get their bearings and unload the wagon of their things.

"Can I help you folks?" asked Harry, moving over to Mr. Harrison's wagon.

"Relax, Mr. Jackson, it is my wagon, and I have no need of your special services," stated Mr. Harrison sternly. They heard his tone change, thick with the animosity that shaded his response.

"Well, if you need me, I have horses and wagons that can be had for the right price." said Harry, pointing back towards the large red barn that was the centerpiece of any town.

"Thank you, Mr. Jackson, for the offer. We will be here for a few days, and we might need to take you up on it," said John, reaching out to grip the man's hand.

Harry shook it, leaving a little grease in the palm of John's hand that had an odd texture. "You can call me Harry, my name is Harold, but Harry is what my friends call me," smiled the older man, not exactly in the friendliest way.

"Call me John, and this is Elizabeth, my wife. Would you please excuse our appearance? It has been a rough couple of days," he said, looking over to his wife, who smiled kindly then curtsied.

"It's nice to meet you both. You will need to excuse me." He turned towards the large doors to address the people inside. "Mrs. Olson, your children, are running out into the street again, and if they get themselves ran down, it will just take that much more time to depart this here city."

"Get back here," yelled the woman who they assumed was Mrs. Olson.

They watched as the woman rounded them up and grabbed the oldest by the back of the ear.

"You'll have to forgive the children. They have been cooped up for a few days while I repaired their wagon. The trail out here is hard on wagon wheels, and I'm the only blacksmith for 50 miles."

"Thought you said?" asked John as he felt the grease on his fingertips that smelled of bacon.

"I did. I own the livery service and do the metalwork for the town. I also do veterinary services as long as the problem isn't too complicated," stated Harry, starting back to the large opened door.

"What if it is too complicated?" asked Elizabeth, giving him a smile that would warm an ice block in February.

"Nothing good, ma'am," he answered, turning and heading into the large door into what looked like the receiving bay.

"Well, good luck to you, folks. Did you get everything that belongs to you?" asked Mr. Harrison, rambling around the rear of his wagon, making his way over to where they stood on the boardwalk. "You folks have traveled a long way just to forget your possessions in the back of my wagon."

"We thank you, Mr. Harrison, for the long ride from Fort Walla Walla," she said.

They had told him their well-practiced story of living in St. Louis for almost a year, working as many hours as possible to make their journey to Seattle.

When they arrived in Yakima City, they had no idea that what was supposed to be a layover would turn out to be a week's stay at the hotel.

"This sure is a busy town," stated John, watching the wagons run up and down the street.

"Oh, they run from nine o'clock in the morning to five o'clock in the afternoon," said Mr. Harrison, climbing on the driver's seat of his wagon.

"Husband, we need to eat and get some items from the shop," whispered Elizabeth into his ear while sliding her hand across his back.

"Yes, but let us get cleaned up a little," whispered John, squirming a little before turning to Mr. Harrison. "Thank you again for the ride, Mr. Harrison."

The man tipped his hat in agreement.

"You have no idea how long we walked. It means a lot to have someone willing to help when no one else would," she said to the wagon's owner. He had found them on the side of the trail, this side of the Columbia River, sitting on a log resting in the shade.

"You take care of your woman, watch over her close in this town. There might not be as many people here as St. Louis, but this town has all the trappings of the big city," he warned, looking over to a place called the Emporium as the wagon started to move.

"Thank you for your advice, and we will watch out for each other," said Elizabeth, pulling at John's shoulder a little while nodding to a Northwest Mercantile just down the street.

They picked up their things and started for the shop. They stopped when someone tossed a man through what had appeared to be a wall across from the livery.

Consortium of Acquaintances

"Look, a dust-up!" exclaimed John, stopping to observe the goings-on in the middle of the street.

"You're not a constable anymore," she said softly so no one would hear one of their secrets.

"I wasn't much of one when I was," he replied as they watched a large man come running from around the building. The mountain man intended to finish the man off but settled for talking to the sheriff, who was standing between him and the human cannonball.

The sheriff had been eating his breakfast by the napkin draped from his neck, but other than that, he was all business when it came to the peace.

Chapter 2
A little earlier.

The Lucy Saloon occupied a storefront a few blocks from the Jackson Livery. If the livery was where the work was done, the Lucy was where the workers were lubricated. During the evenings, the player piano can be heard for several blocks in all directions. However, during the day, it had become a meeting place to get a good meal and catch up with the local gossip.

A fellow named Nigel Lowman, or Lomax to anyone he cared to talk to, wandered in, pushing through the batwing doors. He looked around for his friend that he had stayed in Yakima an extra day to see. "Nelson, it's good to see that you finally made it back."

"Lomax, you are a sight for sore eyes. Come sit and have some breakfast with me. You are hungry?" he asked, wiping his chin of runny eggs that only made it halfway into his mouth.

"I am always hungry," he answered, looking over at the man behind the bar, catching his eye, then pointing to the table in front of him. It was code for bringing him whatever was hot at the moment.

"I hear you're selling your land."

"Lomax, that is what I like about you. You know how to get to the point," he said as Jim, the barman, walked over to the table to drop a plate of eggs and potatoes off.

"I have been asked to talk to you. Certain people want to know why you're selling your land. So as soon as you are finished with your explanation, we can get on over to the Winston for some poker." Lomax had a way with words that when he spoke, it always seemed as if he was yelling, even though he hadn't raised his voice.

"I've seen strange manifestations in that valley. Now, don't be dismissing what I'm sayin' as ramblings of a lonely man. I have spent most of my life alone. In fact I like to be alone," he spoke in a raised voice, not caring who heard.

Lomax patted the table with his off-hand lightly to get him to quiet down. He picked up his fork with the same hand and slipped some of his fried potatoes in his mouth, choosing not to respond either way. He finally motioned with his gun-hand for him to continue before returning it to his revolver that sat in his lap under the table.

"There is a band of Indians that camp up there. Oh, they are nice enough in the daylight, but when the sun fades on the horizon, they change."

"They change, how?" asked Lomax, taking another mouthful of the mixture of eggs and potatoes.

"Into animals."

"So they are hostile. If they are hostile, all we need to do is get ahold of someone at Fort Simcoe. The U.S. Army is gone, but the Indian Affairs Agent can do something," said Lomax with his mouth half full of potatoes.

"No, they ain't hostile," he said with his normal voice before whispering. "They never tried to hurt me. As a matter of fact, they went out of their way to avoid hurting me."

"Then what have you seen that has you so upset that you would want to sell your land and leave for Portland. People are starting to worry about you. The people you don't want to worry about you," stated Lomax being, both direct and cryptic about the consortium in case someone was listening. He looked around to see if anyone was paying them any attention and couldn't pick anyone out.

"I saw their fire a few nights ago, so I headed over to see what they were doing up so late. I walked into their camp un-accosted, right up to their fire pit. There was no one there," he answered, keeping his voice low. "But as I was about to leave, I hear noises from all around. I raised my hands prepared to meet my maker."

"Then what happened?" asked Lomax, pushing his plate away, picking up his friend's beer to wash his breakfast down.

"From all around came howls, first one then more. Wolves, there were large wolves running all around me."

"Were you drinking at the time?" asked Lomax, finishing his friend's beer. He noticed a ranch hand at the next table snicker, then straighten himself.

"No, they never attacked me. The next day they were gone, and I hadn't seen them for a week before deciding to head this way, but I could hear them at night."

"Well, I guess if it were me up there days from nowhere. I would want to head back to town. Speaking of heading places, let us head over to the Winston and play some poker.

"Look, I know I sound crazy, and I know why we are here, trust me, it is not to make money."

"Let's talk about it over a hand of cards at the Winston," said Lomax noticing that too many people seemed interested in their conversation.

The Winston Saloon was a smoke-filled card room catering to an alternative bunch of gamblers who spent their days sitting at round wooden parlor tables, talking about the good old days. It was true the people that visited the card room had seen the death and pain that comes with war, and most missed neither.

This morning, only one poker player table was still playing cards when Nelson and Lomax walked through the opened doorway. The rest of the patrons had long since gone home or just stepped outside to pass out in the alley.

Neither man thought it strange when two poker players made room at the only table. They sat down as the other two headed into the morning light.

The alley opened onto a respectable street towards the west, flanked by the Hummel Hotel and Johnston's Boarding House. The other end opened up into the tented compound where most patrons would lay their heads at night and keep their clothes dry during the day. It was said if you win at the Winston, you turn right and head to the hotel; if you lose, you turn left towards the first available tent.

At the Winston, Nelson was taking his opponents' money with each hand of cards. Lomax was holding his own to the dismay of the other two players.

"Damn, how are yous' winning so much of our money?" asked Tom as he folded, dropping his cards facedown onto the pile of cash at the center of the table. He looked over at his friend Raphael, who sat across from him.

"Speak for yourself. It is as if you fellas want to give us your earnings," answered Lomax, looking at Tom while he gathered the cards into a pile.

"What are you trying to say?" asked Nelson, sliding a stray card over to Lomax as he began to shuffle the cards.

"You know'd what I'm say'n, yous' a cheat'n, I just haven't got the notion as to how just yet," argued Tom as he threw his ante in the middle of the table and leaned back in his chair.

"Take it outside if you're going to talk like that," yelled Billy, the Winston's owner, serving a morning refresher to George. He was a man that was more of a witness than a participant having just walked in the door. He was here for another reason.

Lomax was a large man that carried a commanding presence. He rarely linked more than a dozen words together in any particular conversation unless you were a friend or he had something to say, which was a rarity. At first glance, he looked like a mountain man. It was true he had trapped and hunted his way across the continent, then traveled back east to fight in several battles during the War Between The States. The war ended a few months after he enlisted, so he had decided to take one last look at what the United States had achieved.

He decided he didn't like how crowded the world was getting and hopped on a ship out of New York Harbor, and that is where he met Nelson. It wasn't long before he offered his services as a scout.

"Are you fellas planning on playing cards, or are you going to throw down?" asked Lomax, noticing the malice in both Tom and Raphael's eyes.

"The way I reckon, I'm tired of this uneducated..." said Nelson, not finishing his thought.

"What cat got your tongue?" asked Tom as if he already knew the answer.

Sensing trouble, Lomax picked up what was left of his winnings as Nelson sat in his chair, choking. It was then he noticed the knife that Rafael had buried hilt deep into his friend's heart.

Rafael, up until this point, had been quietly waiting for his moment to strike.

"What you got to say now, smart man," spat Tom, reaching over the table to take the money he had lost.

Lomax had been mistaken not to have taken them more seriously. He jumped back, lifting his revolver from where it sat on his lap, shooting Rafael in the stomach. It surprised Tom, who turned while he attempted to draw his weapon. Lomax pulled the hammer back, pulling the trigger, hitting the man in his gun arm before he could draw.

"Don't kill me, Nigel, I didn't know Rafael was goin' to stab him," shouted Tom as he whimpered about his arm.

Lomax snapped just then. He was tired of losing friends. He grabbed Tom's collar and lifted him off his feet as if he were about to toss out the trash. "Nelson was my friend. He never cheated at anything," he said, calmly as if he was speaking at the man's funeral.

"Please, Rafael was my friend, so maybe we're even," screamed Tom as he felt weightless for the first time in his life. He wasn't sure how it happened, but he suddenly found himself lying in the street of all places. There was a crowd of people around him, suggesting he stay down. He felt weak from blood loss, and his head felt as if it was about to come off.

"I'm not finished with him, damn-it," yelled Lomax, who had been delayed because he had come around the building, but unfortunately, he was struggling to break the grip of Sheriff Miller.

"He killed my friend," yelled Tom.

Consortium of Acquaintances

His complaints were finding no roost to land because Billy, the Winston's proprietor, had already told Sheriff Miller what happened. He opened his mouth one more time and got a boot for his trouble from a man wearing all black with a United States Marshals badge on his vest.

John Springer stared at the wall that looked as if a cannonball had found its way through it. He wasn't sure if he would have believed a man could have been tossed through a wall so easily. "Did you see that, Elizabeth?"

"Yes, I was standing right here."

He found out that both men were hauled off to The Dalles by a U.S. Marshal, who happened to be passing through town.

John and Elizabeth were both amazed that by morning the card-room that had literally broken out onto the street had been repaired and painted over, leaving a smooth wall with no evidence that anything had happened less than twelve hours before.

Chapter 3
Mid-afternoon on April 1st, 1873
Yakima City, Washington Territory

The Jackson Livery was noisy with the Olsons' children running about as the adults were busily readying the blue Conestoga wagon. They had only planned a stop in Yakima for a quick hub replacement, but it had turned out to be most of the week.

"I was going to ask you about the name on the side of the wagon. Were you a Quarry-man?" asked Harry, the livery's proprietor.

"No, the wagon had come to us second hand," answered Mr. Olson, climbing up onto the wagon.

"The men were bad that lived there," answered a little girl, sticking her head out from under the wagon's bonnet.

"Annie!"

"Well, we would like to thank you for the hard work you performed on the wagon. Maybe, one day, we will be back this way," said Mr. Olson, gathering the reins while reaching down to release the wagon's hand brake.

Harry waved them a farewell before saying, "See you soon." Harry began cleaning the receiving bay.

Robert Hinkle and Frank Daniels walked with a purpose down the boardwalk. They had heard a rumor that the Olson family was leaving town. Robert, a thin man in his late 40's, served as land agent for the Yakima Valley. Mayor Daniels was the polar opposite of the other man.

He rarely exercised and smoked four cigars a day. Robert rarely found himself atop a horse. He didn't let that stop him from walking around town most days.

Mr. Hinkle and the mayor stopped a few businesses down from the livery. They waited as the blue Conestoga pulled out of the largest of the bay doors. Four horses pulled it with the words Livingston Quarry stenciled on its sides.

"Harry, was that the Olsons that were leaving for parts unknown?" asked Mayor Daniels, whispering so loud if you were across the street you would have heard him.

"Yes," Harry replied, waving the two men over to the entrance of his business. He removed his wide-brimmed hat, using it to wipe his forehead as he waited for them to approach.

"What happened? I thought they were going to sign on?" asked Robert, not bothering to whisper.

"Come inside. We can talk about it," responded Harry, starting for the door.

"If I wanted to smell like horse manure, I would have moved on to a ranch. Answer the damn question," demanded Mayor Daniels, who by no vote that anyone could remember was the Mayor of Yakima City.

"Frank, they never said yes, and I don't reckon they will sign the loan papers. Not without a little coaxing," rebuffed Harry, holding one hand on his sliding barn door that was swaying a little with the wind.

"Well, Ben and his friends are south of town and won't be back for a few days," stated Mayor Daniels

"That will be fine. The Olsons will get 15 miles out of town and discover the other three hubs on their wagon won't hold up," said Harry, smiling coyly.

"Did you happened to do what we had talked about?" asked Robert.

"Yes, coated the whole bottom," answered Harry winking at Robert.

"What did you fellas do?" asked Mayor Daniels.

"I painted the bottom of their wagon with pigs' blood and bacon grease. They should have an interesting couple of days," explained

Harry, chuckling at the thought of the Olson family fighting off a few coyotes.

"No one, not even your wives, better find out," admonished Mayor Daniels.

"Well, Benjamin wasn't around, and I didn't want them to get away without you giving them some alternatives," replied Harry, elbowing Robert.

"Well, I sure will do my best to convince them that living here is a better alternative than facing the wilds of the cascades on the way to the westside," said Robert, sounding smooth like a preacher on Sunday.

"Relax, Bob," chuckled Mayor Daniels.

Harry snapped his fingers, then pointed in the direction of the mercantile. "There are a couple of new potential settlers that come round earlier."

"Oh really," replied Robert, unintentionally rubbing his hands together.

"It appeared they would be needed a loan," said Harry, nodding at the both of them smiling.

"Even better. How will I know them?"

"He was a tall man, and she was of average height. Oh, and they both had a month's worth of trail dust all over them," stated Harry, taking a step back into his barn, letting them know he was about to close the door. "They headed over to the mercantile for some supplies."

"I will let you gentlemen work out the details; let me know if you need anything," announced Mayor Daniels, also turning away towards the boardwalk.

"Harry, before you close the damn door, did you happen to catch their names?" asked Robert, also stepping towards the boardwalk.

"The Springers, maybe John and Carol? I'm not sure what her name was. You can't miss them; they are taking the town in like it was a breath of fresh air," answered Harry as he closed the door.

Robert nodded and turned to the fleeing mayor, who had managed to make it to the boardwalk. "Frank, I'm going to need a few claqueurs if you want this arrangement to become more profitable. This time, they need to sell how great a place this town is to live. That way, we don't have to paint their wagons or mix sand into their wheel hubs to convince them to buy land," said Robert, nodding at every other word to emphasize he needed help.

"I will see what I can do. You can offer the newcomers a few days in the hotel, but no more than that if they don't show promise. I will talk to the hotel management to set the room up for them," answered Mayor Daniels, then adding. "I also got the deed back for the Nelson property. Had that simpleton that does odd jobs around town get it. Good day to you, Mr. Hinkle."

"That is good news. I will try to sell it to the new couple. Good day to you, Mr. Mayor," replied Robert, starting across the street towards the mercantile.

Chapter 4
Mid-afternoon on April 1st, 1873
Yakima City, Washington Territory

Upwind from Jackson's Livery, John and Elizabeth found themselves at the Northwest Mercantile, examining what they displayed on the shelves stocked with goods from all over the region. The clouds opened up as the raindrops began to fall, causing people to run from awning to awning avoiding getting wet as much as possible. It seemed sunnier despite the rain.

"It means something bad is supposed to happen," whispered Elizabeth into John's ear.

"It means that the plants will grow green like they do every year," he whispered in response. Little did he know that something terrible was heading their way.

The little bell on the front door rattled as another man walked in dressed in a forest green suit wearing a grey bowler hat. He headed for the Springer's as if they were prey.

"Good morning, my name is Robert Hinkle. I am the land agent for this beautiful valley that only gets greener when it rains like it's doing out there this morning," he said with his hand already clasping that of John's.

John was still trying to figure out how the man had slipped his hand into his own, only managing to nod at the boisterous fellow.

Luckily, Elizabeth was a little quicker on her feet even after spending the same amount of time on the trail. "We are the Springers. He is my husband," said Elizabeth, looking at John as if he had one job here, and he wasn't doing it.

"John," he answered her unspoken question before turning his attention back towards the land agent.

"And I am Elizabeth," she said, smiling, giving John's shoulder a squeeze. It was a reminder that if they were to act respectable, he should have introduced them both.

"What can we do for you?" asked John, managing to regain his senses.

"Well, I was over having a word with our town's fine mayor, Frank Daniels, and the proprietor of the livery, Harold Jackson. I believe you met the man earlier this morning," he said, stopping long enough to see if they wanted to add anything. "In the course of our meeting, it was brought to my attention that you folks may be in the market for a new piece of land."

"We are on our way to Seattle," said John, looking back at his wife for support.

"It is true that Seattle is growing but so are we here in our fine settlement of Yakima City. Just out of town, I have some small farms that a couple such as yourselves could make a fine living," he said, pointing out towards the horizon as if they could see the properties if only they were willing to look.

"We don't have the means," said John, figuring they didn't need to share their actual financial situation with the man.

"Well, if you need, the local bank could be made aware of your need for a loan. I am sure that we could come to an arrangement. These deals won't last long, here in just a few years, we will have a railroad from here to Seattle and clear back to Saint Louis," he offered with his well-practiced tongue.

It became Elizabeth's turn to freeze when he mentioned the distance they had traveled, to distance themselves from the very city he spoke of now. They instinctually walked out the front door, followed by the land agent.

As if Mr. Hinkle could read her mind, he tried to salvage his sales pitch. "The railroad will add extensions to the existing ones, surely they won't head directly to any destination," he said, raising a battered satchel. "In here, I have your future, and if your future includes the desire to be alone, we have a few properties that would keep that dream alive."

John and Elizabeth both decided to have a look at his offerings. They stood under the shop's awning to stay dry. He found a property they might be interested in learning about that had recently come available. It had just come into his possession due to the fact the man had died while playing cards that morning. A piece of information that was quietly left out. They mainly were interested because it was days from anywhere.

Now, John liked to imagine he wasn't born yesterday, and the deal seemed too low of a price without there being a catch. It made him ponder over the old saying, a fool and his money soon will part.

Mr. Hinkle could see that they were still unsure about the purchase. "Mr. Springer, it is a great deal. It is almost fifty acres of flat land. This river here flows right into the same river that passes our fair town," he said as convincingly as the land agent had been as he pointed at the map.

"It seems so far. Why is the property for sale so far out of town?" asked Elizabeth. When looked upon, she covered her mouth and leaned back a little.

"That is a great question, little lady. It is an outpost property. Originally, there were plans for a mountain pass to head that way, and men far smarter than I have opened up properties to become waypoints of sorts. This here property will give a man a life and a chance to make a living if a mountain pass is constructed south of Naches Pass," answered the land agent.

She smiled but felt like the was talking talking down to her and was quickly loosing interest. She watched his body movement and listened to his well practiced lingo.

Robert Hinkle was a big man in his waning years. He wasn't a fat man by any means. He was at least 5 feet in height with broad shoulders. When they shook his hand, they felt no calluses, which made them conclude that the man hadn't worked a day in his life.

Consortium of Acquaintances

The man seemed trustworthy, and to prove it, he asked them to inquire around town about him. He even paid for them to stay at the hotel for a week to deliberate over it. They had no intention of buying the property, although the attraction of spending a couple of nights in a bed and having a roof over their heads that didn't smell like cattle was too much to pass up.

They cleaned up in a back alley under a spring shower. The water that flowed off the roof was cold, but getting the grime off their bodies felt good. They had made up their mind that they would not check into the hotel looking like coyotes.

They found privacy to change their clothes in an outhouse behind the Mercantile.

Feeling better, Elizabeth pulled John towards the hotel to register and take the time to clean up properly. "I wonder if they have a bathtub with endless hot running water," she whispered, holding his hand with one hand and carrying the total of everything she owned in the other.

"I doubt it that it's endless by the condition of the hotel," he said, pointing to the tall building that already seemed in disrepair.

"We need to ask around about the property, so if he asks anyone, he will know we did our due diligence," stated Elizabeth.

For the next few hours, John and Elizabeth walked into several shops asking the proprietors for information before bumping into Mr. George Johnson, who looked old enough to have witnessed the signing of the Declaration of Independence. His wrinkles ran criss-cross, only broken by the patches of a white beard. The older man's clothes hung on his body like they had been there for weeks.

The Springers backed away a little as all of George's acquaintances had done until they had warmed up to him. Some would say it was his smile; others would say his charm. The Springers would have said it was his grandfatherly way about him.

"Hello, my name is George, George Johnson, who might you folks be?" he asked, holding his hand out—looking from John to Elizabeth and back—showing his teeth in what seemed like a genuine smile, odious personal habits set aside.

"I'm John Springer, and this is Elizabeth, my wife," he answered, getting a nudge to shake the older man's outstretched hand by the same person he was introducing.

"What is a fine couple like yous' doing wanderin' about town fer' on a rainy day such as today?" asked George, looking as if he needed a bath and smelling as if he needed two.

"We were left to ponder about buying a property that is being brokered by Mr. Robert Hinkle," answered John, pulling his wife a little closer in hopes her rose fragrance would help cover the old man's stench as it got stronger the closer he leaned in their direction.

Elizabeth interrupted, asking, "We were wondering if you might know if the land was worth the asking price and if Mr. Robert Hinkle was a... a...?" she asked, reaching for the unladylike words on the tip of her tongue. However, she had promised John she wouldn't show that side of her personality.

"Scoundrel?" the old man asked, glancing at Elizabeth before returning his attention to her husband.

The Springers looked at one another and back to George, then smiled. Not sure he was sane or the town drunk. Later, she admitted she thought both from the first moment they met.

"Thief?" he announced, grinning from ear to ear, not caring who heard.

"Yes," answered John, who began at this point to believe he was both.

"We really should be on our way," she said as she pulled at her husband's jacket as she attempted to steer him from the smelly old man.

"What did the fine people of Yakima City have to say about the upstanding Mr. Hinkle?" asked George, pulling his hat from his head, fanning himself with it using broad swipes.

"Not much. Oh, the people we talked to had opinions but knew nothing of the land. They would only say he sells a lot of land in these parts," said John, stepping back from the grey-haired man a little bit more.

Consortium of Acquaintances

"There was the guy that declared he received a refund when his wife passed away. It was so he could move closer to town," said Elizabeth, smiling and lowering her head as if she had revealed too much.

"Where is this land, and how much does the scoundrel want for it?" asked George, sounding a little less drunk, or was it a little more sane.

She pulled the map from its sleeve then spread it out on the counter. George followed each trail as they moved through the valley before saying, "I've been up there hunting many times, and the ground will grow just about anything you plant. There is a meadow that could easily become a productive farm. It is worth the asking price, and a good carpenter can use the savings to buy hinges and nails."

"Nails?" asked John as he began rolling the map to replace it in the sleeve.

"It is said tools in the right man's hands, and all he needs are the nails to build a cabin and the hinges to mount the door and some glass for the winders," answered George. "Just keep in mind that it is without a doubt a lonely place, even though it is hard to get help if you were to have an occasion to need it. The last time I was up that way, there was not a neighbor for days."

"What is it like up there? Is it as desolate as Yakima City seems to be with the dry land?" asked Elizabeth, covering her mouth as she spoke.

"Awe ma'am, the Cascades that far up the mountain the trees are green all year round. Oh, there is only a dry spell at the end of summer that lasts no more than a month, and then it rains for a few months. When it grows cold, it snows until spring. The food afoot is so thick that it's hard to miss when you're hunting," he said, sounding almost poetic.

She was in ah of his description of the land. She found herself just nodding her responses. She found herself moving nearer with each spoken word despite the odious personal habits of the older man.

He reminded her of Uncle Sam, causing her to laugh at the notion that he was here, suggesting they buy the land.

That night in the hotel, John laid in bed with his hands behind his head. "You know, we could do it," he blurted out.

"Do what exactly?" she asked, pulling a brush through her hair, making painful sounds as she combed. It had been almost five days since she combed it out back in Walla Walla.

"Buy it and make a life here," he answered, sitting up as if what he said was more of a revelation of things to come.

"You mean you would give up your dream of opening a carver shop in Seattle to live out in the middle of nowhere," she said, raising her voice towards the end.

"I reckon I would. After all, I could still carve. How do you feel about giving up on Seattle?" he asked, waiting for her to mull it over a bit before answering him.

"Well, as long as it was with you, I reckon I would enjoy the peacefulness of the mountains," she declared, smiling softly, envisioning their time on the Mullan Road.

"You know the best part of this trip was the journey from..."

"Fort Benton," he finished her sentence.

"It was just us," she said, pulling the brush through the last of the knots in her hair.

"And all those explosives," he joked light-heartedly.

"We made it without blowing ourselves up!" she exclaimed, setting the brush down and sliding between the sheets.

"We can go to Seattle. There we can find a small house, rent a shop, and we would be in debt to someone. Would we be happy? You hated what you had to do in St. Louis to make a living," he said, moving nearer the bed to the chair to remove his boots.

"So did you. You weren't happy with your job. You know I will be happy as long as you are by my side," declared Elizabeth, looking almost sad stretched out on their bed.

John looked out the window for a few minutes before commenting, "It sure gets quiet in town in the evening."

"You wouldn't want them to haul freight all night, would you?" she asked, not caring if he answered.

"No, I guess not. It's just it seems quiet like everyone went home."

"Maybe they do," she mused, stretching, giving him a direct hint he should come to bed.

"So should we do it, buy the land becoming farmers?" he asked, clumsily turning the lamp down by twisting the knob, so the wick lowered into the burner.

"No, John, you can still carve. Just because you grow our food doesn't make you a farmer. It makes you self-reliant," she said, pulling the covers back so he could get in.

"So you have given it some thought. So answer me this: What would you do up there to keep busy?" asked John, blowing the lamp out and reaching out to feel his way to bed.

"Be alone with you and away from people. I've had my fill. Honestly, I have," she whispered, kissing him goodnight.

"No one will know you here," he offered, cuddling next to her on the bed.

"I see familiar faces whenever I take a stroll in any crowd," she said, almost silent now in her responses.

"So we will do it," he declared as he closed his eyes.

"That Mr. Hinkle sure seemed to want us to sign a note on the property," she whispered.

"Yeah, I have a feeling he will be a little upset when I pay cash. It might cause trouble," he warned, snuggling in his wife's open arms, thinking of their last night at the Blue Wave saloon.

"Do you reckon he will back out?" she asked at a near whisper.

"If he does, we know he is a grifter."

On George's advice, the self-proclaimed town drunk, the Springers, changed their plans and decided to buy the land. They purchased the homestead from Mr. Hinkle. He was oddly surprised when they paid in cash. He then offered a place closer to town on less than an acre of land. It took several go-arounds until he produced the deed, and they were landowners.

They registered the sale with the courthouse, and they were the new owners of the property. The mayor was there to shake their hands, welcoming them to the county. They both felt as though it was a well-conducted event, if not scripted.

Mr. Hinkle introduced the Springers to each shopkeeper, who, in turn, promised to give them a fair deal on any merchandise they needed. Which was a good thing, because as it turned out, they needed a great deal more to homestead the land, but that wasn't half as bad as finding the property in the first place.

John picked up a book for settlers that described essential things about building, irrigating, farming, and even candle making. The book even listed supplies to be obtained and the tools they would need to purchase.

The first sign of trouble was when they asked George Johnson for directions to their slice of heaven. That was when he admitted he would need to look at the map again. Elizabeth pointed out later if he knew the land so well, why would he not know how to get there. When he finally found the property on the map, he explained that it was out east of the settlement of Yakima City.

"And how do we get there?" asked Elizabeth, having trouble holding her contempt for the man. She had struggled with her temper her entire life, and as she grew older, she held it back now like a wildcat on a tether.

George scratched his long white beard for a few seconds before answering, "You can't get there from here." With that, John went from her hero to the zero, at least until they stepped on their new property.

"What do you mean that we can't get there from here?" she demanded, sounding more like his mother than his wife, which caught them both off guard, including the shopkeeper who raised an eyebrow. She shrank from the conversation but in hindsight it made her look like a rattlesnake readying for its next meal.

George took a breath and continued. "Well, it is one of those places that yous' need to goes somewheres' else to meet up with the trail to your homestead. I will show yous' on the map. You will need to buy a donkey to drag a cart up there. Both are for purchase at the livery. That way, you

don't have to haul all the supplies on your backs," said George, soundin
monotone.

"Do you reckon we should purchase a horse?" asked John, looking
little timider than he had a few minutes ago. Thoughts of horse ride
filled his head.

"Horses are fine animals, but you're talking about cutting a trail int
your property. It may take you a week to do that, and a misstep with you
horse and you have a broked' leg."

With that, John's vision of sitting high in the saddle overlooking hi
land blew away like a dandelion in the wind.

Chapter 5
April 7th, 1873
Yakima City, Washington Territory

John and Elizabeth grew comfortable staying in the Hummel Hotel. They kept to themselves when they moved about the town. It was lucky for them. It turned out to be commonplace in Yakima City for people to keep to themselves, especially when they had something to hide.

They were excited about leaving town, even though it would take a few days to gather supplies so they would need for their new lives. They worked from a list that John had found in the back of the Settlers Guide that made suggestions they would need on their homestead.

George was friendly enough to show him some of the building techniques he would use when he reached his land. "Now, yous might want to buy a pulley, then again, if yous could make one as good as the one we have here, yous could take an extra rope with the weight difference. For now, hold your queries so we can get the work we have here done before supper time. If that's fine with you, let's get this up there, pull, and pull," directed George as they helped Mr. Peterson lift his roof trusses one at a time to the second story of his new house.

By the third house that they worked that afternoon, it became clear the George was a great deal smarter than he had believed a few days ago. For an answer to his questions, sure as the sunrise, some chores needed to be done. He learned how to hang a door by walking a mile to install an entry door for a man that George knew.

He did, upon John's request, show him how to use a plow. "Do you reckon you can keep ahold of it now?" asked George, holding his left side.

"Yes, I do reckon, I got an understanding of the plow's principles," answered John as he wrapped a shoulder strap around himself.

George leaned against a shovel, watching him struggle with the plow for about an hour. Only stopping when he had finished plowing the garden, he agreed by saying, "By golly, I reckon you have the gist of it." Nodding several times before John was able to respond.

"Thank you." Looking back at his progress, then comparing it to the rows George had plowed, he asked, "How do you keep your rows so straight?"

"Practice," replied George limping, holding his side, which reminded John of a Kill Deer, a bird that is known to act as if it had a broken wing whenever it felt threatened.

"Thank you for all your help. See you in the morning. We are heading out for our new life on our property early tomorrow. Would you be willing to wake up early and have breakfast with us?" asked John, holding out his hand for George to shake.

"I don't like saying goodbye to people," stated George plainly, disappearing around a corner. The tone of his voice betrayed the words he had spoken.

Later at the livery, they went through their supplies and tools. "It was George's idea to buy all the tools without the handles," said John as he raised the head of a chisel up to show Elizabeth that it had no handle.

"I noticed the shovel and plow heads," she admitted, pointing at the other tools as she spoke. She lifted the ax with a handle to examine its edge.

"With the weight, we saved with all of the suggestions George gave us, we can carry extra seed and those window panes you wanted," he announced, pointing out the fabric and windows.

"I was just happy to see the fabric even though it was a bit of an odd pattern," she said, reaching down and feeling the texture. Letting her fingers trace the floral pattern.

"There is more in the sack here somewhere, the fabric you were eyeball'n when we were buying the supplies yesterday," he said, opening a sack or two as he looked for the fabric. He had only purchased the odd material for padding. He figured his wife would use it for something eventually.

"Well, did you learn anything else?" asked Elizabeth, sitting down at the tailgate of the wagon. It creaked, threatened to come off the temporary blocks it rested on.

"I learned George is smarter than we give him credit for," answered John.

"About building?" she asked, holding her hand out for him to take. She smiled as he did so, and she gently pulled him closer. Their love was born of privacy, and rarely did they show their love for each other in public.

"Oh yes, I'm certain I can build us a cabin," he replied most confidently, letting himself be drawn into her grasp.

"Then it's time to stop paying for a room at this here hotel and start up the trail," she stated, "but first, I will need to take a long hot bath."

"Why is that?" he asked, moving even closer and leaning in for a kiss.

"Remember the Mullan Road, how dirty we were?" she said, kissing him back and lingering near him.

"Yes," he answered, reaching around his wife and patting her back as they spoke.

"The closest bath is the one we are walking away from right here in town," muttered Elizabeth, bonking him on the nose with her hairbrush causing him to sneeze.

Early the next morning, the sun was up but hidden by large fluffy grey clouds. "Might rain today," warned Harry as he helped them pack the building supplies and tools.

"The clouds do show the signs," she said, pointing west and in the direction where the bad weather seemed to congregate.

"He seems knowledgeable in many things for being the owner of the livery," whispered John, looking over to his wife. John didn't judge a person by the way they appeared.

Harry returned with some used chicken wire. "It is for your chickens. Might need to patch a few holes, but it will hold up if you take care of it," he explained, patting the roll and dropping it into the trailer.

"Thank you, Mr. Jackson," smiled Elizabeth as she looked at the relatively large amount of supplies.

"Don't worry. This cart is strong as they come. Its past life was that of an ore hauler. Just keep the wheel hubs greased, and you will be fine," said Harry.

"We thank you again, Mr. Jackson, you have been a great help," she said, kindly to the livery owner.

They looked around one last time as they prepared to leave. "I guess George isn't much for farewells," he said to his wife, pulling on a knot holding everything they owned to the cart.

"How do you know?" she asked.

"He had much as stated so," replied John as they started on the road to their new life.

"Good afternoon, was that the Springers on their way out of town?" asked Robert Hinkle, rather cheerfully.

"Yes," answered Harry, pulling his large door closed to keep the sun from warming the barn anymore than it had already.

"I hope they make a go of it up there. I will want to head up there to see their progress before the fall season begins. If you would be willing to find me a guide that will take me?" asked Robert.

"If they don't come running out of the mountains after the first sign of wolves, I will take you," answered Harry, attempting to clean his hands of bacon fat.

"There is a clause in the sales contract that they must live on the land for two full years before they can sell or move off of it. It will revert to the trust if they don't," he said as he heard riders making their way up the street towards the livery.

"Smart," said Harry, also turning.

"Well, after the trouble with Nelson, I thought it best."

Harry nodded.

A man known as Benjamin "Binky" Keys rode up with two other men hanging back to watch the street. Most anyone local would know his horse, who was called Tuffy. As for the man, he was built strong and with a hardened look about him. He never went anywhere without his brown Kansas City flat top that sat on his head as if tailored to fit. His sudden appearance made most people head indoors, even on the hottest of days.

"Robert, Harry," greeted Binky as he swung his leg off his horse and walked a little stiff-legged over to where they were standing.

"What can I do fer' you?" asked Harry nervously.

"Say as long as I have you here, Lomax won't be around for a while," said Robert, moving away in the direction of the boardwalk.

"And why is that, what is my father having him doing?" asked Binky.

"He killed a man in front of a United States Marshal over at the Winston, then threw another through the wall into the street," answered Robert, pointing over where Lucky sat on his horse.

"Why?"

"They killed Nelson," answered Harry.

"Well, I will say good day to you both. I'm heading down the street to settle up with the hotel," announced Robert so that every passerby would look in his direction.

"Hinkle! If you take a step closer to the street, you won't need to settle up with anyone," exclaimed Binky, resting his hand on the butt of his Peacemaker. He watched the man stop and turned to Harry, asking, "You hear of a family named Olson that came by here?"

"Why, yes, we did. I offered the Olsons a great package deal and sent them on their way," answered Robert, looking over at Harry.

"They had a bad hub. I repaired it like new," said Harry, wiping his hands with an old shirt.

"When did they leave?" asked Binky, plumb out of patience with them both.

Consortium of Acquaintances

"A few days ago, and you won't need to worry about anything. sanded three of their hubs. They won't get too far," replied Harry, sti trying to get his hands clean with an old shirt.

"Don't try to do my job. You're sure to piss me off when you do admonished Binky, and with that, he slid a leg over his horse and pulle himself into his saddle. He nodded at a woman holding her son's han that blocked the dramatic exit he had planned.

"Ma'am," he whispered, waiting for the lady to move out of the wa so he and his men could ride out of town.

"How did he know where they headed?" asked Robert of Harry.

Harry shrugged as he disappeared into the smaller of the two doo of the large red barn.

Chapter 6
April 10th, 1873
Yakima City, Washington Territory

John and Elizabeth headed out on the road north of Yakima City. John walked alongside, and Elisabeth sat in the wagon using a box as a seat. It was his penance for the trip from the Columbia River to Yakima City. She would let him sit once she was tired of sitting.

The wagon reminded him of the one he used to haul trash, making a dollar for a week's worth of effort. Over the years, John had learned to hide it within and ignored the muscle pain he felt with hard labor. His mind drifted away from his last occupation when he heard the sound of hoofbeats on the road behind them.

"John, did you pay your bar tab?" she asked nervously.

"Funny, I'm sure we are too close to town to be worried about highwaymen," he answered, helping her pull the wagon over and into the next wagon rut.

"Morning ma'am, mister," shouted the first rider.

They could hear the horses breathe deep and quick as they passed. "Morning," they both shouted back.

The other two riders passed with a little more caution but sped up once they were clear. Neither of them said anything.

He released his hand from his rifle that was next to Elizabeth in the bed of the wagon. "Well, they are in a hurry," he whispered, moving from beside the wagon to in front of Nana the burro.

Consortium of Acquaintances

Soon they were moving again and trying to keep their wagon out of the ruts with increasing difficulty. The little wagon seemed ridiculously small compared to the wagon ruts made from the heavy Conestoga wagons that passed this way each day.

"Look at the wagon tracks that curve in and out like the driver was up all night drinking," he said, pointing at the wagon tracks that didn't follow the much deeper ruts made by the Conestogas.

"What caused that? Are the wagon drivers drunk?" she laughed.

"I would guess it's the smaller cargo wagons like Mr. Harrison's. When the wagons are light, the bumps make them bounce around, but they are full of supplies for Yakima City on the way back to Fort Walla Walla. By the condition of the streets in town, there are a lot of empty wagons," he said, glancing over to his wife.

She was now looking at him as though he was possessed. "Why was Mr. Harrison's wagon almost empty?"

"The wagon was full of crates," answered John, kicking a rock out of the way of the cart's wheel. "What you say'n?"

"Whatever was in those crates, they didn't weigh much."

"Why do you say that?" asked John.

"I lifted one or two of them," replied Elizabeth, glancing over to her husband. "Now, don't be gawking in my direction like that. I just wanted more room for my legs."

"Yeah, well, let's not get into trouble with these people," he whispered, smiling briefly, getting lost in her eyes.

"Where did you learn about wagons?" she asked, giving him a strange smile.

"What?" he asked, laughing at her strange look.

"We have been staring at the same tracks since we left Walla Walla," she answered on the verge of a rant. "How did you learn about the ruts?" She pushed at his shoulder playfully.

"Oh, George," he replied, beginning to laugh again. "That might be the point. These types of ruts only occur around Yakima City."

"What does it mean?" she asked.

"I don't even know why George pointed it out. Maybe, it was a puzzle he was having trouble with figuring out himself.

"He isn't as simple as he seems?" she asked, holding on to the wagon as the burro bucked a little, trying to head up a small hill.

"George is a deep well of information. It's just hard to draw up that information before you die of thirst."

As promised, the road wandered westerly, and soon they had come to a river crossing. Luckily, the spring rains hadn't swelled the river to the point of flooding. When they crossed, they could sense the potential of the power of the river.

Around lunchtime, they heard the same riders again coming from behind. The lead rider greeted them, "Good afternoon," he said, slowing enough as not to spook the donkey.

"Good afternoon," answered John; his heart jumped as he heard the trigger being cocked on his rifle. Elizabeth could handle the gun as well, if not better than himself.

Soon the riders had passed, and they watched as they became only a dust-cloud up-ahead. It wasn't long, and even that faded.

They came to an old fort that neither had heard anything about late in the afternoon. The front gate had fallen into disrepair.

"This isn't Fort Simcoe, is it?" asked Elizabeth.

"I should hope not," responded John.

"Why?" she asked.

"Because if it were, we went completely in the wrong direction," he answered, smiling at her as she looked around.

"But, what if..."

"It's not! The place is a school. There would be Indian children wandering around," he answered, choosing not to laugh.

The fort before them was made of wood, smaller than most that they had visited on their trip from St. Louis, with only a small building in the center of the stockades.

"It seems to be at a crossroads of sorts," said John, as they set the tent and readied the campsite within the old fort.

"It sure is a lonely place. I wonder why they built it here?"

"George told me the hills are crisscrossed with trails. I would guess that it is on a trade route that has gone unused for a while."

"This appears to be a river crossing. The fort was left to the elements?" asked Elizabeth, pointing across the river.

"Haunted," he joked, regretting it as the word left his lips.

"John Will Springer, you want to be walking half the night to find a better campsite, you best be stopping that noise right now. This place is spooky enough that you don't need to add to it."

They stopped another night further west in the valley, each time setting up a tent and watching the sunset behind the mountains.

"I believe I'm... I'm in love with you," she whispered with an affectionate smile on her lips.

"I have always loved you," he said, kissing her lips.

"Do you still believe running out on your people was a good idea?" she asked, kissing him again.

He started to snore as she kissed him.

"John?" she asked.

He let out a deep breath and snored a little more.

"Good night, honey," she said, falling asleep in his arms.

They woke up early, noticing the weather was colder than in Yakima City. It would warm up quickly, and then the afternoons brought stormy weather. The trail they were on dropped into a valley, and by mid-morning, they came to a junction connecting them with the Naches Trail. It was a joyous time for them both as they again turned to the west.

They got up early each morning, switching positions every couple of hours with one walking and one riding. On the hills, they walked and helped Nana pull the wagon. They noticed by doing this. They could travel further each day.

The Naches Trail found its way over the Cascades, over the famed Naches Pass. They had read about the pass in the ads posted on the Walla Walla bulletin board placed there by the people of Tacoma.

"It seems no one uses this trail anymore," stated John, stepping over a sage bush that was growing in the middle of their path.

Well, George did say take the Naches Trail at your own risk," said Elizabeth, stepping over the same bush.

"It was sure strange that they advertise Seattle this way, but they tell everyone that if they want to go to Seattle, they will need to turn around," he said, looking up at the tall hills that loomed to the north and south that seemed to close in on them at the head of the valley.

"Are these the Cascades?"

"They are tall and imposing, but the ones we will be skirting today are just the foothills," answered John with confidence.

"How do you know? Is it on the map?" she asked.

"No, George told me," he answered, letting out a chuckle.

"You sure learned a good deal from that drunken-loon."

"Well, according to him, we cross the river and head up the south fork from the Naches River about a day's hike into the valley," he said, repeating the directions that he memorized.

Once they crossed the river, they found the old trapper's trail used by the Chinooks for hundreds of years before any European had laid eyes on the area. As they walked, they saw properties surveyed and readied for sale, yet no one lived here. "It is so odd to see the places back on the hillside ready to be settled with no one on them," she stated.

"Well, maybe it is like you were saying this morning. People in Yakima City are promoting the area so much that they have readied the properties for future sales."

They stopped for a break near a small settlement that was not much more than a collection of shacks to look at the map. "I wouldn't buy those without a good source of water. Do you reckon it's the lack of water?" asked Elizabeth, watching him look at the map with a bit of concern.

"I am not sure. The cutoff from this river is just up around the bend. Maybe an hour to the cutoff from there a day or two, to the property," he answered, folding the map, placing it back into the pack that was sitting on the wagon.

"What is your opinion about stopping at the settlement across the river," she asked, pointing at the shacks on the other side of the river.

"I reckon we should pass them up, the water is swift here, and i would take a half-day to get there, with little reward," he answered pulling at the donkey's reins to get the wagon moving again.

"That is a good point," she said as she watched the shacks disappear knowing it was best to avoid people unless they had a reason due to the way they left St. Louis.

They crossed the river near the end of the valley and turned south for a mile to follow the Tieton River. John stopped as the trail again turned west. She watched him scratch his head, acting confused.

"What is the matter, Mr. Springer?"

"Hmm," he muttered.

"How much further do you reckon we have?" asked Elizabeth a little louder.

"Well, they told us we needed to buy a burro and cart to make it into the property," he stated, glancing up the trail and back the way they came.

She nodded, not that he noticed.

"Then why are there wagon tracks in the mud. Back over by the river, there are too many rocks to notice, but here I can see a set of tracks heading up the trail."

"Do you reckon someone is lost?" she asked.

"Maybe," John answered.

"Why did you want this cart?" asked Elizabeth, finally taking the time to ask a question that had bothered her for a few days.

"The bottom of the cart is made from a walnut tree. Each of the planks can build a strong door that we can use on the cabin, might even have enough to build a proper table," answered John, as he started down into a small draw that looked like it would cross the river up ahead.

"So that is why you spent the extra money on this wagon?" she asked, chasing after him.

"Well, you want a door that a bear might take more than a minute to get through, right?" he asked, looking back.

"Well, yeah, I would rather have one that takes a little longer than that," she answered.

"Well, a minute is a lot of time to defend your home. You can load the rifle then shoot the bugger between the eyes in a minute," he said as he came to the top of the slight rise over a patch of basalt. He stopped suddenly above a depression, whispering, "Be silent."

Which they both knew would not last them long. Elizabeth was one opinionated woman, and if he didn't want her opinion, he should have married someone else. For some reason, she chose to listen as he picked up the rifle.

For the life of her, she wondered why she didn't have a rifle of her own. She watched as he slowly moved forward, and he motioned for her to stay close.

"Indians?" she asked, noticing what he was concerned about as she came up beside him.

"Be quiet if ever you listened, you listen now, do not scream," he said directly into her ear.

The trail widened into a small meadow, where a blue Conestoga wagon with two broken wheels was sitting tipped on its side. He could see at least three bodies lying within a few feet of the wagon.

Elizabeth poked him and pointed toward the river. There, not far from the water's edge, were three more. "What happened here?" she asked, covering her mouth with her hand before he did.

He answered by pointing at a woman's body with a torn dress stained with her husband's blood. He had died protecting his family. No more than a few feet from the bodies was a wolf on its back with two legs pointed toward the sky.

"It does appear that they killed one," he declared.

"John Springer, I am more concerned where the rest of the wolves ventured off to," said Elizabeth.

They heard rustling in the grass above them on the hillside and in the trees behind them. They turned their attention towards the noise and away from the massacred family. Over by the wagon, a body slid from view before they could turn back around.

"What was that?" asked Elizabeth as her voice echoed on the canyon's walls.

Consortium of Acquaintances

"I have not the foggiest," he said, patting the air in front of hi suggesting she should panic a little quieter.

"They are just hiding, but they will be back. They always cor back," answered a soft voice on the wind.

It was that moment he completely lost his calm as he raised the rif aiming in several different directions. "Who is out there, Eliza?" asked, still shouldering his rifle, letting a name slip that his wife longer used.

"I told them that this was the wrong trail. I told them we needed larger fire and someone to watch over us, but no one ever listens to me whispered a voice almost as soft as the first time.

He pointed his rifle into the dim evening and was about to pull tl trigger when she called out his name, "John," pointing to a pine tre Halfway up the tree, where the branches become unstable for climbin was a girl of around eight or nine years old.

John wandered back over to his wife. "Can you climb down and te us what happened here?" he asked, looking up into the tree. It was question they would not have answered for eight months.

"No."

"Wait, no to the coming down or the explaining of current events. he asked matter of factly.

"Yes."

"Honey, can you come down?" asked Elizabeth.

"No."

"And you won't tell us what happened?" he asked, already expectin what her answer would be.

"Umm, yes?" said Annie as confusion started to set in.

"Well, that clears that up," he chuckled, moving to the back of th wagon and picking up the ax.

"John Springer, what in the hell are you planning to do?"

"She won't come down, so it's just easier to drop the tree then picl up the pieces, so to speak," he answered as his chest made contact witl his wife's.

54

"Would you like to explain to me, where on this trip you lose your mind? Maybe we can walk down the trail yonder and retrieve it?" Elizabeth asked, with a fire in her eyes that just could not be ignored.

"That's fine, we can do it your way," he declared and would often wonder where he was standing with a rifle in one hand and an ax in the other it was he who backed down to an unarmed woman of half his size. Then he would remember that Eliza was a scary one to deal with even on her best days.

He checked for survivors, moving over by the wagon. Most of the supplies looked like they ended up in the river or maybe dragged off. He thought about burying the dead, but it was close to nightfall, and this meadow was growing scarier by the minute. He gathered canvas from the wagon and a couple of blankets, dropping a third due to a bloody stain.

He walked back to his wagon, so he could watch over Elizabeth as she coaxed the little girl from her hiding spot.

"Her name is Annie. She told me while you were checking on the others," said Elizabeth, pulling the girl into her arms.

"Put her in the wagon, then let us leave this place because there is nothing we can do for these people. The wolves will be out as soon as the sun drops below the horizon."

"How far do you want to make it tonight?" asked his wife.

"Until I feel safe," answered John.

"So we are going back?" she said, making a nervous joke.

"It's three days back, and less than a day ahead, we did not come here to quit. Besides, Mr. Hinkle told me that he would be happy to repurchase the property for almost the asking price if we changed our minds within two weeks," he warned, already moving ahead with his rifle in his arms. Nana could sense the trouble for the rest of the trip, and they had to pull her along to gain headway.

"What if we take a month to get back?" asked Elizabeth.

"He takes a percentage the longer we take to change our minds."

"I'm starting to see the grift we got ourselves involved with," said Elizabeth, watching for movement as they steamed ahead into the great unknown. "I didn't know wolves hunted like that, did you?"

Consortium of Acquaintances

"I know almost nothing of wolves, but wild dogs will hunt human without fear of a rifle," whispered John.

"Are you saying these are special?"

"I'm saying that these wolves have no fear of us, no fear of my rifle they only see us as food."

Annie started to cry.

Elizabeth raised her hand and threatened to slap John's beard off.

He noticed the red stain on her hand. "Are you hurt?"

She shook her head then pointed at the little one, "She had a little cut. It's not bad."

"It may attract wolves if it's bad."

Annie cried harder.

"Maybe we should stay quiet for a while," he warned, pulling the donkey hard to get her to climb the rise.

As the trail crested the hill, he looked back, suddenly feeling cold a a lone wolf called out to the rest of his pack. When finished with hi lonesome song, the rest of the wolf pack called back as if to tell each other their location and it was safe to return to the meadow.

"There has to be at least twenty of them," he said before he knew what he was saying.

"Remember the properties down the hill. You reckon it is the wolve that keep them vacant?"

"Maybe."

Chapter 7
A few Days earlier

The Boardwalks of Yakima City were stirred up as Benjamin "Binky" Keys, and his men made their way down Main Street. They were passing cargo wagons as if they were standing still.

With a whip in hand, the drivers would make suggestions as to the riders about the origins of their mothers. That is until they realized they were talking to Binky and Lucky. Their attitude changed quicker than a field mouse noticing the new house cat.

One after the other, they pulled their wagons to the side as if the volunteer fire department was racing up the street. Everyone knew Binky's reputation, and they didn't wish to add to it.

He had been in town for less than a year but had a reputation that blew in with the mail. A wanted poster and a newspaper clipping from a town no one could recall fueled the rumor-mill and sewing circle's gossipers for months.

They picked up speed on the outskirts of town and brought their horses to a gallop towards a place north of town. Where they had left most of the gang about four days ago, they came upon a small wagon two miles out of town, a man walking a donkey pulling a woman on the little wagon.

"Good morning, Ma'am, mister," said Binky moved over as he passed them but did not bother to slow down.

"Good morning," replied the man.

Consortium of Acquaintances

Lucky charged ahead of Drake, passing the couple without a word. When Drake caught up to Lucky, he looked over and nodded as if to say whatever has their boss so upset, it must be a big deal.

A few miles north of town, the Yakima river came through two ridges and was joined by the Naches River on the other side that ran west to east. The Yakima then splits the valley as it makes its way south around Yakima City through Union Gap and into the Lower Yakima Valley.

They took the less traveled right fork when they came to the fork in the road near where the two rivers became one. Then walked their horses into a dried horseshoe lake that was once part of the river. They picked this spot because it was easy to defend and even harder to find unless you had been there once or twice. By the time Lucky caught up with their leader, he was already off his horse.

"Wake up, Willy," shouted Binky, kicking the older man's foot to stir him from his slumber.

"Well, there you are, what a sight for sore eyes you turned out to be," said Willy, rising from his resting spot. He coughed and struggled to stand. His beard caught the wind and waved around like a white flag.

"Where is everyone?" asked Binky, looking around the camp noticing the lack of bedrolls. He handed the older man a canteen full of water.

"Well, when you ran south to The Dalles, a bunch of us went into town, yah see, it was Frank that pull a few of them aside. He told them he had a new job for them," he answered, taking that moment to take a long pull on Binky's canteen.

"Why didn't you go?" asked Lucky, causing Binky to glance up, however, he chose not to say anything.

Somehow Lucky knew he had asked the wrong question.

"Too old, I suppose," he answered, sounding a little depressed. "You know there was a time. I used to be important. I handled the messages of the Calvary and before that I walked every stream and river in these parts. Long before the Calvary even came to these parts." He took another drink and handed the canteen back to Binky.

"What was the new job?" asked Binky, glancing over at Lucky, who nodded in understanding.

"They headed up the south fork towards Mount Rainier in search of Frank's Eldorado. Whatever that is? Like I was say'in I know these parts better than anyone."

In town amongst the Consortium, there had been a rumor that Frank had drug them across North America to find something precious. Some said it was gold; others said it had to do with the Fountain of Youth. Binky didn't believe anyone would be able to guess his father's motivations, including himself.

"How long they been gone?" asked Lucky, this time receiving a nod from his leader.

"Right after you left, a week at most," answered Willy, reaching back with both arms and stretching his bones cracked like kindling.

"I am going to head up Naches Pass. I need to find the Olson party. They should be halfway up the pass by now."

"What is so important about that wagon?" said Lucky, this time looking over at Drake, who had moved closer to hear the answer.

"Because it's our job," he answered. Lucky's eyes flashed with excitement. It was a moment that Binky didn't miss.

"I will come with you," said Drake. He was a man of few words.

"Sure, we can come with you. You are returning?" asked Lucky, but by his tone, he was still wondering about Binky's motivation.

"I am," answered Binky, nodding his head.

Lucky seemed to relax with his answer.

"Well, if you don't mind, I am going to take a nap and then wander into town for some supplies. Don't worry, I knows how to keep my trap shut," said Willy, at least being honest about the heading into town part.

"Now, Willy, Frank doesn't need to find out where we are heading. We can handle it," said Lucky to Binky's surprise.

"We can handle this and be back in a week provided we can fix the wagon and get it back to town," said Binky.

"You just need to get it back to Flint's place. He may be a little off, but he knows how to fix wagons. Harry has given him plenty of

practice," said Willy, kicking some dirt into his campfire then goin
about rolling up his bedroll.

"Didn't you say you were heading for town later," said Bink
slipping onto Tuffy's back as he waited for an answer.

"Yes, but the thought of a steak at the Lucy is going to keep m
awake," said Willy, picking up his saddle and walking over to his horse.

A few minutes later, they were on the trail again, kicking up dus
When they passed the man and woman once again, he about laughe
surprised they had made it as far as they had. "Good afternoon," he sai
as he passed, slowing down a little more to keep from spooking the burr
this time.

By late afternoon, they were near Flint's place. From the road, the
could tell he had no company. Part of him wished the wagon had broke
down. They had found travelers that had limped to Flint's little cabin i
the past. The other part of him worried about his companions and wh
Lucky seemed to get excited when he said he wanted to follow th
wagon up here.

They followed the river west and came to the Tieton River tha
forked south from the Naches.

The sun was hanging low in the sky, and they would need to cros
the river at least two times before coming to a decent campsite.

"The only fortunate thing about the Naches trail is you see mor
coyotes than wolves," whispered Drake passing Lucky as he took th
time rolling a cigarette.

"Don't be careless and drop it into the dry grass," said Binky, passin
him to keep up with Drake.

Chapter 8
Well into the evening, April 12th, 1873
25 miles Northwest of Yakima City

The full moon high in the sky sent light weaving through a mixture of deciduous trees, painting spider web shadows on the ground as they headed up the trail towards their land. The only sound heard was the occasional cricket playing a love song.

It went on like this for a few hours as John walked slightly ahead, holding the rope of Nana the donkey with his left hand and his Spencer Repeating Rifle in his right.

"Have you heard anything?" asked Elizabeth, rising from where she had been sleeping, holding the little one.

Looking back at his wife. "What should we do about her?"

"We could keep her," she blurted out.

Listening to the wagon that had started to make a squeaky sound while they had been talking to one another, "What we need to do is find out if this property is worth having, make some decisions and if this was a grift, maybe gets some payback."

She turned around to look into the darkness. "You reckon it is safe to stop for the night?"

"The moon is up, and I reckon it will fall behind that ridge to... Well, that direction anyway," he replied, pointing with the rifle.

"Moon sets in the west even out in the middle of nowhere," laughed Elizabeth, starting to tease.

"Yes, but the hill as well, even the large hill should be wester] smart, uhm, woman," John said, stumbling upon his words. He tried explain the tall canyon walls climb so high that they caused the sun a the moon to rise late and set early.

Little did he know she had thought of it hours ago and decided not explain it to him. "Might want to grease the wheels," she said.

"Let's stop for the night, we can fix it tomorrow," he said, noticir the wheels had started making a little noise as they stopped.

"You are not going to leave her like that, are you?" asked Elizabe leaning Annie back into the cargo then slipping from the makeshift se that was a case of ammo.

"I want to get a fire started," he said, tying the donkey to a tree.

"We going to set the tent?" she asked, twisting to loosen her back u letting her dress spin and catch air.

She caught him staring before he continued to ready the fire.

"No, I will make a fire. Will you keep watch? We can put our back against that log," he said as he pointed to a large log and rocky groun that looked utterly uncomfortable.

"On those rocks?" she asked, waking Annie as she became agitated.

"Over there gives us a good field of visibility, giving us th advantage. Over on the riverside gives the wolves the advantage. S where would you like to lie down for the night," he said, raising his voic because of the screams that were coming from the little wagon.

"Hush, she isn't even awake. Come now, little one you're all right, she said as she gathered her into her arms.

"What's wrong with her?" he asked, moving the blankets along wit anything soft to help with the rocky ground.

"She is just having a nightmare," declared Elizabeth, picking th child up and moving her over to the pile of blankets.

He started throwing rocks into the middle of the small clearing. H cleared the ground and soon had a small firepit. He hummed while h worked. It was his way of coping with stress. Such as when wolves are a your heels, driving a wagon full of explosives down a mountainside, o carrying bodies down the back alley of the Blue Wave Saloon. He looked over at his wife and wondered what made her hum.

Elisabeth tossed some small pieces of wood in the pit and readied the fire. She watched John walk back to the wagon to get a box of matches. In moments, the moonlight had been replaced by the dancing fire. He walked around and quickly gathered more wood. Not like how rare it was on the Mullan Road with the traffic from people coming west.

"Well, I do like your fire-making skills," complimented Elizabeth, holding the girl reaching for his hand to come and lie down.

"I will as soon as I give Nana a little freedom and some water."

"Did you feed the chickens?" she asked.

"Earlier, but they are quiet now, we should let them stay that way," he sat down, leaning up against the tree next to his wife. He closed his eyes for what seemed like a moment.

John's eyes snapped open when the rooster they had brought with them cleared his lungs. He jumped up onto his feet, looking around for Elizabeth, who wasn't anywhere to be found. He slapped the grass, looking for his rifle, which was also missing.

"Elizabeth?" he asked, stopping all movement to listen to the forest noise made by the struggles of the wind.

"Morning," smiled Elizabeth, walking back from the river edge.

"Where did you go?" He asked, offering her a hug as if he had no concept of time.

"I needed a few minutes to myself," she said with a wink.

"I was just worried when I woke, and you were gone. Oh, and where is my?" asked John, holding his hands out as if he held an invisible rifle.

"I set it back in the wagon because I was leaving, and you were asleep. Oh, you have noticed that Annie is gone," she said, pointing to the blanket lying next to where he had awoken.

"Well, yes, I was just worried when you were missing," he answered, trying to cover for the fact he had forgotten about the extra passenger. She didn't give it away if she noticed his bluff.

"She was asleep when I got up," said Elizabeth, moving over next to the wagon. "I am willing to bet she hasn't gone too far."

Consortium of Acquaintances

He watched her place her index finger in a shushing manner covering her beautiful lips. 'She is my Angel,' he thought.

"Annie?" she whispered.

"I'm hiding," came a muttered response from under the tarp.

"Why are you hiding?"

"He was growling," answered Annie with a tiny voice.

"Who is he?"

"Him," she answered with her raised hand pointing at John.

"He was snoring, dear?" asked Elizabeth, randomly tickling under the tarp covering their charge and the supplies.

"Stop, stop," pleaded the little girl, who giggled for more.

"We should be going," he stated, slapping grease on the hub before vowing to check it at least once more before they reached the property.

"What about breakfast?" they both asked, laughing at the fact the had asked at the same time.

Annie's laugh came without a smile.

"I'm not convinced we should take the time to heat food and raise stink that could be smelled by anyone," he whispered.

"What?" asked Elizabeth, putting her arm around his neck.

"He is afraid to attract more wolves, but the bad wolves only com out at night," warned Annie, looking into the hills.

She pushed him playfully. "Then why didn't you say so? Try bein plainer with your words, so maybe we can follow what you're saying."

"I was trying not to say that in front of the child," he answered looking a little picked on.

She hopped up on the little wagon next to the child, "So husband how is that working out for you?"

"Not too well," answered Annie, sitting on the box of ammo.

"Now, don't you go ganging up on me too."

"Morning," called out a man riding a raft down the river, not twent feet from where they stood. He looked to be the definition of a mountai man. They only had time to nod the reply and wave goodbye at the ma on the raft.

"I bet he walks up into the mountains and rides a raft back to civilization," yelled John, turning back to his wife and Annie.

"Yeah, I'm just glad I wasn't squatting over there when he went by smiling and waving," laughed Elizabeth, a little red-faced. It was amazing how she was still able to blush after all she had been through in her thirty years of life.

"Well, at least he will see the bodies and let someone know." Once it left his mouth, he wished he could have left it unspoken.

The girl sniffled, "My mommy." She took a moment to look back into the canyon and then began to cry.

"Gee, husband, do you want to maybe pull it back a little," admonished Elizabeth, reaching into the cart and rubbing her back.

'With that, I'm a hero to zero,' he thought, not bothering to explain she had just told him to be more direct.

"Ah, John?" she asked when he looked as though he was in a fog of his own. "Annie, we may have broken him."

He stirred from his thoughts to answer her. "Either way, we need to get going." He untied the rope holding the donkey.

"Shouldn't you at least feed the chickens," said Elizabeth, still rubbing Annie's back comforting the child.

Annie continued to sob in little outbursts that would last the rest of the morning. She only stopped to watch John toss some food in with the chickens. "I'm an orphan, does that mean I have to take a ride on a train?" she whispered as she fell asleep.

"What is she say'n about trains?" asked John with an odd smile.

"I don't have the foggiest notion. It's not like the girl came with a manual," answered Elizabeth, covering her face with the blanket.

Three hours later, they came to a campsite at the edge of a large meadow. Someone had been there less than a week or so ago. John began to smile as he realized the significance of where they stood. "We are here!" he exclaimed, having trouble holding back the excitement that stirred within him.

"Where?" they asked, glancing again at each other.

"Well, if I'm right, this meadow is our piece of heaven."

Consortium of Acquaintances

"I thought it would take longer," she declared, looking up.

"I want to see," said Annie, who had been quiet for the last hour tucked under the canvas he had salvaged from the Conestoga.

"Well, let us walk into the middle of the meadow to have a gander at our new home," said John, generally pointing to the west.

A few minutes later, they stopped the wagon to take in the grassy meadow watching as the wind serenaded their ears with a natural melody. The light greens from the grass and the pale yellow wildflowers moved and swayed with the wind.

A forest of dark evergreen foliage encircled the meadow. Three ridges surrounded the valley. Annie pointed at the stream that meandered through the middle of the property.

"Paradise," whispered Elizabeth, breathless as tears started to flow.

"Oh wait, might be the next valley," said John, looking at the map.

"What?"

"Really!"

"I'm joking, this is it!" he screams, running into what seemed more like a painting than their new home. Elizabeth and Annie chased after him through the field of flowers. Their intentions weren't immediately clear what they had planned to do with him.

They stopped after a few minutes, now upon their elbows taking in the sun-soaked meadow, the smell of wildflowers, and the sound of the trees moving ever so slowly. Whispering to them a message too faded, too removed to hear, a message that has brought man, beast, and everything in between to this valley surrounded by tall peaks for a thousand years.

Chapter 9

Construction of the cabin was on the mind of John as he stood in the field of wildflowers. He took the time to dig a hole while Elizabeth and Annie spent their time investigating the stream. He found that the soil would grow almost anything given enough care.

He could hear them throwing rocks into the stream. The occasional laughter gave away their location as they wandered around. He returned the dirt into the hole, patting the ground with the back of the shovel. Their voices grew louder as they returned up the slight rise from the edge of the stream.

They watched wild rabbits dart around without fear of humans. They learned this because Annie was holding two of the little gray critters after a few minutes.

"The rabbits will be a problem and will need to be considered. If we ever hope to grow enough food to support a farm," said John smiling at how quickly the child had befriended the wildlife clutched in her arms. He looked over at the small child holding his wife's hand with one hand and a tentative bunny with her other hand.

They had planned what they would do the first day, from picking a location for their new cabin to surveying the land. Then, once they calmed down from the initial excitement, they were left with several decisions to be made about their future. "Do you love the property?"

"Yes," answered Elizabeth.

Consortium of Acquaintances

Annie just nodded her response, not being sure if she was part of the overall conversation. After all, she was a newcomer to their partnership and she was unsure of her status.

"So we should keep the land?" he asked, keeping the straightest face he could muster, pulling his bowler hat lower to hide his eyes.

"Yes," replied his wife, smiling at her husband's playfulness, turning to look down towards Annie.

Annie only moved her head as one would nod to a passing friend. She didn't feel she had a right to have an opinion.

"It's fine. You have a right to cast a vote," John said, watching for her reaction, combing her loose hair with his fingertips.

"Yes, then, I like the meadow and the stream and the little hill and the trees and big mountains there, there and there," she answered pointing to the three small peaks within eyeshot.

Both Elizabeth and John turned to each other to make a silent arrangement.

Elizabeth spoke first, asking, "Darlin' would you like to live here? We would love to have you until your family comes round." She knelt to make Annie a little more comfortable.

"You could help out with the chickens and maybe the rabbits," stated John, pointing out a little one bouncing into his field of vision.

"Oh, he is cute," declared Annie, her smile dropped as soon as it arrived, thinking back on the last few days.

"It's fine. You can have a few days to contemplate over it while we get settled, said Elisabeth, laying her hand on Annie's shoulder.

"I will stay, at least until my father comes for me. I was trying to figure out how long it will be," whispered Annie, moving away chasing the bunny.

"Well, it is settled. We are here to stay," announced John, taking a moment to form a plan. He felt his wife's hand near his, instinctively opening his, intertwining with her fingers.

"I don't know why. However, it doth seem right," said Elizabeth leaning closely to kiss his cheek.

He drew the land out the best he could on the ground with the handle of his ax. It shows where he believed the field would do best due to its flatness and location to the stream. Then he drew a little canal from off the map showing where the water would come from to water the fields.

"What about the cabin?" asked Elizabeth, pointing to the field and following the canal with her finger.

They could see little trees poking up all around the meadow.

"Well, we can set the tent up for the first month and make some decisions at a later convening of a family meeting," he replied while walking over to pull on the closest sapling, and with an audible pop, it came out of the ground.

"Just need to do that, what two hundred more times, and we have a field," she said, wiggling her nose like a cat that is about to pounce.

Annie drew a house on the map on the property's southeastern corner, close to the stream.

"Why would you want to build it over there? I'm not saying that it's a bad location?" questioned Elizabeth, hoping not to offend little Annie's attempt to plan the farm.

"Hmm, you know it's not that bad of an idea," answered John, getting a stern look in return from Elizabeth, one that said to her husband, you better not be making me out to be the bad guy.

"If you have company and you want a path to the door, you won't want to take up the flat land to do it," she muttered, not daring to look up.

"Plus, if we can figure a way to build the house down there, we can save that much more farmland for crops," said John, smiling and reaching out for both of them, bringing them into a hug.

The simple little thirty-minute meeting would set them on a course for the next six months. In the first month, they stayed in a tent on the upper part of the meadow. They did this because they spent just about every waking minute working on the field.

The first week, he fell all the trees in the meadow and the trees near the planned home site. He left them where they fell so that they would dry out. After a few attempts, he made handles for the small two-person saw.

"You need to work together. Annie, you push the saw back when Elizabeth pulls, then you pull it back," he said, showing them how to remove the limbs from the fallen trees. Later, he showed them how to debark the trees needed to build a small cabin and a much larger one later in the season.

For the next few weeks, he went to work, making the handles for the farm implements. He was using the plow behind the donkey, which, as it turned out, was a great deal easier than dragging the hand-plow over the field. That day, he noticed his neighbors, who had seen him on the trip to the property. They waved, and he waved back. "They seem nice," he said aloud but to no one really, which came as a surprise when his wife spoke.

"Does this mean there will be trouble?"

"I don't reckon so," he answered, watching a dozen or so Native Americans walk back into the forest on the other side of the creek.

"They seem fit," she said, then quickly recanted, "Oh, don't gawk at me like that, you know what I mean to say. They look healthy, unlike the ones we saw on our way out from Kansas City," she argued.

"I do agree. The Natives up here do not appear beaten," he said.

A few days later, they got a hopeful sign. Three goats showed up tied to the stakes, 50 yards from where they saw the hunting party. "Well, I would take it that these are a welcome to the neighborhood gift," said Elizabeth, leaning her head over onto his shoulder.

"How do you know that?" asked Annie, pushing closer to see if the smallest one was friendly.

"Well, what we would have received if they weren't trying to welcome us would have been a great deal different?" he asked, putting his arm around her shoulder, reminding her that her husband needed a bath.

"I suppose," she looked at him and nodded as she fed some grass to the little one.

"Look how they are eating the grass down to the roots. We should water them and move them around the field. It would make it easier to clear the field," he said, pointing at the large circle around the staked goats.

"Do you reckon that was the real gift here? To teach us to stop moving the food to the animals and bring the animals to the food," asked Elizabeth as she swung the rake around.

"The rake's handle is funny looking," giggled Annie, making fun of the branch that was straight when he made it into a handle but now seemed to have a twist as it dried.

"Well, that is why we want the trees to dry out before we build the cabin," he said.

Years later, he would find himself staring at the rake with the twisted handle, daydreaming of this first year.

"Are you fixing to do some work?" mused his wife.

He went about letting the goats eat the grass low before he removed the roots. He had a quarter of the field uncovered by the end of the week.

A week later, he took the time to till the soil with a hand plow and added the crops' rows. They weren't all that straight but following the contours of the land. Elizabeth couldn't help laughing at his effort playfully.

Early on, they built pens for the animals. They ended up putting the chickens in with the rabbits and tying the donkey to a post until they could make a larger pen.

"You see that rabbit that is pestering the chickens. This one rabbit is liable to upset them so much they will stop laying eggs," said John, turning to Annie and asking, "So what do you reckon we should do with him?"

"We eat him," she had answered his question with action.

Elizabeth jumped when a pitchfork suddenly impaled the rabbit. "What the hell are you doing?"

"Well, you answered two questions," declared John, patting Annie on her back. "What to do about the rabbit and what was going to be for dinner."

Consortium of Acquaintances

"You could warn a gal when you're aiming to do something lik that," yelled Elizabeth, holding her heart like she was about to faint. " thought you liked your rabbits."

"Wife of mine, she loves the rabbits, but she loves the eggs evei more," he said, trying to make light of the situation.

"And if they stop producing, we will have to eat the rabbits and thei the chickens," she added with no remorse for the loss of the rabbit.

What John hadn't told his wife was that he had a previoui conversation about the economics of raising rabbits and chickens. Ii hindsight, he decided to inform his wife before their 8-year-old charg dispatched another animal. He believed she would choose to go for walk the next time, and you know he was not wrong.

They planted the rest of their seeds and used kitchen pots to water. I wasn't long before John had dug a little ditch that diverted stream wate onto the planted field.

Annie had three jobs: tending the rabbits, feeding the chickens, an that of the farm's scarecrow. She watched over the field during the da' and set traps at night for the offending rabbits.

"You sure work hard on catching rabbits. Why is that?" sai Elizabeth, smiling at her morning's collection of small gray rabbits tha shrunk from her attention.

"I want to catch them because I don't want my rabbits to end up in stew," answered Annie, giving Elizabeth a small smile as she handed th four rabbits over for eating.

"John, you sure she isn't a boy?" she asked in jest, although she wa starting to see a trend in Annie's behavior. She was becoming more hi daughter than hers.

It wasn't long before they had the makings of a fledgling crop, sign of sprouting out in the field, and a log cabin of around 12-feet by 10-feet It wasn't much bigger than the tent. It had the benefit of not worrying s much about the wolves, which could be heard late at night singing thei sad songs.

"Once we get the cabin built, we should build a better hutch for the rabbits and chickens," said John, not realizing saying this in the middl of a wolf's rendition of a love ballad was just a bad idea. Annie and Elizabeth pushed him over the next few days into building a hutch onto the cabin that would keep the chitters safe.

They ended up staying in the tent for an extra few days because of it. They were happy with the results. "It is a fine chicken and rabbit hutch. Is it safe to stay so close to the chickens?"

He started the construction on the larger cabin the day he finished what would become the barn.

Every week or so, he would see a deer wander onto the property, after several attempts by Annie running from the field to tell John. They figured out a strategy that seemed to work. Annie watched over the fields, and when she saw a deer, she would pull on a long rope and just hold still.

"She is signaling with the rope," declared Elizabeth, already moving towards the field.

"Let me get the rifle," he said, watching the rope rise and drop to the ground over and over.

They both reached the top of the rise leading to the field to find three deer sniffing around at the ground about 100 yards out. It was a mother and two fawns. He aimed towards his targets.

"Husband?"

He shot, splitting a tree in the edge of the field in two and scaring the deer from sight.

"What, I'm not a monster," he grinned.

Water flow problems, he soon needed to build a small weir dam on his property's headwaters. Completed in a week, with the water's added benefit, it overflowed into a smaller ditch that watered the animals before returning to the river.

The food was simple in the summer. Deer was shot and smoked for later use as well as for dinner for days after. Fish when they took the bait. Eggs and flatbread for breakfast. Beans were served most meals until the potatoes ripened enough to eat. When they caught rabbits, they skinned them and either smoked the meat to preserve it or ate it for lunch; most nights, their stomachs were full.

Consortium of Acquaintances

They settled into a rhythm for the next few months as John and Elizabeth dug a terrace into the embankment and used the dirt to level the ground out where the front of the cabin would stand.

Once the walls were up, he built supports inside to use the pulley that he brought along. Taking the time to wind the rope around and back through, he tied the tree off, then wrapped the ropes around it ten times. With the help of Elizabeth and Nana, the donkey being coaxed by Annie with a switch, he rolled the three mighty pines over to where the cabin walls stood to become the roof joists. It took a day for each tree to be moved into the right place and another week to finish the walls.

He was getting up when Annie screamed, coming from outside.

He jumped from the bed, not bothering to get dressed, and barged outside, Spencer in hand. "What is it?"

"Nana is gone," she replied, sounding shaken.

"What she ran off?" he asked, with a foggy brain.

"No, John, she is dead," answered Elizabeth.

"Come quickly," said Annie, without a way of explaining that Nana had managed to break her neck in the middle of the night.

She was like a relative, so they collectively chose to take her up on the hill and lay her to rest. Annie used his carving-brace and carved Nana's name and a date on a cross.

It was legible, and that was all that mattered. John's daughter did take notice of his carvings then. He had a plan to make storm shutters and had painstakingly carved the story of his travels from the riverboat journey up the Missouri River to the Ammo wagons. Elizabeth hadn't seen them, and he planned to give them to her once he had completed them. Depending on how long, he would call it an early birthday or late anniversary present.

It wasn't long before they had a visitor, a trapper named Barbie Hanover, who showed up one night and ended up staying for three days. He came back at the end of the month with an extensive collection of furs, of which a few made a nice coat for John. They had quite a few rabbit furs that Barbie seemed interested in with him. He traded a couple of traps and knowledge on catching the mink and beaver that made their home in the area.

He explained the wolves were only in the area when they followed the deer and elk herds. He then explained that the natives used this land as a hunting camp for possibly a thousand years. "I've seen some bizarre occurrences while trapping up here. Packs of wolves numbering more than a man can count. I've seen cougars running in packs of six. I know most people say I'm crazy for passing that bit of information along. After all, cougars don't run in large packs like the wolves. But something is different about these wolves and cougars. I once saw them running together. There is a place between here and Yakima that the wolves gather. They killed a family last spring, but don't worry, they never come up this far unless they are chasing the herds."

When he mentioned Annie's family, John and Elizabeth looked at one another, then down to Annie, who was fast asleep. "I'm going to put her in bed," whispered Elizabeth, standing and, with the help of John, carried her into the cabin.

"You ever notice the Native Americans around here standing on their toes?" asked John, poking the campfire as he spoke.

"Can't say I have. You saw this with your eyes?" asked the trapper, holding a pipe between his lips.

"My eyes?" asked John, looking confused for a moment.

"I mean, did you see it," he answered.

"All of us have seen them," said John, looking off into the night as a wolf called out as if to remind them they were still around.

"Interesting. During the day, I've noticed, it's fine to hunt with a rifle, but if used too late in the day, the wolves come," he said.

It was strange having someone else around. It was even more bizarre when the trapper left without saying goodbye. "Maybe he is like George in a way. He didn't like saying goodbye either," said John.

"Maybe he is just rude and doesn't want to be invited back."

By the end of the summer, they had more company on the southern side of the creek. It was a parcel of orphan land that didn't have much use and was prone to flooding.

Consortium of Acquaintances

A hunting party of Yakamas made camp and stayed for two weeks hunting higher up into the mountains. They never bothered them, and the Springers never thought of chasing them off the land. He treated them as neighbors and waved at them as they came back each day from their hunts. He was never up when they left, so that was the only time he saw them. They noticed that these men were not as healthy as the men they had seen camping all summer long.

Elizabeth was first to point out that they walked around like everyone else, not making a point of walking on their toes.

John looked up from his work and noticed a Yakama man standing on the river bank. "Say Elizabeth, what do you reckon he is pointing at?" he asked, nodding in the hunter's direction.

"I have no idea, he was pointing towards the upper field, and I don't have the foggiest notion as to what he was saying."

"You reckon he wants us off his land?" asked Elizabeth, grabbing hold of her husband's arm.

"No, because the town is the other direction," he answered.

"Maybe, it's Drake. He lives over there," answered Annie, pointing towards where her imagery dragon lived while playing with her doll who she called Mister Nickels.

The Yakama hunting party left the next day, and life went back to normal on the farm. The days started to get longer, and the nights got colder. John put the notion of the man's warning about dragons out of his head.

Chapter 10
The afternoon of August 24th, 1873
Yakima City, Washington Territory

Late Summer in Yakima City is hot, sweltering, like folks waving fans, drinking water on the porch kind of hot. The streets were dirty and, if the wind blew, clouds of dust would find ways into every crack and crevice imaginable. A man could paint his fence in the morning and come back in the evening to see the paint sandblasted down to the wood grains.

The heat and lack of any help from mother nature put the average citizen understandably on edge. When the wind decided to blow, the relief was overshadowed by dust storms that choke the life of every living creature that encountered it. When the rain fell, it was light and caused the streets to get a thin muddy coating that made everything slick.

Inside the Northwest Mercantile, the proprietor, Mr. Charles Dumas, was no exception, having let the teenager that helped him in the afternoon go home early for no other reason than he wanted to be left alone. He hadn't seen a customer for a few hours, and somehow he liked it that way.

The likes of Barbie Hanover darkened the door left open in hopes the temperature would drop a degree or two. He dressed appropriately for his occupation as a trapper. Some would call him a mountain man. Some would dismiss him as a vagrant. Mr. Dumas was of the latter notion because, simply put, the man never brought a dime into his shop.

"Oh, do my bones hurt, my friend," announced Barbie Hanover holding his bundle of goods with both hands while twisting to see where he was going. He was the kind of man that would claim an item was twice as heavy to boost the asking price. "Oh, the work I put into this lot it's sure to bring in a nice tidy profit for your lovely store." He looked at the five sets, again trying to decide if there was a profit in making them 'If there were, there wouldn't be five sets leftover from last year.' he thought turning his attention back to the shops owner.

"I don't need anything," declared Mr. Dumas, only looking up for a few seconds before returning to his shelves to dust his wares with a black feather duster.

"Oh, you say that every time I come in here," said Barbie Hanover noticing someone had recently dusted the snowshoes.

"Yet, you still find a way to weasel some of my ammunition or my flint or my tobacco," said Mr. Dumas, pausing for as long as it took to speak and went back to work dusting the jars of fruit.

"I have quite the haul this time. Not as good as it was ten years ago although this still be a mighty fine haul," said Barbie Hanover, laying his furs onto the glass counter covering the two matching Peacemakers.

"I didn't say you could drop your goods in here," said Mr. Dumas already moving over to the counter to have a look at the trapper's wares Barbie Hanover had his bartering tactics, and he had his own.

"You know this is going to be the last year for a haul like this," stated Barbie Hanover, sounding a little crestfallen. The truth was the mountains were getting taller as he got older. He wasn't the man he used to be and felt it with each winter's passing.

"Are you planning on retiring, maybe heading off somewhere cooler?" asked Mr. Dumas, flipping through the offered furs. It occurred to him that Barbie wasn't looking healthy these days. He didn't need any animal furs unless he found one that stood out.

"No, it is getting a little crowded up my river. There are settlers planting fields in the middle of my trap line. Oh, they seemed nice enough even to invite me to sit with them for dinner both on the way up and on the way back," answered Barbie, choosing that moment to slide his pack off and lean it against the shelve of dried goods.

"They sound like nice people. Putting up with the likes of you. How is that a problem?" Mr. Dumas asked, finding a nice beaver pelt that was unusually large.

"Yes, they are growing crops and planning to have the river dammed up above their place," stated Barbie, thumbing the counter as he spoke.

"Barbie, you were still able to bring all this in," he said, stopping at a white fur briefly before quickly moving through the rest. He had found the one that would make the lot worth having. He only hoped Barbie hadn't noticed.

"You don't get it. The more people up there, the wildlife will move on or get killed to make the homesteaders slippers or whatever they want," stated Barbie, walking away from the counter in frustration. Fixating on the five sets of snowshoes, he wondered who would buy another man's snowshoes. After all, he could make a set to use for the day then break them up for kindling.

"So, how is this a problem?" asked Mr. Dumas. 'What he was wondering was, how does this affect him?' Used to changes, and change had been good in town for the most part.

"Problems, might I inquire about these problems?" asked Mayor Daniels, a short stalky man in his fifties with a face that closely resembled a buzzard.

"No problems here, Frank, Barbie was just telling stories again," said Mr. Dumas, waving the trapper over to the counter.

"Well, I love stories," said Mayor Daniels, coming into the store.

"Did you hear the one about the band of Injuns that walk on their toes?"

"No, I haven't. Where were they the last time you saw them?" asked Mayor Daniels, who looked as though he had won a prize.

"Barbie, I will give you the supplies you need if you leave now," announced Mr. Dumas, holding his hand out for the trapper to shake.

Consortium of Acquaintances

"Deal," said Barbie Hanover, spitting into his hand and grabbing Mr Dumas's hand in a firm handshake before he could jerk his appendage away. "I will be round later to pick up my supplies if that is good with you?"

"Fine," answered Mr. Dumas, wiping his hand into a bright green rag.

"Do you mind telling me what that was all about?" asked Mayor Daniels, watching the trader head outside and pick up another bundle of furs and head off to the north towards the Lucy.

"It was about him complaining about how he finds fewer and fewer critters in his traps, and I don't want to hear about it again. It is a haggling tactic. He talks until I relent. Say, maybe I should ask him to run for mayor," answered Mr. Dumas, reaching for his duster with the intention of going back to work.

Mayor Daniels just stood watching him for a moment with an internal conversation that had to do with buying Charles a drink. He walked out the door and down the boardwalk without so much as a howdy-do.

Mr. Dumas walked over to the door and glanced down the street. As he closed the door, he said, "I hope you trip and fall, you buzzard." He turned to his sweeping as the wind came up, and in the distance, he could see a dust storm coming this way.

Three blocks down, people were finishing up their business taking cover inside the saloon and anywhere that offered a little protection.

"I say, good afternoon to you, Mr. Hanover, may I speak with you if you want a touch of whiskey. I can help you, depending on if you were willing to help me?"

Barbie Hanover nodded once and motioned for him to go on.

"What you were saying to the proprietor at the mercantile?" asked Mayor Daniels, pointing at the barkeeper and raising a finger.

Barbie Hanover mashed his lips in anticipation.

"Good sir, may we have a bottle over here." He turned back to the trapper, asking, "Can you wait here? I have a man that I would like to hear your tale."

James D FarnWorth

Barbie Hanover sat bellied up to the bar after drinking five fingers of whiskey when he started to feel a little numb. It was funny, he never thought of himself as a lightweight, but here he was, almost unconscious. It had been thirty minutes since the mayor had requested that Barbie wait for the mayor's man to come. So he could complain about his troubles. He was beginning to wonder if he should call a full retreat before a need to call for his complete surrender, and by surrender, he was about to hit the floor and await someone to cart him away to sleep it off in the alley.

"Are you feeling your drink, Mr. Hanover?" asked Mayor Daniels, propping the old trapper up for the moment.

"I'm in need of a Doctor," he managed to get out. "This liquor sure, hic*, sure, does taste funny."

"Well, here is the man that I wanted you to talk to," said Mayor Daniels, motioning over to a darker-complected man who had been sitting in the corner.

"Finally, hic*, where you been, boy?" asked Barbie, belching his words.

"Take Mr. Hanover to the wagon?" asked Mayor Daniels, winking at his man, one Thomas Drake. He was the mayor's specialist in all things rotten.

"Come on, old-timer. We will find you someplace to lie you to rest," said Drake.

"Are you of Yakama stock?" asked Barbie, putting his arm over the tall man's shoulders.

"I'm what whites call an Eskimo," answered Drake.

"Well, you look Injun, hic*, what do they call you?"

"Drake," he answered, loading the older man into the wagon.

"Well, Drake, you and I can be friends. I like all kinds of people. Just get me some more of that whiskey, it's so good, hic* please."

Drake walked back into the saloon. No one had even noticed him take the old trapper out to the wagon. He didn't fall under the sign over the mirror behind the bottles shelved behind the bar, barring Native Americans and Mexicans from coming into the Lucy Saloon. He worked for the mayor, and no one crossed Mayor Daniels.

Consortium of Acquaintances

"What is it you want me to do to the man?" asked Drake solemnly.

"Ride him up and down the street until 5 o'clock this afternoon ar then head out of town towards the west until you can't travel any furth and find out where he saw the settlers, then you know what to do."

"I have my shovel this time," said Drake, pulling his gloves over h knuckles.

Barbie Hanover became just a memory. He was missed only b Charles, whose inquiries into the missing trapper went un-investigate Weeks later, even he lost interest, finally restocking Barbie's goods ar supplies.

Chapter 11
Fall, 1873
Springer Ranch, Washington Territory

The Springer Ranch, as Annie had named it, was the little depression of land that her adopted family had made their home in just six short months. When they first came upon the property in April, the hillsides teamed with wild game, and rivers held an alarming amount of trout.

They knew then that this land could be cultivated, compared to most of the places they had seen since crossing the Great Divide. In April, the snow was still high up in the Cascades; by late June, it had retreated under the north-facing ridges of the upper elevations. Then by July, the snow seemed to disappear almost overnight. The green grasses began drying up and turned a light tan as the long hot summer days took their toll.

The creek began to dry up in August, but it kept just enough flow to keep the farm irrigated to the Springers' delight. He sat looking at the creek one night and turned to Elizabeth, saying, "We need to build a series of ponds in the upper valley. It will help with flooding, and in times of drought, we can open the ponds up and feed our needs."

He began that day, making the first of many. He knew that there wouldn't be a chance of filling the ponds this year, but that was of no concern. If he started when the crops were in the field, he could use his spare time for pond building that he usually spent carving his wife's storm shutters.

Consortium of Acquaintances

She married the dreamer, designer, and achiever. She wished the past didn't creep its way back into her thoughts. She didn't understand what was making her sad as the days grew shorter. She seemed to grow distant, but John and Annie didn't notice what bothered her the most.

They watched as the snow returned into the upper elevations. Even their little charge noticed each morning, Annie begged her foster parent to take a walk up there and play in the snow. "Please, can we go? It is just right up there, it can't be that far?" she asked, looking up at her father with puppy dog eyes.

"Annie, I already told you, we can't," replied Elizabeth, holding her arms out for the little one. "There is just too much to do around here."

"It is not as near as you imagine. That is close to 30 miles there and back. Not to mention, the snow will come to us if you give it time," said John, holding out his arms for Annie, who was already jumping into his lap.

Elizabeth could see that Annie was becoming her daddy's girl and wished she could have made the same connection that her husband had made. She felt rejected watching them work on the farm. She did her best, even though hard work wasn't her strong suit. Every noise in the forest caused her to jump and John to investigate. The short days were becoming more noticeable, and the nights only made the fear come alive.

"Daddy, will the trees turn colors?" asked Annie, releasing him and returning to her chair.

"Some they turn yellow, some lose their leaves altogether. However, most of the trees around here stay green all year long. If you watch, you can see the signs already that winter is coming," he answered, looking over to his wife, who seemed to be brewing something behind her false smile.

"Like the creek drying up and the grass on the hill turning brown," said Annie.

"And the birds heading south," added Elizabeth, returning from wherever her mind had sent her to smile at her husband.

"The trees in the distance that are turning yellow," said John cutting the last of his meat and shoving it into his waiting mouth.

"And temp-pour-achew," added Annie looking from parent to parent as they laughed.

"Temperature," corrected Elizabeth looking over at Annie.

"Yes, you are right, as the temperature drops, we will edge that much closer to winter. The night becomes longer, and the days shorter. This also brings me back to my point that we need to be in the field gathering our crops and digging up our potatoes that we grew this summer," said John, looking over to his wife for some support. She was thinking about the past again. He could tell because she would get that look of sadness that came in the form of a false smile. Her depression was contagious, but he dared not let on.

A few weeks later, on the night of the first frost, the Springers rested, having worked hard to bring their crops in as they readied their cabin for winter with wood, split and stacked, making a tall wall on the windward side of the house. They weatherized the walls with a clay and straw mixture found along the stream bank and painstakingly brought up in the water buckets. It wasn't the first time they would miss Nana, and it wouldn't be the last.

John often wondered how his donkey had died. They supposed it was a cougar that scared her so bad she jumped into a tree, breaking her neck. It was like most mysteries around a farm. It would have to wait to be solved until the work was done.

The meat locker had turned out nicely, standing twenty feet tall with a small box large enough for their needs. It was ready for deer and elk that seemed to frequent their little valley and the valley northwest from their homestead. John looked forward to filling the locker once the temperature dropped below 30 degrees. They smoked the meat on a low flame close to the river and away from their house until then.

The shed that they once called home stored 300 pounds of potatoes in roof bins, dried meats, and yams. They were well underway to declaring their homestead a success. He sat on the porch after dinner and rested his feet up on his carving stand.

Consortium of Acquaintances

"I see you're hard at work, husband," said Elizabeth playfully as she strolled out of the cabin. The sky was orange and had traces of red, herald of some distant fire.

"Yeah, I am just enjoying the evening," he said, resting his pipe between his lips.

"Why do you still suckle the pipe when you are free of the need of tobacco?" she asked, coming to a rest next to him on the bench made from a half-sawn log.

The carving stand that his boot rested on was built and designed for John's needs as a woodcarver. He had made the dishes, bowls, and utensils, both big and small. For the farm, he used the table to hold the handles that he carved.

"Should we be worried about the sky?"

"What about the sky?" he said, looking up for the first time. "Oh well, I suppose we need to glance around. Examine clouds for signs of smoke." He looked around and sniffed the air.

She watched him in silence as he looked around and sniffed the air.

"If it is a fire, it is 50 miles from here. If we start seeing animals running and smelling fire, we will worry."

"You are always scientific about how you see the world."

"I try to be observant and then act logically when I approach a problem," he said, looking into her eye, seeing the reflection of the sky inside, making her eyes seem as though they were aflame.

"I sometimes believe you are too good for me. You never give up," whispered Elizabeth.

"Look at how far we have come, leaving St Louis in the middle of the night. We steamed up the Missouri River by mountain boat, jumping and found our way back to Fort Benton. We crossed the Rocky Mountains on wagons full of explosives to end up here sitting on this porch, watching this beautiful sunset in your eyes, and you know what?"

"I have no idea what my charming husband is about to say next," she answered, letting a genuine smile replace the fake one she had been wearing for days, if not weeks.

"I couldn't have done it without you."

Tears welled up in her eyes, and the sadness faded for now. She could tell he meant every word. She had learned the skill from Mags years ago. "You know what you should do?"

"What's that beautiful wife?"

"Write a book about our adventures," she answered, choosing that moment to kiss him.

He thought about it for a moment before dropping his pipe into his empty tobacco pouch and turning to his wife. He asked, "I wonder how George is fairing?" It was an apparent change in the subject.

"I was asking myself that a few days ago," she answered, leaning into her man's shoulder.

"I asked, do you think of George a lot?"

"No, just when I need to bath," she answered, remembering that George wasn't one she wished to stand behind in any line.

"So all the time then," laughed John as they started to run.

"Springer, you come to bed smelling of tree sap and sawdust almost every night, and you suggest I am dirty. Maybe, instead of carving your trinkets, you should carve us a bathtub," yelled Elizabeth, turning as the cabin door swung open.

Annie came running out of the cabin as Elizabeth stood in front of John. He had his back up against the shed. In her hand was a bucket of water. She was aiming to get her daddy John wet.

"Take it back," she demanded as she swirled the bucket of water in a somewhat threatening manner. She looked into the bucket and smiled at her husband. It was a different smile than before. He was about to get wet.

"Oh, I apologize that I suggested you think of George all the time," he said, smiling over at Annie as the contents of the bucket were let loose into his chest and neck.

"Oh, you are going to get it," he warned as he began chasing his wife around the little yard.

"You two are so funny," yelled Annie, as she watched daddy John pick her mommy off her feet.

Consortium of Acquaintances

"You are the cleanest woman I know," he exclaimed as he wrapped his arms around her in a loving embrace. Suppressing a smile that he harbored away.

"I'm the only woman you know, let alone the only one you have seen in six months," she said, hugging her man once again, breathing hard into his chest.

"Oh, well, then you are the most beautiful I have ever kissed."

"I'm not sure how many women you've kissed, but I will assume the number is in the hundreds."

He laughed.

She glared.

He stopped.

They headed inside once the last of the sunlight faded from the sky. A short time later, the cabin's three windows were like a beacon in the night, slowly dimmed, and only the half-moon in the sky lit the small dale.

Upon the hillside stood two men dressed in dark clothing. They had watched them for a few days now. They saw them bring the crops in and store the fruits of their labor into the little barn. They saw the chicken coop that had been built.

"I apologize," muttered one of the men.

**

Darkened windows glistening with condensation flickered the reflection of two candles and an oil lamp. Such was life after the sun disappeared behind the tall ridges with overhung snowy caps. Winter was coming, and the Springers bundled up inside their finished cabin.

John sat at the table scraping the last few bites of his second helping of dinner while Elizabeth and Annie worked out a stitch that his wife was in the process of teaching the little one.

He was starting to get a handle on farming, hunting, fishing, and most importantly, being a father. He hadn't thought about raising a family. The first of the summer, he wondered if it was right to keep

Annie. He had thought about hiking into town. Walking up to the sheriff to ask if he knew anyone was looking for her. As the months went on, that thought faded as he saw how important she became in both their lives.

"No, that isn't quite right. It is important because when you do it correctly, it sets you up for the next stitch without offering a loose thread," said Elizabeth, with more patience than he would have given her credit.

"Like this?" asked Annie, obviously losing her patience. The frustration was apparent in her responses.

"Yes," answered Elizabeth, "that is correct, now see how the next stitch, its already started?" She helped her complete a couple of stitches and handed her the needle and thread.

"Yes, I reckon I do understand now," answered Annie, giving Elizabeth a long affectionate hug and taking the fabric and returning to her chair.

He finished his supper and cleaned his bowl out with a small spoon. He was looking forward to carving tonight. He had almost completed the second window's shutter. He had carved each night to make something special for his wife. On each slat, a reminder of their adventure coming out west. Starting from the day, they met to escaping the Blue Wave to their trip onboard the steam-powered boat, the River Lady. It was a mountain paddle boat that they had worked on for six weeks. It took a while convincing the captain that having the extra crew on the way back was terrible for business. Then the Mullan Road and shipping the two explosive wagons for Fort Benton to Fort Walla Walla. In his carving, he was halfway down the Mullan Road.

"Whatcha pondering?" asked Annie, looking up at her adopted father. He had an awkward smile as if he thought something was funny.

"Oh, how it will be good to carve for a while tonight," replied John, leaning over the counter to grab a little piece of cloth to wipe his hands.

"What's that?" asked Annie, pointing at the window.

He looked and didn't see anything.

Consortium of Acquaintances

"Husband!" shouted Elizabeth as she looked out from a different angle.

"What is it?" he replied, turning to the woman of the house and standing up, knocking the chair into the corner.

"John, get yourself outside!" she exclaimed, standing and letting everything drop from her lap.

He picked up his rifle and started for the door but stopped when he noticed the flames licking at the sides of the barn. He sat his rifle back on the table. "Get pans and the bucket, and I will grab my shovel," he said as he disappeared out the door and around the side of the new cabin.

"Here," responded Elizabeth, giving a bucket to Annie and following John outside.

As soon as they were outside together, they pulled water from the creek and threw it on the flames. It wasn't long, and they realized just how useless it was becoming because there was no hope to save the barn.

"Look up there," said Elizabeth pointing to the embers floating toward the new cabin.

"Start putting out the embers that make it to the roof," he said coughing as he ran around their home to climb onto the roof. The cabin was built into the earth on the windward side. He had let the contours of the landscape fill in three of the walls. The roof of a thatchy sod of the meadow would burn if it were dry enough.

He used his shovel to put out two small blazes on the roof before checking on his wife. She was splashing buckets of water on the porch. Annie was using hers to put out tiny ember starts on the sides of the cabin.

They both carried up buckets from the creek and helped whenever John asked. He turned and had to put out a couple more upstarts before he could come down and survey the damage.

"The fire is almost out," declared Elizabeth, splashing the porch with the contents of her bucket.

"Let's have a look at it."

"Are the chickens all right?"

"Stay over by the house, Annie," he stated, stopping next to the chicken coop. He could tell the chickens were dead, and the rabbits that shared the yard with the chickens were missing.

"What about the goats and rabbits?" asked Annie in a tone that suggested a fit was coming on.

"No, the goats must have broken out, and the rabbits got out of a small hole in the enclosure. Fire is a strong motivator," he answered, holding up his hand, asking her to wait before throwing herself to the ground.

"Well, at least we can catch them again?"

"I suppose," answered John, walking to the barn that they once called home for the last few months.

"Is all the food gone?" asked Elizabeth, taking a step forward, forcing herself to stay back.

"All the potatoes on the top layer are burnt, although it seems a couple of layers down they are just cooked on one side. So they will need to be used first."

"Nothing else, husband?" asked Elizabeth, leaning a little closer when he glanced back in her direction.

"No, I will need to make handles for the tools again, at least the ones that were in the barn," replied John, picking up the burnt remains of a hoe.

"What happened?" asked Elizabeth, standing still a ways away.

"Maybe the lamp fell?" he whispered, moving closer.

"How did that happen? Did you leave it lit?"

"I don't know," he answered. He had left the lamp on more than one occasion, and so did his wife. He looked back, and both of them were sitting exhausted on the log bench on the porch.

"Pardon me," she apologized as she folded her arms around Annie.

"It wasn't anyone's fault. The lamp broke. I'm not sure how it fell from the table," said John, moving his eyes over to the fallen chickens.

"What do we do now?" asked Annie.

"We pluck chickens and clean them, most of them we will eat over the next couple of days; the rest we will smoke and eat over the next couple of weeks," he stated, opening the burnt coop that was attached t the barn.

"Well, let's get started," said Elizabeth, standing up and heading fo her kitchen to get what they needed.

"Are you going to be all right helping with the chickens?" aske John, looking towards Annie.

"As long as none of the rabbits are dead, I am fine with pulling th feathers off the chickens," answered Annie frankly, pulling a large pa from under the bench and walking over, holding it out for someone t load it with chicken carcasses.

Chapter 12
November 26th, 1873
Springer Ranch, Washington Territory

Building the cabin and bringing the first crop in was nothing compared to that of losing the barn. It was like getting kicked in the gut by a mule on your birthday.

As they salvaged the chickens, John went about making extra racks for the smokehouse. He looked over at the burned-out ruins of the cabin. He was wondering if this was the end of their dream to be self-reliant. Would he be able to feed his family this winter?

The course was set. John would need to go to town and be back before winter set in. He would need to buy beans and rice for the next few months. There were other things that they needed to survive. What concerned him the most was the cost of the supplies.

"The money is almost all gone," he said. He walked to the waterfall, as Annie calls it. A place where the stream dropped a foot or two in three stages. "What will I do?"

"What will you do about what?" asked Annie, startling him.

"Never sneak up on a man while he is contemplating, girl," he admonished. He wasn't furious. He could never be mad at such a beautiful child who brightened a room just by walking into it.

"Pardon me for I was concerned about you," she apologized, walking over and hugging him around the waist.

"Funny you should say that I'm also fretted about you, and Elizabeth, and the farm, and the price of tea in Scotland.

Consortium of Acquaintances

"Why tea, why not kilts?" she asked.

"Just a little joke," he whispered, finally returning her hug.

"I was consta-plating about our problems."

"I was contemplating, also," he said kindly, smiling and putting on what he believed was a brave face.

"If we need supplies, we should go get some," said Annie.

"How would we buy these supplies? With your good looks?" he asked, almost sounding as if he was upset.

"No, I was reckoning you could sell something," she said.

"Such as?" he asked. He was intrigued at how simplistic Annie saw the problem and the answer. 'If only she could help,' he thought.

"I was wondering if we could sell Miss Elizabeth's present. They appear to be valuable, and I'm sure someone could use shutters," she said, putting on what could be interpreted as a brave face.

He mulled it over, first dismissing the idea then again resurrecting it just as quickly. "No, there is only one shutter that could be useful. What we need is several items to sell," he said, staring into Annies' big green eyes.

"I'm sorry," she apologized, feeling as though she had failed.

"No, Annie, you have nothing to be fretting about," he said as he knelt and matched her height. He ran his fingers through her hair and pulled it away from her eyes, all the while smiling.

"What are you happy about?" asked Annie, leaning her head to one side with the oddest look upon her face.

"You saved us, Annie. Let's go tell Elizabeth," answered John, grabbing her by the hand and heading off back to the cabin.

Elizabeth sat at the table, looking at the shutter, pondering how it would save them. He pulled a few slats from his bag and laid them on the table. "What do you see?" he asked.

"A crazy man with some carvings," chuckled Elizabeth, looking over at Annie as she spoke.

"Valuable carvings."

"But not as a shutter," said John, arranging them as a square.

She leaned forward to get a better view, "A picture frame?" she asked, tilting her head to the side as if to get a better point of view. She finally looked up at him for the answer.

He nodded, "The corners don't match, and if I cut them, so they match, it would ruin the carving," he said, pointing at an elk on the carving closest to him.

"So what will we do?" she asked, running her finger across a horse on one of the carvings.

"We make corners for the pieces, and I take them to town and glue them together. Sell them to whoever wants them," answered John with a small grin and reaching over and ruffling Annie's hair.

"I forget you're so talented," she said, looking a little glum.

"Why are you sad?" asked Annie, moving closer.

"I didn't get you anything or have time to make you anything. All I have given you is grief for wasting so much time with your little carvings. All the while, you were making something for me," replied Elizabeth, sniffling and wiping tears from her eyes.

"Well, if it helps, I don't have anything for you now," he laughed and reached for her hand.

"It is a good idea, and yes, it does help," she blew her nose and looked over at the carving in his hand. John, can I keep that one," she asked. It was of the place she once felt like a lady and where she had started to feel safe for the first moment of her life.

He flipped it over and handed her that one and others of equal emotional weight. "I thought you might want these. We can make a frame for the photo in the chest." He was referring to the picture they took on the River Lady.

"Brilliant!" she exclaimed.

"It was Annie's idea," he laughed.

"Well, we already know she is brilliant," declared Elizabeth, finally breaking out into a smile.

For the next few weeks, they ate smoked chicken and potatoes before they spoiled. The frames looked perfect, Annie and Elizabeth cut the pieces to make the corners, and he added four matching animals carved

on each corner. Once they had enough corners, they laid them out, ar
they looked beautiful.

"Husband, you really made something here. You say this was mea
to be a shutter?"

"Yes, it was supposed to be a Christmas present," replied Joh
flipping the slat over in his hand.

"What do we do next?" asked Annie.

"Next, we build a raft, like the trappers use to go back to Yakin
City. I can launch it right here and be in town in less than a day
answered John, again with that spark he got when he was making a pla
for them to follow.

"It sounds like you have it all planned out," she said, showing him
brave smile all the while her insides were screaming in fear.

"You are going to leave us here, alone?" asked Annie, already with
pouting face.

"Only for a few days, maybe a week. Depending on how soon I ca
get there and get back. Besides, you will have it easy here, and it will b
safer," John replied, taking them both by the hands and leaning over an
kissing Elizabeth.

"I've heard that before," whispered Annie, looking even glummer.

The next day, he opened his Settlers Bible, a book on all things t
know about settling the land. He had noticed that more than once,
looked as if the later chapters were unfinished and, unfortunately, raft
were in the before mentioned sections. "Rubbish," he said, closing th
book and looking over to his wife.

"So, what knowledge can be gleaned from the text?"

"The definition of a raft and where you might need one, along wit
several knot suggestions," he answered, flipping back to the page an
showing it to his wife.

"Well, at least, you know what knots to use," laughed Elizabeth.

"It literally redirects me to see Knots, page 63."

"Well, there you go, we will have a raft in no time," she stated
letting her eyes wander over the page.

"Except the drawings are not clear and the directions say to see Illustration next page. So I suppose there will be a lot of trial and error," he said, closing the book with an audible thunk.

"Then we work it out, and we get the supplies, you can do it, you can do anything," cheered Annie, this time walking over and hugging him around the waist.

"Thank you, you're right, we need this, and I will figure it out, we will figure it out," he corrected himself, letting a sneeze out that nearly knocked him to the floor.

The next morning, he woke up before the break of dawn. He was determined to use every hour of daylight available. He was out the door and into the southern tree line as the sun peeked over the horizon. He wouldn't see the sun for almost two hours due to the high hills and low valleys that scarred the landscape.

He was looking for cedar trees about seven inches in diameter. John would have liked to use larger poles, but he simply could not bring the number of trees back to camp in the time allotted. As it would turn out, the stream wasn't deep enough to use anything more extensive. He coughed several times heading out, but he was coughing regularly by the time he had the material for the raft.

"John?"

"Yes, my love," he answered, coughing after he addressed her, all the while removing the bark and limbs from the trees.

"Come inside and have some lunch," she demanded.

"No, thank you, I need to finish up this part by nightfall."

"It wasn't a request. We can limb and debark the poles. You have some lunch and get warm. You're looking downright pasty," she admonished and then stared at him until he handed over the ax.

He took off one last piece of bark before heading into the cabin. It was more of a point of pride to say, 'you don't scare me.' An act of defiance even though he wasn't even sure she noticed. "Love you," he said as he paused in the doorway. He tried to kiss her but coughed over her shoulder instead.

"You made a wise choice, John."

"Coming inside?" he asked, turning back to her.

"Not coughing in my face," she laughed, walking over to the ben and dragging one end out to use as a brace.

He nodded his approval from the window before heading to the tal where a bowl of soup was waiting for him. He picked it up from table, choosing to sip the soup in front of the fire.

With the help of her charge, Elizabeth cleaned the logs and was the house before sundown. "We are done!" exclaimed Annie, runni inside the door just ahead of her mother.

"We thought you would have come out after lunch. However, as turned out, we didn't need you," said Elizabeth as she closed the do and pulled three sweaters over her head, first a blue, then a red, and last yellow one leaving her in a sleeved undershirt. She looked up to s Annie standing between the fireplace and her husband.

"He doesn't look so good. He might be dead," said Annie.

Elizabeth's heart skipped a beat and hurried to his side, reaching f his stomach checking for fever and other signs of life.

"Honey, John, John!" she yelled, only to see an eye twitch ar turning upwards to notice her.

"Well, at least he is alive," said Annie, moving off and sitting dow in her mom's chair.

"Don't sit down, go fill the bucket with snow; we need to warm u some water for pine needle tea. It will help with your cough," state Elizabeth before bringing a cloth towel and warm water over to clea him up some.

Soon the tea was ready, and he was at least talking, although he wa not himself, "I just need a little rest," he coughed twice and sipped hi tea.

"You were unconscious until a few minutes ago," said Elizabeth excitedly using a cloth to dry his forehead. "You had a fever. You're staying put, you hear me."

He tried to rise to his feet. "What the hell," he muttered, looking down and seeing a mess of knots holding him into his chair. "When di you have time to tie me down, woman."

"John, you were delirious and probably still are. You have been asleep for several hours, and we have had this conversation twice. So you just sit there and when you're ready, just untie yourself."

He sat there for a few minutes, mulling over her words. Generally, holding his tongue knowing full well, there wasn't anything he could say once Elizabeth had made up her mind. He reached down and could feel the knot and slipped his left hand, pulling the rope, loosening the knot, and letting it fall to the side. He followed the other rope down the side of the chair to find it. This one would only be loosened with one hand. He was tired and decided to rest for a few minutes.

"John, are you in the mood to eat something?" she asked.

"Now, don't distract me from my task. I need to untie the rope." He felt the knot on his lap that had been retied. "When did you have time to retie the knot? I just untied it," he said, looking over at her and Annie at the table, noticing Elizabeth pointing at the giggling Annie.

"She tied it back up about an hour ago, after you fell asleep again," announced Elizabeth, pointing at his lap.

Still pale as a sheet, he looked down and then glanced back up sometime later, saying, "I would like to eat, woman, untie me from this chair."

"John, you're not tied to the chair," she laughed, smiling cheerfully.

He looked down and felt the ropes, and they were tight. So he attempted to stand, and bindings were just tucked under his legs. They fell away as he stood up.

"I told you that you were out of it," she said, taking a sip of her tea.

"Are you feeling better?" asked Annie, who was eating on the other side of the table nearest the window.

"Yes, I still don't believe I should overeat; my stomach is feeling under the weather."

Using the wooden spoon, his wife filled a small bowl and set it in front of him. "Well, eat a little, and then you can head to bed."

"I need to eat and finish the logs. They need the limbs removed and debarked," said John.

"We did it already," declared Annie.

Consortium of Acquaintances

"The sun went down hours ago. How are you feeling?" she asked, taking another sip of tea.

John moved to the table and sat down to enjoy a bowl of soup. "Fair to middling, I reckon. How long have I been asleep?"

That night, he lay in his bed, coughing and turning over and over, never really finding the spot that was just comfortable to fall asleep. He woke up tired and spent the day warm inside while Elizabeth and Annie took care of the chores. It went on that way for almost a week until Elizabeth and Annie opened the door and drug in two logs and a bundle of rope. "What is going on here?"

"I know you have been contemplating on heading outside and lashing the raft together. Well, unless you want to spend the next few days tied to the bed, you will just make do in here learning your knots you want to use on the raft," replied Elizabeth, handing him the bundle of rope.

"Well, this is smart," he said, reaching out for the rope and pulling up a chair. "Can you get me the homesteader book? Maybe I can figure out what knots they used from the drawings?"

She pointed to their foster daughter, adding, "It was her idea." She moved to their small library and removed the thick book. "She has been helping out around here since you have been sick."

"You will figure it out," said Annie, "and I'm glad you are feeling better." She walked around a chair and pushed it over closer before turning it around to face John's project. She then plopped herself into the chair to watch him work.

It took a couple of hours, and he had all but one knot figured out. He decided at that point to take his wife's advice and keep resting. As for the weather, the mountain tops seemed to have more snow each morning, making them stand forth as white monoliths contrasted to the deep blue skies. The sun hung low, casting long shadows that moved with the wind.

Day after day, the snow moved down the mountainsides until the hilltops around the cabin were covered in snow. It had not snowed at their elevation, but everyone knew that winter was coming.

"It's cold, are sure you want to be going outside today?" asked Annie.

"I'm fine, and I need to lash the raft together before the weather worsens, or I will be doing it in the snow," he replied, slipping out the door and looking around at the sky and the hills noticing all the sudden changes of winter's approach.

He lashed the raft together by dinner and even moved it closer to the stream bank. It floated and only took a little effort to pull it out far enough to test the buoyancy.

He noticed Annie standing not ten feet from him on the bank. "What is your opinion of the raft?" he asked, tying it to a tree and turning back to the little one.

"It appears to be like the old trapper's raft. Will it make it to that town?" said Annie, who walked over and stepped onto the raft.

"I should hope so," John replied, laughing a little.

"It took him two hours to build it," said Annie.

"He knew how to build one; the next time I build one, it will take less time. It's a little like that stitch that Elizabeth was teaching you to use. Once you understood how to do it and the importance of each step, you don't take hardly any time to do it."

"I don't understand why you gotta' leave us here alone, pappy?" Annie asked, trying another nickname on him in hopes to strum at his heartstrings and let them go to town with him. Her lower lip plumped up.

"With the cold weather and us losing the crops in the fire, someone needs to buy some supplies and bring them back here," he answered, strapping down the last box.

"I know," she muttered with the beginning of a sob letting her lower lip slip between her teeth. She had thoughts of her father leaving her mother and her at a train station to fend for themselves. She sobbed because she couldn't put her feelings into words. He hadn't gone away, and she already missed him.

"Now, Annie, you have to be brave for your ma. She will need you to look out for her and the whatnots around the farm," said John, crossing the yard and scooping his daughter up and spinning her around. Her sobs broke out into a case of the giggles.

"What's going on out here that could not be accomplished in front of the warm fire?" asked Elizabeth, using the tone reserved for mothers and sisters of the Catholic faith.

By the tone of her words, he lowered his daughter to the ground, then they both walked back into the cabin.

"Are you packed?" his wife asked, knowing the answer but feeling the need to be involved.

"Yes, I am planning on departing in the morning, shouldn't be gone more than a few days, and..." he stopped watching as the rays of light from setting sunset Elizabeth's reddish-brown hair aflame.

"You're so pretty," he said shyly, reminding her of the day they had met; it seemed a lifetime ago.

"Springer, what has gotten into you?" she asked, playfully slapping her husband with a rag as if he were a stranger on the street.

Annie giggled at the performance.

"Annie, it's time for bed," whispered John, taking his wife in his arms and planting a kiss on her lips.

Chapter 13
December 19th, 1873
Springer Ranch, Washington Territory

Elizabeth and Annie sat on the porch, observing John as he worked on the raft. He placed the crates in the middle of the raft and stepped off. He was concerned about balance and readjusted the cargo several times.

"Why are you spending so much time moving the crates around?" asked his wife, tucking her knees up to her chest and wrapping her blanket around both of them.

"You're warm," whispered Annie.

The wind called out and what it was saying was winter was coming. Elizabeth knew what it meant, Annie felt the chill, and John knew what he must do if they were to survive.

"It must be less than 40 degrees this morning," he said, stretching his arms back. He meant to have gone earlier in the month, although his health wouldn't allow him. The moist air of October and the hard work had led to a nasty cold that was more of an annoyance than anything. Still, Elizabeth refused to let him go while he was sick. She had often seen how a simple cold led to pneumonia, and pneumonia usually led to death.

"Do you have all the money?"

"No. I do have enough that I can get a place to stay and some supplies," John answered, patting his waist where he had sewn it into his watch pocket. "The way I figure it, I sell them, or I will buy what I can and get back here even if it means having to head back down next month."

"But," retorted Elizabeth.

"Don't worry, I can sell the frames and get what we need." he said, "then make my way back up here."

"Do you have the list?"

"Yes," replied John while he pulled at the crates, checking if they were secure.

"Do you want Mister Nickels to go with you?" asked Annie, holding out her doll with two nickels that were used as buttons on the doll's vest. "He has money."

"No, you keep him," he answered, walking back to the porch.

"Are you ready?"

"Yes, I need to leave while the weather is still above freezing," he said, looking up at the bright sun.

"Wish I could come," whispered Annie, who started to pout.

"You know I do too, and you know that. Yet, there is no way I'm taking both of you on the raft's maiden voyage," he answered. As the words left his mouth, he wished he could have taken them back.

"It's not really safe, is it?" asked Annie with tear-soaked eyes.

"Yes, however, that is why I balanced the load. I can control the raft better this way. Once I do it a couple of times, then we can do it together," he answered, looking at Elizabeth's worried eyes.

"You better be careful and remember I need shoes," she said, reminding him again and holding Mister Nickels tightly in what would have been a death grip if he were alive.

"You need warm clothes," warned Elizabeth, grabbing her and pulling her into her loving grasp.

"Shoes, shoes most of all, real shoes," reminded Annie again, holding up her plank sandals, which like the name suggests, were carved from wood that did little to keep her feet warm.

"Yes, new shoes for you," he replied with a smile, holding out his arms for both of them.

"Daddy John, I had a dream about you and George. You can trust him; he will do what is right, eventually," declared Annie, looking up at both her foster parents.

"I will take it under advisement," kissing them both, Elizabeth on the lips and Annie on her forehead as he pushed off. He watched as they followed him for a while.

Truthfully, he had no idea if his plan was safe. Last April, he watched a trapper use the river to get down out of the hills. All he knew was he was a better swimmer than either of them and didn't want to lose them over a trip to town.

"I didn't even know she knew George," he said, looking one last time at the little valley he called home before slipping into the trees and basalt formations.

The plan was simple: he pushed off with his pole and let the current do the work. Only he hadn't realized that the current would not take him over three sandbars. Three times, he stepped off the raft into water that had been snow an hour ago, walking along, guiding the raft over each obstacle.

It took an hour to make it the first couple of miles. "Next time, I'm going to build the raft at the last sand bar," he said aloud.

Not far beyond the last sand bar, the stream narrowed and picked up speed. Whitecaps replaced the ripples. He bounced off large rocks covered with frost that was in his way and slowed his progress.

"Wow, now we are talking," he yelled as the stream flowed into the much larger Tieton River.

The raft crafted from cedar and 100 feet of rope lashed tightly with 90 knots creaked as the rapids twisted and turned through the tight canyon. The current always threatened to toss him from the raft as quickly as Annie tossed Mr. Nichols into the air.

"I'm never telling Eliza about this," he yelled over the sound of the rapids. He was having the time of his life. He felt for rocks with the 12-foot pole held tight by his hands made strong from the years of carving back in St. Louis, and the last six months of farming only made his muscles more defined.

When the water slowed, he watched the old-growth pines sway in the wind. He could even hear the creaking the trees made as the cold wind from the higher country blew down through the ravines that seemed to open up to the north and south.

About the time he started getting comfortable, the river would begin to drop in elevation, and the canyon walls would close in, rocking the raft once again. He had learned quickly that he needed to hold on for his life.

Around a point on the map named Wolf Bend, the river settled down once more, turning calm as glass reflecting the morning sun. He took advantage by sitting on his cargo and pulling his pipe out, wishing he still had tobacco to smoke. It seemed comforting somehow to leave the pipe between his lips even when it wasn't lit.

He was drenched in the freezing mists of the Tieton River. His bear coat was frosted but was keeping him warm. He sat for a few minutes catching his breath and talking to himself. He had always had conversations with himself. "How else would a man figure stuff out by himself?" he asked the trees.

He waited for the answer and noticed an elk overlooking the strange contraption floating down the river. "Hello," he called out. The elk turned and disappeared only to let loose a rockfall sending rocks into the water and splashing John and his little raft.

"Well, that's refreshing," he said, looking back at Wolf Bend.

"At least the wolves are not here to greet me as they were last spring on our way in," he said. As if by cue, he heard what sounded like a ghost on the wind. It sent chills through him, and he steered the raft to the other side of the river.

Paying too much attention to where they had spent the first night with Annie caused him to almost flip the raft. In hindsight, he would wonder if he could have done anything about the three-foot drop, which was only a guess as he was holding on for his life.

The raft went almost vertical, and he thought his life was over. Just when he was about to take his first lung full of water, the raft righted itself after scraping the bottom.

"Now, Eliza, that's why you take the time to balance your raft," he yelled as he looked back at the waterfall and exclaimed, "Yahoo!" The word echoed three or so times before the sound from the river seemed to swallow his words.

"It truly is an exciting time to be alive. Yes, it is," said John, finding it was just easier to answer himself.

He smiled at how far he had dropped in the last waterfall. Then the smile dropped from his face as he came near the Olson's last camp. He wondered how much Annie remembered from that night.

He could see the small tree Annie had spent the night in, waiting for someone to come to the rescue.

He was happy to have her in their lives. However, how she came to be theirs was no way for any child to lose her family.

As he passed the camp, he could see that someone had done the Christian thing and buried the family's remains. As he floated by where the family was massacred, eight mounds of melon-sized Basalt rocks memorialized by eight crosses not far from the water's edge.

He hadn't gotten a straight answer from Annie about that night. When asked, she would begin to cry and change the subject. He guessed it was her story to tell, and he was a patient man. He believed she would tell her story when the time was right.

He had felt guilty for not staying and fighting off the wolves and burying the Olsons. "I had my wife and my newly acquired ward to consider," he said in a half-whisper, knowing the real reason was he was scared for his life as well as his family's. He knew no one would ever blame him for leaving them. He felt regret just the same.

He also noticed the camp had been picked clean; however, that was the way of the west. "Give a man a Christian burial and say a few words over his grave. Next thing you know, you're loading up all of his assets," he yelled, the word "assets" starting a new echo before the raft began to buck from end to end.

He looked up to see another set of rapids, and as he recalled, these were the last set before the river flowed into the Naches River. It was swift but manageable.

Consortium of Acquaintances

About an hour from where the river forked, he passed the abandoned fort; it looked like a large basket from a distance.

Where the Naches River dumped into the Yakima River, he knew he was making his final approach into Yakima City. John reached down and tugged at the bindings of the cargo. He worried that he wouldn't have enough money to purchase the supplies needed to make it through the winter if he lost his frames.

The only choice he would have is to take a loan out on the land. "Heck, no," he yelled.

If only he had known that a large tree had fallen into the river, he would have been prepared and gotten out early and walked the last four miles to town.

Clearing the last rapids seemed easy as to what blocked most of the river. Grabbing the pole, he poked in the mud and attempted to guide his little raft to safety. In a last-ditch effort, he pulled too hard on the navigation pole, causing it to snap, and he almost impaled himself coming inches from ending his life as he neared the finish line of his journey.

The unforgiving Yakima River pulled and pushed at his raft, giving him only seconds to act. He jumped into the river and swam to the muddy bank. Looking back, he watched his future get caught up by the elm tree, eventually flipping over before continuing down the river without him.

"Balanced," he yelled, cold and exhausted, sitting on the river bank. Tears fell as he thought of his wife and daughter starving because he couldn't do a straightforward thing. He retched water from his lungs and hit himself for no other reason than to make his outside hurt as bad as his insides felt.

"Are yous' right in the head, Mister," called out a voice from the rise not far from the bank.

He looked up and got an eye full of sun and a silhouette of a man. "My life is over. I've wasted my last chance to help my family," he answered with his head lowered in shame.

"Well, John, yous' might feel better with a warm set of clothes and some beans in your belly."

"George?"

"Yes sir, so when yous' done whatever yous' are doin', come up by the fire and get yourself warm before yous' freeze to death," warned George, walking away and out of sight.

"Beans," he uttered, clambering up the rise and almost beating the old man back to his riverside camp.

"Where you been?" he asked, serving up a bowl of beans and serving the soaked man.

"I've been up on my ranch," he answered, taking the bowl from George with steady hands and slurping the thick hot broth.

"Ranch, what are you raising, mountain goats? There is a fella named Flint in the foothills just before the cut off to your place. He raised sheep until he forgot where he was grazing them," stated George, adding some more broth to the starving man's bowl.

"No, just rabbits. We had a herd of them until someone released them last month."

"You know the town folk thought you dead. We had a funeral and everything. Wait, you said you raise rabbits; you know that doesn't make you a rancher, right?" asked George, sitting on a rock.

"Why did they believe we were dead?" he asked with a full mouth.

"They found all those bodies up the river. They told everyone they were all eaten up," answered George, now almost in tears.

"Well, we did not die," he declared, taking a bite, and then he noticed the old man wasn't eating. He swallowed hard and coughed.

"Yes, I guess," he said, snorting something up into his throat before spitting it into the coals of the fire, making a sizzling sound that reminded them both of eggs and bacon.

"Won't you eat some. It is your lunch after all?" he asked, with his mouth full.

"I only gots one bowl and wasn't expecting the resurrection of... of John Winger," he answered as he adjusted his legs to get a little closer to the fire.

"Springer," corrected John, looking at the bowl in his hand.

"No, I'm pretty sure the names were spelled, WINGER," corrected George, with all the confidence of a hooker in church.

"Well, who would I talk to in Yakima City to clear this up?" he asked, standing and sweeping sand and muck from his legs.

"I reckon that would be someone in the courthouse," answered George, dipping the bowl into the beans and taking the same spoon and poking at his lunch.

"Well, unless you know of a reason why I can't talk to anyone?"

"I wonder who the Wingers were?" asked the older man stretching and picking up a pan and using it to store what he liked to think of as his cooking supplies.

"Were they not part of the Olson's party?" asked John, picking up a ladle and passing it to George.

"No, there were too many of them to be just the Olson's. That's why we thought the Wingers died," he answered, gathering his things and loading his pack board.

"Springers."

"Yes, I did hear you say that, but the bodies up there will always be known as the Wingers. Due to the misprinting of their names."

"You foretold something about clean clothes?" asked John as he looked around for a tent or some sign from George as to where he would find a set of fresh clothes that had been promised.

"Well, I really don't have a set. I was suggesting you could sit by the fire and dry yourself," answered George as he glanced up at John, who now found himself without a reason to stand.

"So they believe I'm dead? They believe my wife and I died on the trail last, what was it, April?" asked John, as he sat back down on the log, doing his best to let the warmth of the fire dry his clothes.

"Yes, sir."

"How cold you reckon it is today?" raising his dirty hands to the fire to warm them up.

"It's 45 degrees, give or take a few degrees," guessed George.

John nodded in agreement and stood up to warm his backside. "I need to get into town and explain I have not died. First, I destroy my cargo, wrecking my only chance to get supplies, and now, I find out I'm dead," said John as he became more agitated.

"Well, it's good because I thought you were dead most of the time you were gone. I've been grieving for yous' and yours for six months," said George as he became increasingly unhinged.

"Well, I am sorry to disappoint you, but it was almost eight months since we walked on to our ranch," he corrected, letting out a laugh that made him ponder the fertility of crying over the cargo. After all, at least he wasn't dead.

"Yes, suppose it was eight months," said George nervously. He thought about the last time he saw them and looked towards the tree, blocking half the river.

"What are you pondering over there?" asked John, adjusting himself on one of the logs that wrapped around the fire pit.

"Oh yeah, I just remembered why we don't need to hurry back to town," said George as he finished his lunch, cleaned out his bowl.

He waited for the old man to explain his revelation for about a minute before breaking the silence, asking, "Why is that?" He stood and turned to let the fire warm his backside.

"It's Friday," answered George, nodding into the air in front of him like Friday answered everything.

"No, I reckon it's a Thursday," he said, cleaning his hands.

"No, it's Friday. I know it because half the town takes the day off for fishing on Fridays," declared the old man before continuing, "That's why I was out here."

"So we talk to someone on Saturday," suggested John, attempting to mimic George's head nod, which was more of a bobble, as he recalled it.

"Well, you could try, but no one will be there to listen on Saturday and Sunday around here."

"Why, won't they be open today?"

Consortium of Acquaintances

"Well, today is a fishing day, and before you ask again, only 400 people are living in Yakima City, and there isn't enough Court'n to do, so they take Friday off."

"Well, all righty, may I have another bowl for another dip of beans?" he asked.

"Certainly," answered George, dipping the bowl into the beans and handing it back to the younger man.

"So, how many fish have you caught?"

"Well, I do not have a line in the water," answered George, glancing at the large tree across the river.

"Then why did you walk four or five miles from town to sit in this depression by the bank?"

"I didn't want people to think I wasn't going fishing; after all, it's Friday," replied George with a smile from ear to ear.

"You are a character," he said, finishing off his second bowl.

"Thank you, John."

"I didn't mean..." he started to say before George cut him off.

"I know, it is not the worst I have been called," said George, looking towards town lost in thought for a few seconds.

"I guess, just be you," holding out the bowl.

"I can be no one else. I wouldn't know how," replied George, standing to find somewhere to relieve himself complaining about his back as he walked behind a bush. "Give me a moment."

Chapter 14
Probably Friday, December 19, 1873
Few miles north of Yakima City

The walk from the river to the town was a chance for them to catch up on current events. John spent the time telling George all about the farm and their new child. He paused, lost in thought, reflecting on their struggles the last few months.

George cleared his throat, and John looked away before meeting his friend's eye.

He continued explaining how they built the tiny one-room cabin. How they just recently moved into the larger cabin built half into the embankment. The area was thick with wild game and the mountain men they had seen and met on the farm.

George seemed to hang on John's every word, occasionally glancing back to hear the younger man better. "So what happened with your fruit cellar?" asked George, picking up a small rock and turning it over in his hand.

"Fruit cellar? Oh, the barn, well, I'm not sure. One minute everything was fine, and then the barn was on fire. It almost took my new cabin and my meat locker," answered John, stopping to admire the mountain he hadn't noticed on his last trip to town.

"What is a meat locker?" questioned George, who expressed an odd confused look upon his face.

"It's a box on a tower that we built tall. It has a ladder that's not built as strong as the legs. That way, if a bear climbs up the tower to get to your meat, the ladder will break, and the food is safe," answered John, matching the older man's footfall for footfall, quickly feeling the strain in his legs.

"I was wondering what that was," said George.

"Excuse me?"

"What a meat locker was? I never required one. What if a small bear climbs the ladder?" he asked, wondering in the back of his mind if he should explain that bears don't need ladders to climb.

"Then he wouldn't be strong enough to break the door off the hinges without falling 20 feet to the ground," answered John, looking out over the tan and brown hills that surround the valley. His eye caught a large black patch that covered the ridge south of town.

"Yous' should put a bell tied to a string inside the house to let yous' know when something is messing with it," he said, breaking into a single formation to climb a rise and waited for John so they could finish walking into town. An image of a bear up a fine tree with his claws buried in a beehive came to mind.

"George, that sounds like a great idea. Maybe you should come up and show me ways to improve my ranch. Maybe explain the fruit cellar idea?"

"Well, it is kinda like what yous' have already done. It would be best to build a shed back into the rise and cover the roof with dirt. The temperature should stay above freezing in the winter and below 60 degrees in the summer. That is if yous' and yours can keep the door closed up during the day," said George, what the younger man was staring behind him.

"Hey, was there a fire or something this summer?" he asked, looking up at the darkened hillside.

"Sure was, for a few days, everyone in the town was up there fighting that fire. It was a fear that the wildfire might take Yakima City down to the root cellars."

"Where we heading now?"

"Just thought I would drop by my tent for a few minutes to lighten my load and get a fresher set of clothes on that's all," answered George, as he stepped onto a wider road that went from east to west towards town.

"Yeah, you sure have a large pack. Were you planning to stay down there by the river all week?"

"I aimed to be prepared this time of the year."

"You stay in a tent year-round?" stopping to notice the snow-covered mountain toward the west.

"Rainier, the snow as you can see never melts off the monster," declared George, stumbling a little because of his redirected attention. "You know if you were to climb that mountain, you would need to know how to build a snow shelter."

"What is a snow shelter?" asked John, helping him up and steadying him. He noticed the older man was in good shape under his warm jacket, and by the way, he took off at a near gallop. He again followed his friend to the west into town.

"Well, you dig blocks out of snow and build walls and slant them in to close the roof off," answered George as he started to pass a small apple orchard.

"That sounds cold."

"Not as cold as sleeping in the elements."

"Fruit any good?" asked John, stopping to point at a tree with hanging apples.

"Helped pick the crop last month before the first frost," answered George. "Be particular, and you can find a worm-free apple or two," replied George, as he picked a few for snacking on later.

"Worm-free?"

"Worms are free, John," replied the old man as he snickered. "Mind the worms."

Still hungry, he picked four and looked around the apple before sinking his teeth into the red treasure. He wasn't sure if the first two bites had the worms; however, he would have liked to think it was just the rest of the apple that had worms.

"How is it?"

Consortium of Acquaintances

"George, that is the first apple I've eaten in at least a year. It tasted like heaven even though it looks like hell inside."

That elicited a long belly laugh from the older man. "Young man, you are a funny one to know," said George, turning and coming to a white canvas tent, which looked like army surplus. The side walls were faded, and an advisement of some defunct business was printed on the side.

"This your place?" he asked, looking at the dozen or so tents in the vacant lot behind some business and possibly a card room.

"This tent is my mansion, but the land doesn't belong to anyone. We stay here working for the town in one way or another. If a business buys the lot from the land agent, we move one lot to the east," he replied, opening the tent flap and inviting him inside. It was about the same temperature as it was on the outside.

"This is about the size of the tent Elizabeth, and I shared this summer before we built the smaller cabin. Oh, speaking of Robert Hinkle, where can he be found?" asked John, setting his things on a box next to the stove.

Using a tone reserved for the passing of people from this world, he replied, "He is gone."

"What? That is unfortunate to hear that. What did he die of?"

Someone passing by the tent announced, "Some say lead poisoning."

"What happened?"

"No one knows for sure, but as you can hear, most believe he was taken out of town and shot," George answered, looking a little glum.

"I know what lead poisoning means. What happened?" asked John.

"About a week after you headed for your property, Binky rode into town and dropped a flour sack over Robert Hinkle and Harry Jackson's heads right out front of the livery. Threw them over a horse, and no one has seen them since."

"Why?"

"Because Binky doesn't need a reason. He had a problem, and he took care of them, and what's funny is no one has bothered to arrest him for it. They have had plenty of chances. Even the United States Marshal from Spokane had been here in Yakima City four times since then, and he hasn't lifted a finger," answered George.

"He is protected, you know that," announced someone passing the tent, and by the sound of it, there were at least six others with him.

"Who are they?" asked John, nibbling on another wormy apple, being a little more precise cutting around the resident critters using his small carving knife.

"It just the men coming back from working all day. It must be just after five o'clock. Do you want to eat more than a wormy apple?" asked George.

"I need to watch my spending."

"That's fine. I know of a place that we can work for a while, and the owner will feed us."

"I bet you do," laughed John, taking a moment to reflect on the last time George tricked him into working for him.

"It is just across the street at the livery. Gilbert Jackson has horses to put away and take care of before the sun goes down any more than it has already."

When they left George's tent, he could see the stark difference between when he had entered and come out. The sky looked grey, and it seemed like it was about to storm.

"We better hurry before it starts to rain."

'Or snow,' he grimaced, thinking of the trip home as they walked over to the livery.

Fourteen horses brushed and put up for the night, and their stomachs were full of stew and sitting across from Gilbert, a man in his late twenties and full of energy.

"Thanks, boys. I'm glad to share a meal with you for all the help you provided," said Gilbert, finishing his bowl of bean stew.

"Thank you, sir," said John, scraping his bowl clean.

"Anytime," replied Gilbert.

"Say, where is the missus?" asked George, looking over Gilbert's shoulder.

"She had a church meeting or something," answered Gilbert, obviously not knowing where his wife was or when she would get back.

Everyone stood there awkwardly for a minute before the old man spoke up, saying, "Well, we better be getting. We need to stop at a couple of places in town before we head to bed." When they stepped out into the night, it was dark, and only a few lanterns lit the way. He noticed that there was little wagon traffic and the boardwalks only had a few evening strollers, mostly heading to the northern part of town.

"If the Winston is in the alley down that way, what's lit up down that way?" asked John.

"The Lucy," answered George, pointing to a well-lit business just up the street.

"Lucy?"

"Yeah, there is a squaw that sits on the boardwalk most days in front of the saloon. She doesn't harm anyone, and no one really notices her. But the ones that did began to call the saloon Lucy's, and the name stuck," answered George, suddenly sounding a few degrees more lucent than usual.

"I'm not sure I want to go into the Lucy Saloon."

"You want to stay a ghost, or would you like to be declared alive again."

He just stared at the crazy older man blankly.

"John, the mayor is in there, and I want you to meet him and ask him to fix your death certificate, and it would be in your best interest to be seen."

"Oh, I get it. Fine, let us proceed."

"Just trust me: when we get in there, if your ranch comes up, let us not mention the rabbits, let's just call them long-eared sheep."

"It will be fine, if you reckon it will make a difference, I will trust you," said John, suddenly missing home and feeling guilty for entering a saloon while his family sat home with dwindling supplies.

"If you want people to take you seriously, it does."

One hour later and the mayor bought him two drinks to make up for any hardship he endured from the misfortune of being declared dead

John shared the top-shelf unique whiskey with the older man. Both of them thought it tasted funny. So when asked by the mayor if they wanted another, they said they were happy with the one.

Twenty minutes later, they were walking down the middle of the street as if they were in a three-legged race. The clouds were moving in, and there was a threat of rain as they made their way to the tent. John noticed the movement and had to look down, "What was in those drinks?"

"Don't know, but they do, does, did, um Wut' was the question?"

"I don't know, hic* I forgot, wait, George, hic* isn't that, hic*, the way back to your man... hic* man... hic* -sion," he stammered, letting free a volley of laughter.

"No, I reckon we had better find a more invitin' place tonight," answered George. "And don't be making fun of my tent, you, you, rabbit herder."

Both let out a laugh that nearly caused George to lose a lung and woke up at least three people who lit their lamps and peered out shrouded windows.

***

Not a half block from where two noisy drunks held their three-legged race, a man stood behind the livery and leaned up against the fence. He was of French descent, and he spoke English as well as most mountain men. He had inherited his looks from his mother, but his height he got from his father. When he came to the territory, he was often confused for a Native American. He grew tired of explaining he was just darkened from the sun.

"When you see him, you make sure he doesn't see you and sneak up and bury a tomahawk in the back of his head. After it's done, make sure you carry him down near the Union Gap. We will blame it on a drunk Yaka-man."

Consortium of Acquaintances

"Yes, but I was born in Nantes, France, we don't carry tomahawks, carry an ax, and who is paying me?" asked Kentucky Bob not to b confused with Ohio-Bob, who was a bouncer at the Emporium.

Kentucky-Bob was a bearded man with a lean body. He turned t look generally at the fence and the person hiding on the other side. "An what about the other one?" He brushed the snow from his bearskin coa and fur-covered boots, making him look more like a mountain man.

"You will get your money, as you always do, and if he gets in th way, you can do the same for him at the same pay," stated the shadow figure behind the fence.

"That will be fine," replied Kentucky-Bob, wondering just how h was roped into standing in the street the first night he was back in town.

"One last item. No matter what happens tonight, you will say nothin to anyone about this job, you understand?"

"I understand. I will wait across the street," answered Kentucky-Bol before realizing he was alone and the person with the epicene voice ha abandoned him to do his virulent actions.

Chapter 15
December 20th, 1873
Yakima City, Washington Territory

The sun has been the greatest alarm clock the world has ever known, from flowers to ground squirrels, from deer to the wolves, and from the farmer to the town drunk. According to the latest scientific held belief at the time, the sun had woken the world for at least 6000 years, and today was no exception.

When the sun peaked over the tan sagebrush-covered ridges east of Yakima City, beams of light entered the windows of the Hummel Hotel and into the bloodshot eyelids of John Springer. He rolled over onto his side to face away from the sunrise. He blinked twice as he noticed the lump of someone else in bed with him.

An image of the women of the Blue Wave saloon sprang into his thoughts, waving friendly-like in support of their endeavor, whatever that endeavor was last night. His mind raced while trying to remember what had happened the night before.

He rolled over to face the day once again and wondered if this was even his room, all at the same time wondering, 'Where in the hell are my trousers?'

Now, until this point in his life, John was known as a good man in at least three states when most men had trouble with their reputation within their own household. He had been only with one woman, the love of his life, Elizabeth. He only had eyes for her, and he could not fathom having eyes for any other woman no matter how drunk he managed to get,

which was a rarity in his relatively short life, having taken to the bottl
fewer than a dozen times. His mind pondered how he would sneak from
the bed and find the before-mentioned trousers before his companio
would wake and that he could not bear.

He slowly lifted his leg and slipped it from the patchworked qui
and noticed something that made him take pause and gave him th
overwhelming urge to re-examine his present predicament.

He lifted his blankets and looked down the length of his body. "Wha
is going on?" The mystery of his trousers was solved. He had not take
them off, which was even more of a rarity than taking to the bottle. Eve
further down, his muddy shoes were still on his feet. They were a har
contrast compared to the white linen that was on the bed.

He lifted the patchwork and examined the person next to him. He
arm was thick and hairy. He then noticed the smell of feet. The foc
attached to the hairy leg lifted and rubbed him from his chin to hi
forehead.

'I don't know if you have ever been on the south end of a northboun
Texas longhorn, but surely you could imagine that it smelled a touc
better than his bed companion's foot.'

It may have been an exaggeration to warn husbands about infidelit
and karma as to what transpired next. However, for years it would b
talked about in local taverns and hair salons.

"Ack," heaved John as he bailed off the bed as if it were on a
unbroken horse. 'Oh, how I wish I had a horse,' he thought befor
heaving one more time. He was breathing hard, coughing, making hi
attempt to rid himself of the smell of infected feet.

"What in the 'ell?" yelled George as he too bailed out the other sid
launching himself into the dresser planting his foot into the meta
chamber pot. He fell back, kicking the chamber pot over the bed and int
John's open arms, splashing him with its contents.

He looked briefly at the rim, noticing the ornate design before hi
eyes betrayed him by focusing on the contents swirling within the pot. I
less than half a second, the smell made its way into his nostrils, forcin
him to dry heave once again. He had the oddest thought in the briefest o

moments, asking himself, 'Whose contents are these held in my palms and all over my thumbs?'

Before he came up with an answer, he did as any other man would do and tossed it back at George, who being a man of many years, reached out and completely missed his turn with the hot potato, and it was unfortunate for him, the dresser and the bed.

John lost the remaining contents of his stomach. He swore off alcohol between heaves and was curious to know just whose room this was, secretly hoping the hotel did not know who he was. I looked up at the painting and missed his cargo even more than before they started to drink.

Cough.

"Yak "

Cough!

"John?"

"Morning, George."

"Morning, John."

"How's your morning going so far?" asked John, already knowing the answer. He was just wanting to hear his take on waking up only to play hot potato with the chamber pot.

"I wish I could say that this was the worst morning I have had the misfortune to be present fer," answered George as an image of a cesspool came to mind that quickly was overshadowed by another of far worse implications.

"How is this not the worst morning of your life?" asked John, moving away from a small mound of dubious substance in hopes he would leave the smell behind him. His hopes were dashed as he noticed the excess from George's stomach contains flowing like a river in his direction from under the bed.

"I would say that it was the fourth-worst morning of my life. Not counting personal tragedy, which seems to intensify the pain one feels with their heart," George answered, sounding almost philosophical about the matter.

Consortium of Acquaintances

It would be years before the older man shared the worst thre mornings in detail. He suspected it had to do with the War Between Th States. George didn't say, and he didn't ask.

There are long roads in life, each man and woman needs to take thei own journey to get where they're going, and it's their business what the want to share along the way. John could hear his father explaining that t him as if he stood behind him now. He was glad that his father didn't se him like this. He was afraid of what his father might have said.

George struggled to sit up and fling some half solid from the back o his hand. He had no wish to investigate further, figuring it was better nc to know.

John was lying back against the bed, avoiding the mess from him an the chamber pot. He looked over and noticed the older man was sitting i roughly the same position, except it looked as if he had not missed any o its contents.

"Say, George, why were you in the bed backward?" he asked wit his first moment of clarity.

"Well, I'm not sure yous' understand, you're a married man of younger age," he answered, half slurring his response.

"Go on, George. I'm listening?"

His voice strained as he answered, "Yous liked to put me into cuddle, and I didn't believe it was proper you being married and all, said George, holding a straight face for the moment and sounding as if h was stricken with a case of congestion. Later John would come t understand it was George speak for I just got one over on you.

At this point, some would say he cried. Years later, he was hear saying that he had laughed so hard that he broke into a coughing fit.

Just then, someone pounded on the door, that luckily someone ha thought to prop a chair against the knob. It was buying precious time t find an alternative to explain George and his appearance withou registering downstairs.

John glanced back at where he had last seen the older man sitting and he was gone. "George?" he whispered, looking about the room fo his friend.

"Hush," said the old man as he opened the window and took to the balcony.

"Whose room is this anyway?" he asked, feeling as though he was committing some infraction of the law.

"It's what I call an open win-doe' room," he answered, snorting to clear his nasal passages, which he suddenly regretted as he could again smell the general aromatic quality or lack thereof in the room.

John grabbed his bag and boots before following George through the open window and down the trellis. He didn't know whether to laugh or cry.

"OH! My Lord, who has done this," exclaimed the manager as the door swung open, knocking the chamber pot under the bed and into the dresser.

"Well, I'm a good man in at least two states," he declared, walking a step behind him in one inch of snow, struggling with putting his boots on and keeping up with the old man as he darted through the crowd along the boardwalk.

"Awe, yous' a good man in my book in any state of being," he answered, looking back from time to time to make sure he was still behind him.

"Thanks, George," he replied, not feeling as though the old man's comments helped.

"You're welcome," he said as he directed John into a tented business.

He had been a customer of bathhouses when the need arose, but this didn't feel right. Yes, there was a tub, and there was a towel somewhat questionably clean. He glanced around as the large tent's walls flapped like a spoiled sail in the wind.

It was the water in the tub that bothered him. He looked hard at the tub for a few minutes, even as he watched the older man go first. In disbelief, he asked politely, "Say, how far is the river?"

"It's about a half-mile, over yonder," answered George, pointing toward the east and the rising sun.

"Thank you," he said, slowly turning towards the door.

Consortium of Acquaintances

"John, don't be bashful, I've seen them man parts before," mused the old man with a tongue-in-cheek grin.

"George, it not me man parts, I just feel the point of a bath is to get clean," he stated, looking at the scum-lined tub the old man was sitting in.

"Well, law-dee-da' yous' don't have to use the same water as thi here tub. Yous' can just step over into the next room and pay the lady tw bits for a clean tub of hot water. That was when John realized that ther was more than one room for baths, and he was standing in a private roor watching a man take a bath.

At this point, he wasn't sure if he should apologize or just hang hi head and seek the promised warm bath waters of another room. He chos the latter and slipped from the room into a curtained hallway.

"You want a bath, would you like extras?" asked a woman who ha lost the battle with gum disease sometime before.

"Extras?"

"Girl to do your back, young man," answered George, with that sam little stress in his voice when he was trying to be funny.

"No, I don't reckon so, not today. I mean, I'm married to a lovel girl. No, wait, I mean a lovely wife. No, woman. I meaning to say, I wi have just the bath," stumbling on his words, already listening to th banters of several bathers, especially George, who had started to sing th Southern Hymn of the Republic. Which he thought was odd because h thought he had fought on the Northern side. He made a mental note t ask the crazy older man later.

"Quarter first, and then we will bring you your bathwater," sai Virginia, holding out her hand, waiting for the quarter.

"Here you go," replied John, setting the quarter in the outstretche open palm of her hand.

"Would you like a clean towel for five cents?" she asked with th same palm opened in front of him.

"Yes," he answered, adding the shiny shield nickel into her palm which she closed like a vise and disappeared behind the curtain.

In just a few minutes, he was sitting in a hot water paradise. It felt like he had slipped away to heaven. He thought about what he would tell Elizabeth and then decided he would need to avoid the details of his trip. Adding a bath to the list, he had already started, almost drowning and getting falling-down drunk being just two of the things he regretted.

He felt like a new man slipping from the tub and drying off. He looked at the clothes, and they looked as though he had crawled from his grave. He was just glad more people didn't know him in town, or he could have scared the freckles off of the locals.

He pushed his dirty clothes into the water and rubbed out the worst of the stains. He wasn't sure they would ever be clean enough to wear into any law-abiding establishment, although, if all went right, he would be heading out tomorrow.

"Say, George, is there any place I could buy some used clothing?"

"Nope, we can try the church tomorrow. They have some set aside for charity and might get a good meal out of it to boot. As long as we are willing to do a few chores," answered George, as he spits water out like a fountain and begins to pull himself out of the tub.

"George?"

"Yes, John."

"You do remember the condition of that water when you jumped in and the condition of yourself when you departed the Hotel?"

Silence.

"George?"

"Yes, John."

"What are you contemplating over there?" he asked, wringing his clothes out.

"Just my life choices, John."

"We should find some breakfast. You reckon the livery would have a little work?"

"Best not be talkin' bout no food at the moment," said George, already struggling with keeping the contents of his stomach in place.

John stared at the curtain wall that separated them. The silence was deafening and finally broken when he asked, "George, are you all right?"

"I hope so. I might need to see the doctor. If any symptoms presen themselves," answered George, sounding as though he might end u adding to his troubles.

"Whatever doesn't kill a man outright only makes him stronger, said John, already in the curtained hallway heading for the front door.

"Can not be true, John."

"Why did you say that?" he asked.

"Because I should be a Greek god by now," answered George.

"A man cannot argue your logic," he muttered, stepping through th faux storefront and onto the boardwalk where the morning air assaulte him. He was surprised that it could be so sunny and still below freezing His clothes felt as though they were freezing to his body. 'Maybe i wasn't a good idea to wash my clothes,' he thought, then it occurred t him there was no good outcome; either way, he would have bee uncomfortable.

Chapter 16
December 20th, 1873
Yakima City, Washington Territory

There were no hard and fast rules when it came to building towns in the west. Sure, you could form a settlement with more churches than saloons, but try organizing one without a watering hole. The people needed a place to meet up and burn off the excess hostility frequently found in the garden variety homesteader.

Yakima City was no exception. There was the back alley, Winston card room, the Emporium where they sold kindness, and then there was the Lucy, which was all the above, just a little watered down for the respectable crowd of ranchers and townsfolk. Their double doors are only closed for Sunday morning service. They served food for a reasonable price that kept most people coming back.

In the back corner of the Lucy Saloon sat Sebastian and Lucky at a round table. Both had steak and eggs sitting in front of them. Lucky sat with his back against the wall and watched the patrons come in, sit down, and leave twenty minutes later. It was like that during the day at the Lucy. People would come for breakfast and slip in for drinks here and there. However, no one had stayed as long as they had, quietly nursing their drinks and eating breakfast.

Lucky had come to the territory four years before without so much as a nickel in his trousers. It was said, he fought for the Grays during the war and came west to lick his wounds. No one even knew what part of the country he was from or even his full name. It was just the way he liked it. He once told a co-worker how he lost his family during Northern aggression and how he was lucky to be alive. The story spread like wildfire, and his name became that Lucky fellow, then just Lucky.

"Why are you not eating?" asked Sebastian, speaking softly into his plate. He was thin with dirty blond hair and lacked a beard. He was often called an open book, not because he was easy to read. It was because the younger man never knew when to hold his cards to his chest. If it was on his mind, sooner or later, it dropped out of his mouth.

Lucky sat across from the younger man. He was older and second in command of the gang. His beard hung so low it touched his eggs as he ate. "Because we were just supposed to come and see what Frank had for us. We were not supposed to take the morning off sitting on our asses in the Lucy. You know he is liable to whip us both for takin' so long, answered Lucky, looking into his glass and what passed for whiskey in these parts.

"How do you know he didn't expect us to eat breakfast?" asked Sebastian, holding a small piece of steak in a corralled egg fusion mess on his plate, only to slowly bring it into his mouth and slip it inside. It was as if he took pleasure in the act of eating.

Lucky found his method of eating somewhat detracting, making him ponder his answer. "Because he told us, and I quote, 'look dumb-asses get the desired information, and find your way back here. Don't be stoppin' to eat breakfast and drinkin'. He was very clear." He made a great impersonation of their employer. He even got the hand motion correct.

"What can we do?" asked Sebastian softy as he cut his steak into smaller portions in a way that could only be described as dainty.

Lucky took a deep breath and started into his breakfast. "Eat. Damn Seb, this steak is really good," he finally answered, cutting a large piece and pushing it into his egg yolk and then attacking it as a badger would.

One of the other patrons laughed and looked Lucky's way.

Lucky dropped his cigarette, which rolled across the table and under Sebastian's plate. His fork fell into his eggs and kicked up yolk to come to rest in his aforementioned beard. "What are you gawking at, you

Gibface hedge-creeper? I will knock that smile right off your face, if you laugh one more time," he shouted, pointing his left index finger at the man while dropping his hand to his lap where his pistol already rested. He had cocked the hammer back before they delivered his eggs.

"Good morning, Lucky, and you're, well...never mind, you won't be here that long," said Mayor Daniels, only glancing at the younger man for a moment before turning his attention back to Lucky. "Tell Binky that the job I sent him last night is becoming a problem. He needs to take care of it." He glanced back at the younger man, realizing he knew him from somewhere.

Sebastian was too busy looking for the reason his plate was smoking to notice Mayor Daniel's concern.

"Now, if you gentlemen are done threatening innocent townsfolk. Would you head out before you cause my day to become difficult," he said, turning back, obviously alarmed at the fact a new face is never supposed to be recognized, especially in his line of work.

Sebastian's plate was cleaned off, and his side of the table looked as if he hadn't been there at all. He stood up, looked over at Lucky, who leaned forward and stabbed his fork into the steak. "I'm taking the steak with me," he said with disdain dripping off each word.

"Fine, but leave the fork. They do not grow on trees," declared Mayor Daniels gruffly.

Lifting the wooden utensil to his lips, he picked the steak off its tip with his teeth, and it flopped to his dirty chin. Setting the fork on the table before telling Sebastian, "Take your gawkers outside and take a measure of the street and make sure we can walk out of here." He let the steak flop around as he spoke. He grabbed the pistol off his lap, stood, and came within six inches from the round man. His side of the table looked like a five-year-old child's finger painting.

"I assure you, it was just for show," whispered Mayor Daniels, pulling on his gloves.

Lucky pulled the steak out of his mouth and held it with his left hand, "I assure you this is not just for show," whispered Lucky, leveling the revolver waist high with his right.

Consortium of Acquaintances

"Just go," said Mayor Daniels, letting a single bead of sweat fall from his temple down to his lapel.

Lucky walked straight out of the bat-winged doors, letting them swing on squeaky hinges. He paused next to Sebastian, who was noticeably smaller in every way that was important. "Everything good out here?" he asked as he slipped his pistol into his holster and chewed on a large piece of the steak.

"Were you going to shoot him?" asked Sebastian, kicking the snow around as he walked out.

"Nah, I like him; anyone that makes me money is worth liking. I was just feeding the gossipers," answered Lucky with a yellow-toothed grin noticing the playfulness of Sebastian's gait. The kind of walk a man got when he had spent too many hours in the saddle.

"Did he know that?" asked Sebastian, walking over to his horse and throwing a leg over it.

"Naw, that's what makes it fun," answered Lucky as he sat his cheeks into the saddle.

"What now?" asked Sebastian, shifting his body weight, making the horse turn around in a tight circle threatening to toss him from the saddle.

"Now, we ride like we're being chased before Binky comes for us," answered Lucky, spurring his horse in the belly, making him almost leap into a full gallop.

Chapter 17
December 20th, 1873
Yakima City, Washington Territory

Nightfall in the city is like living on the homestead out west. In the town, oil lights burn on every corner. Men and women crowd the boardwalks on their way home. Except as the sky fades on the farm, there are no lamp posts. All the tasks that should have been completed hours ago now become a frenzy of activity. The darkness envelops the homesteader as they finish their chores and head inside.

This annoyance compounded on a night such as this on the Springer Ranch mainly due to the weather. As Elizabeth pulled the meat from the smoke rack, she stopped when she realized her daughter was standing still with her head back and her tongue stretched out, looking like a complete loon.

"You looked as though you have lost your mind. What are you trying to accomplish, young lady?" asked Elizabeth, readjusting the smoked meat so it wouldn't fall to the ground.

"Is this snow? It tastes like water and smoke," replied Annie with a question, talking as though some unseen force was holding her tongue. Her eyes met her mother's, and she grinned. She knew what snow was but was never allowed to play in it.

It was then that Elizabeth stopped rushing and started to pay attention to the little snowflakes mixed in with the rain. She answered her then, "Yes, but surely you have seen snowflakes," she answered,

sticking her tongue out at first to mock the child, then she realized th
cold snowflakes were beautiful, so she kept doing it.

'Why do the snowflakes landing on my tongue remind me of m
childhood?' she asked herself. She struggled to remember as Annie'
giggles woke her from her internal query.

"It's wonderful," declared Annie. It was then that the snowflake
became more extensive. Like some magic trick or maybe mother natur
was just showing off, the larger flakes began to dance around on sma
wind funnels.

"Annie, we need to retreat into the cabin. There is a storm comin
in," warned Elizabeth, walking quickly inside and dropping the smoke
deer meat onto the wooden carving platter. She glanced back the way sh
had come, and her child was not behind her. She leaned towards th
window to see outside and still standing enthralled by the beauty of th
falling flakes.

Annie screamed and then giggled, waving her hand as if to sa
goodbye.

"Annie Marie Springer Olson, get inside this cabin before you catc
cold," she yelled, running outside without waiting for her to answer. Sh
rushed to pick her up, carrying her to the threshold before letting her g
only to watch her affix herself to the window that looked out over th
porch.

"What's wrong?"

"We are going to have some bad weather tonight. It's called
blizzard," answered Elizabeth, picking up a knife and cutting one of th
last pieces of the deer John had shot more than a few days ago. In th
back of her head, she hoped that it was still fresh. She rechecked it onc
more, giving it a sniff.

"Is it still good?" she asked, looking back to the candle then back t
the window.

"There is but only one way to find out little one," she answerec
smiling in the girl's direction, holding a piece of freshly cut and freshl
sniffed.

"I hope it's good," Annie said, looking back to the candle and then back to her mother.

"Why are you turning to the candle?" she asked as she tested the meat by chewing it more than usual before swallowing it.

"I can't see out the window, only the reflection of the candle," she answered, moving toward the table and pulling the larger chair away from the end of the table. She settled into her father's spot and smiled again at Elizabeth.

"It is fine if you sit there, but if he gets home tonight, you're going to have to move," said her mother before coaxing another smile from her daughter.

"I hope he isn't out there tonight. It is too cold and wet. He would freeze to death and then get eaten by the wolves," announced Annie, leaning over her plate, examining the aroma for herself, and reaching for her favorite fork.

"Me too," muttered Elizabeth, forcing back tears and making herself continue to smile even though her insides felt like they were collapsing. She had already been worried that her husband would be out there if not tonight in the next few days.

Annie volunteered to pray, and while she did so, Elizabeth hid her eyes in what passed for a kitchen towel.

When she was done, Elizabeth stood up and hugged her. "We should bolt the door. The wind may blow it open tonight. They both had noticed the wind whipping over the cabin, dragging brush from the countryside up and over the roof.

"There, it is bolted," she said, locking the large beam horizontally across the door.

"That seems heavy. What happens if daddy does come home?" asked Annie as she tried to cut her meat.

"The beam is solid, it is like the rest of the cabin, and he will just have to knock," she answered, pausing next to her little one to cut her meat into child-size portions.

"Thank you," she responded, leaning back in her father's chair and watching as her new mama cut her meat.

"I forget that you are not as old as you appear," stated Elizabeth filling two water cups and setting the smaller one in front of her daughter.

A squeak echoed inside the cabin as a gust of wind blew that seemed to reverberate about the small cabin.

"Nor are you," she laughed, leaning back and picking up an early prototype of her father's design of a fork. It had two prongs, and it looked a little too long to be a fork.

"Would you like another one, Annie?" asked her mother, just now sitting down at the table.

"No, ma'am, this one reminds me of Daddy," she answered, poking a bit of meat and placing it in her awaiting mouth.

"How is it?" asked Elizabeth

"Chewy, but really tasty, I like it," answered Annie, taking a potato chunk in her mouth and began chewing.

Another squeak sound echoed from somewhere close as if a tree branch was scraping the side of the cabin.

"We should be safe inside the cabin because your father knows how to build cabins strong," said Elizabeth, taking a drink from her cup to hide her face from the child. She hoped not to scare Annie with a single look of worry.

"I wish daddy would have made shutters for the windows," declared Annie, picking up her cup and taking a drink to wash the potato down.

The noise sounded again, and they both laughed. If Annie and Elizabeth could see outside, they would have seen the snow was falling faster and with larger flakes. By the time they finished dinner, the snow was four inches deep.

"We can clean up in the morning so that we can save the candles," suggested Elizabeth, stepping from the table and reaching out for her daughter's hand.

"Yeah, we wouldn't want to burn the candles too long," Annie responded, giving her a wink.

"No really, we have the tallow from the deer, but I have only made candles once. I'm hoping daddy comes home soon to make some new nes. Besides, if we are careful, we should still have enough to last," she said, thoughtfully hugging her daughter before pushing her playfully in the direction of her bed.

"Oh fine," said Annie, changing from her dress to one of John's shirts that were modified for her.

Elizabeth did the same, slipping into her nightgown. She hurried to get ready for bed as the candle dimmed as it was reaching the end of its usefulness. They laid in their beds, looking out at the darkening one-roomed cabin and the shadows flickering overhead.

Elizabeth rolled onto her side, letting the stress escape her body and inviting sleep to come to take her to dreamland. She felt so comfortable looking out; knowing the beam in place made the cabin feel so much safer.

Her eyes wandered over to the solid hinges and stopped on the turning doorknob as the candle faded out.

Squeak.

Her eyes snapped open, and her heart threatened to jump from her chest. She slipped from her bed and crawled to the fireplace. Her eyes slowly adjusted to the light as she reached for her husband's Spencer.

Gripping the stock awkwardly, she slowly pulled it off the hooks that held it to the wall. Her hands shook as the rifle slipped from the rack and made its way into her arms. It was then she realized someone was behind her. She could hear them breathing.

Squeak.

"Why are you holding daddy's gun?" asked Annie, holding her head cocked to one side.

"My Lord! I believe I just peed myself," answered Elizabeth, reaching up and pulling Annie into the shadows next to the fireplace.

"Are we playing a game?" asked Annie.

"Yes, honey, it's called keeping the monsters out. Do you want to play, too?" asked Elizabeth, burying the fright and the anxiety deep.

"Yes, ma'am, of course," answered Annie, in the sort of way you would talk to a fool, not quite condescending. However, the child's sarcasm was developing nicely.

Consortium of Acquaintances

"Now listen, what we are going to do is cross the room and pret[e]nd that the fire is a monster. We each take turns and make sure that [our] movement casts no shadows," said Elizabeth not more than four inc[hes] from her face to Annie's.

"Oh, I've played that game many times," she whispered as [she] lowered herself to the floor.

She watched her daughter slither away and had to admit she [was] good at wandering about in the darkness of the cabin. She would have [to] make a point of talking with the child about being out of bed when [she] was supposed to be asleep because obviously, she had to have a gr[eat] deal of practice to be this good.

A squeak echoed louder.

The noise was genuinely unnerving her as she followed her noctur[nal] explorer into the shadows. They reached the other side of the ca[bin] behind John's chair and peered out.

"What are you looking for?" asked Annie calmly.

"I am making sure the monster hasn't seen us," answered Elizabe[th] peaking around the chair.

"I don't reckon it is a monster, I believe it's Drake, and he has be[en] watching over us for a long time," said Annie, sitting down and pulli[ng] her knees up.

"Little one, please be silent and let me ponder our situation," s[he] demanded, holding the Spencer at the ready as she tried to form a plan.

'If I shoot out a window, I would have to fix it. Then again, if I h[it] someone, I would need to bury the body before the wolves catch th[e] scent. What an odd statement for my daughter to say?' She stared o[ut] into the darkness, lost in thought for a moment, then turned towards h[er] daughter.

"Honey, how do you know who is out there?" she asked, lookin[g] back where Annie sat leaned up against the back of her father's log chai[r.]

"Because he told me so, I wasn't supposed to tell," she answered.

"This must be what a stroke feels like," Elizabeth muttered befor[e] asking her daughter to describe the monster, "Baby, what does th[e] monster look like."

"He is not a monster even though he smells like one. He is a man a little shorter than daddy. He likes dogs and avoids wolves and bears because they scare him," answered Annie as if it were the most natural conversation to be having with her mother.

"And," muttered Elizabeth, wondering if anything could be more frightening than what her daughter just confessed. She patiently waited for her to continue.

"Oh, and he doesn't like it when you sneak up on him and jump on his back," answered Annie humorously, nodding with a cute smile that reflected the light from the fireplace.

"Yep," muttered Elizabeth, now gritting her teeth.

Squeak, Squeak.

"Ann Marie, you mean to tell me you are talking to a total stranger fifty miles from the nearest neighbor and you haven't dared mentioned it once," said her mother, breathing hard and barely holding back the anger.

"I told you about him loads of times, his name is Drake, and he plays in the woods," said Annie as if this information would somehow clear it up.

Elizabeth suddenly remembered the apron talk of her child. When she was busily making dinner, her daughter talked about her imaginary friend who played in the woods.

"Drake?" she asked as she stood up and shouldered the rifle.

Nothing but the wind responded.

"Drake," she screamed louder, moving closer to the door.

Squeak.

"Drake!" she yelled as her fear turned into anger.

"Yes," replied the muffled voice of the stranger.

Her fear attempted to take hold once more, but it was beaten back by the anger she felt for this man.

"Yes?" he answered, sounding unsure of himself and as though he had moved away from the door towards the window.

"Drake, you have been watching us and stalking us and talking to my daughter. This stops tonight. I have killed two people in my life. One was because I was forced to, and the other, well, he pushed me too far. He got what he deserved. If you walk away, there will be no hard feelings, but you darken my porch one more time, I will shoot you through the nec and drag your carcass out for the wolves to eat. Do. We. Have. A understanding?" demanded Elizabeth, pausing at each word to mak herself heard through the thick door.

"Yes, ma'am, my apologies, ma'am," answered Drake, moving awa from the door by the way he sounded.

She could hear the footfalls of their stalker as he made his retrea back into the woods.

"Now, young lady. We are going to talk about strangers an imaginary friends and especially being out of bed once you are suppose to be asleep," barked Annie's mom.

"I sorwie' mommy."

Chapter 18
December 20th, 1873
Yakima City, Washington Territory

The Milky Way spilled onto the western horizon in the clear night sky above the lonely group of men camped on the Ahtanum Creek. A bend in the stream halfway to the St. Joseph Mission from Yakima City. It's quiet, with only the occasional coyote howling into the night sky to remind them they were not alone.

The gang set camps in several places, moving from time to time for weather or just for the whim of it. They chose West Camp, where they were now, because they felt marginally safe with a posted lookout and the cover of the willow trees.

They had names for all their camps. It was kind of a code for when they were talking in town. Places they referred to as North Camp and East Camp referred to other sites they felt safe. Wide Hollow wasn't far from Cowiche Canyon, yet another place they could hold up, especially in the winter when it went unused by hunters and trappers.

Binky had retained his leadership of the gang of petty thieves. Their territory extended east to the Columbia, west into the Cascades, and as far south as the Yakama Tribal lands.

Binky looked up from his spot by the fire. "So why didn't he just tell me to take care of him last night?" he asked, holding his gloved hands over the campfire. The fire reflected from his blue eyes, giving him a supernatural look.

Consortium of Acquaintances

"That Jollocks wouldn't tell us why he had brought us to town. ' sat there waiting for him for three hours," answered Lucky, movi closer and leaning towards Binky, almost touching his boss with beard.

"Yeah, and we had to sit there drinking and eating all mornin, admitted Sebastian, looking down when Binky turned towards him. told people of his family, but he was an orphan and lacked the courage stand up to Binky, let alone tell him the truth.

"I'm sure you did," said Binky, looking eagle-eyed at the young man who shrunk as he spoke.

"We had to fit in, after all, it twas' Frank, that ratbag threatened to. said Sebastian, stopping when he saw several of the others shaking the heads just out of the line of sight of their leader.

"To do what," Binky snapped, moving fast, pressing close

"Easy, he is young and hasn't a clue how to keep his mouth shu whispered Lucky, noticing the look in Binky's eyes.

"To do what?" he asked again, this time without the hellfire.

"The threat was mostly implied," he answered, stepping back.

"Yeah, it was strongly implied. However, the implication wasi exactly clear," answered Sebastian, nodding as he spoke as if to kee time to some song only heard by him.

Binky and Lucky looked at each other for half of a second befo turning to Sebastian and saying at the same time, "Shut up!"

Binky turned and found a place by the fire to warm up.

"I was just trying to help," complained Sebastian, walking back ov to Kelly, also a new member of the gang.

Lucky watched him get out of earshot. "What should we do about th problem?"

"Well, it is Frank's problem," said Binky as he dropped a little moi wood onto the fire.

"Yes, it is. That is exactly what I was saying on the way back from town," said Sebastian, yelling his response from 20 feet away.

"Boss, should we just put a bullet in the man?" asked Lucky ignoring Sebastian's comment.

Binky stood at the fire in contemplation, warming his backside. "No, we could use a man with good ears like his for eavesdroppin'. We might even get someone to teach him to be a fair safecracker."

"No, Boss, I was talkin' about Frank's two-legged problem, not that numb-nuts," said Lucky, already pointing his finger at Sebastian so he would stop responding to their conversation.

Sebastian took that moment to move to the other side of his horse to count his change.

"I don't care about his problems. However, we did align ourselves with that S.O.B., and that means his problems become ours," he said, looking to his men, making sure they understood.

"So you are going to take care of it?" asked Lucky, now leaning closer to hear his response.

"No, I'm going to send you with Sebastian, Kelly, and that skinny fella that rode in with Lomax last week, ah," he answered, looking around and snapping his fingers.

"Joseph," suggested Lucky with one of his eyebrows raised.

"Yes, that's his name, Joseph. Where the heck is he?" asked Binky, looking down at his feet, dropping tailings of his tobacco tucked in his cheek near his right foot.

"Looking for firewood," answered Lucky. "Wait. Why would you send me with them?"

"No one knows them," answered Binky, turning away so he could continue warming his hands above the small fire.

"You know why no one knows them?" asked Lucky.

"Why is that?" asked Binky with a half-smile.

"Because no one wants to," answered Lucky, nodding his head as if he was head butting the words as they came from his mouth.

"Well, you could just ride into town and hold up in the saloon drinking whiskey and eating steak," said Binky, trying to keep a straight face.

"See, see! I just know'd you were mad about that," said Lucky, picking up a quarter-sized rock and pitching it at Kelly, hitting the younger man's backside.

Consortium of Acquaintances

"Who the hell did that?" yelled Kelly, grabbing at his butt.

"Just go into town, play it by ear, and listen for a chance to f Frank's problem fer' good," said Binky over Kelly's outburst.

"Well, you know I could use a night of drink'n," declared Luck watching Kelly rub his bottom and wander over to the fire.

"You wanted me, Mr. Lucky?" asked Kelly as if his feelings we mashed a bit. He was Irish, and his accent revealed it.

"You and Sebastian better go and put your big boy pants on, then g find Joseph; we have to head back into town," he answered as he starte to gather his bedroll and what he would need in town.

Joseph Pettigrew took that moment to make his appearance b falling out of the short scrub-brush and into several horses that started general ruckus amongst the rest of them. It was remarkable that he hadn dropped the armload of wood for the fire; however, any admiration th could be gotten from that was overshadowed by the fact he had droppe his revolver.

Lucky rushed over and picked up the short-barreled Colt-44 ar tapped him upside his skull with it, "Do you have any idea what wou have happened if this went off?"

"It's unlikely," answered Joseph, leaning closer and offering h holster to Kelly. "It isn't loaded."

"Why is that?" asked Kelly, spitting his words, checking th revolver's cylinders, and then sliding the unloaded handgun into Joseph awaiting holster.

"It was my idea. The boy dropped it on our way from The Dalles an almost blew my head off my shoulders. I just thought it would be safe for everybody concerned if he kept it unloaded until it was needed, answered Lomax, standing up from the fire and moving uncomfortabl close to Lucky.

"Load it, for tonight, you shall need it," said Lucky, walking awa towards Binky.

Chapter 19
December 20th, 1873
Yakima City, Washington Territory

The wind caught the flap as John entered the tent with an arm full of wood. He had to admit it was warmer inside this thin-walled structure than out in what stood for a front yard. He looked back and watched the snow blow along the ground as a snake would crawl.

"Young fella, yous' needs to close the flap before we freeze to death. This isn't a well insulated structure as you have managed to point out more that a time or two," George said, bundling up and pulling his hat down practically over his ears. His clothing made him look like a skinny elephant.

He reached out in the wind and brought the makeshift sail under some control before tying it into place with a few quick-release knots. He wasn't sure what to call the knots he made but guessed it would be alright if they held.

George stirred the beans and pushed the meat bits down to the bottom of the iron skillet to catch the heat from the little sheepherder stove. He then poked at the fire that was in need of stoking. "Yous' mean to tell me you're making your pretty wife cook on the hearth when you could have one of these."

"Wait, what did you say earlier?" asked John, realizing George had made a suggestion a ways back in their discussion about whatever came into George's mind that didn't seem all that important at the time. After all, George was the type of friend to spout random facts all day long, and if a man didn't keep a scorecard wouldn't know what was essential and what was a smokescreen.

"Yous' talking about the stove," he answered, sort of pointing with his wrist in the direction of the blue sheepherder stove in front of him. The door was ajar, and the flame seemed to lick the outside of the furnace as they spoke.

"No, about the cargo," he said, attempting to hide his frustration as he moved closer to George and the stove.

"The Yakima River comes from the north and exits the valley through the Gap to the south. Then it slows down some on the other side," he answered, waving his arms as he spoke as if a person could see the river and its flow if only John would look.

"You mean to tell me that the whole river is snagged with timber and stumps," he practically yelled.

"Well, I thought yous' know'd about it," he answered, looking disheveled.

"You understand you're saying it wrong, it is you not yous'," he said finally taking the time to correct George as if no one in the history of George Johnson had mentioned the grammar errors that burst from his mouth every time he took a breath.

"Well, young man, if you are going to be hurtful, you can just find somewhere else to sleep," warned the old man, turning to the stove and hiding his face.

"George, please just tell me. Do yous' reckon yous' knows where my raft is," he said as a big smile came across his lips.

"Well, I am sure it's in the snags, but your goods must be ruined by now. The dry goods and the potatoes have to be ruined by now," said George rattling his head a bit with each spoken word.

"Well, my new best friend. What if my cargo wasn't food, dry or fresh?" he asked in the language of George.

"What kind of goods would yous' have brought down from the mountain. Gold? Did you find gold?" asked George, maybe a little too loud as the most bazaar look came over him.

"Did someone say they found gold?" came a voice from a tent or two away back further in the lot.

"Who found gold?" questioned another.

"That new feller," answered yet another man in the distance.

"No! I didn't find any damn gold," he yelled so loud that his voice cracked.

"Yous' shouldn't mention the gold so loudly," warned George, stirring his beans.

"George, there isn't any," said John, who could feel his face flush over.

"Oh, there is no gold," he announced, then winked at John.

"My father, from the day I was born, made a living at carving. He worked day and night, working with fine woods to make art sold in his little shop. He taught me the trade, and I earned the coin by selling what I carved out of wood to people that came into my father's shop." He looked at the older man for any sign of an understanding of his meaning.

"I'm not sure what value you can put on whittlen' out here in the ass-end of nowheres," said George, with a blank look about his face.

"I'm an expert carver just like my father was a master of the art," said John, pulling his father's knife from his belt. The handle was carved from the hilt to the butt with the body of a wolf. Its claws hung over the bolster. The paws faded into a mountain ridge climbing high to the shoulder, where a wolf called out to the full moon, which was carved into the neck. The butt formed the wolf's head, which represented the animal searching for prey.

"Expert carver," said George, slowly descending into laughter.

Flipping the knife, so the blade slapped into his hand. "Look at the knife's grip."

"It looks pretty nice," complimented George as if he were talking to a numbskull.

"There are picture frames in my cargo that I used to get three dollars each back east where frames are easy to come by. Do you remember the frame on the painting in the hotel room?" asked John, moving uncomfortably close to the older man who looked slightly confused.

147

Consortium of Acquaintances

"No, but the painting was pretty," he answered and took a step back

"Well, my friend, there wasn't a frame around that pretty painting whispered John, a foot from George, who had backed up against the wa of the tent.

"Do you have gold inlays because that would be valuable," he sai giving the younger man a wink.

"How far are the snags?" he asked, looking as though he was abou to have a seizure.

"About two miles south from the Gap," came an answer from a ma the next tent over.

"Thank you."

"You're welcome," said the perfect stranger.

"George, why the heck do you live in a tented collective? You hav less privacy than, than, than a two-seater outhouse," he said, headir back to his bed before George had a chance to recover and throw hir out.

"Well, first of all, we do our business over yonder, and usually w don't have big mouth guests visiting overnight, so again, if you want t use the outhouse to sleep, then keep talking," warned the older mar returning his knife.

"You tell him, George," called out yet another voice in the darkness.

"Help me find my cargo, and I will buy you a steak dinner, whereve that serves the best food in town. I didn't mean to complain about you tent. It really is nice for a tent," said John, pulling off his boots an rubbing at his corns.

"We'll give it a try, now eat your beans and meat."

"Meat, George?"

"If you don't ask, I won't lie to you," answered George, which migl have been the most honest advice he had shared with the young man a day.

"All right," said John, nibbling at the morsels of meat bits and bean all the time, wondering, then hoping it was just squirrel.

They talked about everything imaginable and steered away fron such topics as the War Between The States, politics, and the cargo, no wanting to give any more hints to the tented neighbors listening for a chance to find treasure.

George reached for his coat. "So, are you finished with your dinner?"

"We aren't going out drinking tonight, are we?" he asked, almost complaining.

"No, we still need to get a few supplies that can't be retained during the day," answered George, pushing his arm into the warm sleeves of his jacket.

"What can't be retained during business hours?" he asked with furrowed eyebrows.

"He means to take something without asking," called out his neighbor who spoke perfect George.

John hurried with his boots while the older man stoked the fire and blew out the lamp.

They stepped out into the cold night, and his nose hairs seemed to freeze in place. He took a moment to wrap his face with his scarf and then catch up to the older man, who walked quickly away from the tent camp.

"George, where are we going?" he asked, struggling again to keep up with the older man.

"We need to equip ourselves properly if we are going to get the gold from the snags," he answered in a near whisper, stopping their progress and explaining his actions.

John didn't bother re-educating George about the cargo and just chose to say, "Please continue," motioning for him to keep walking.

They would need to stop at three places before returning to the tent, first at old Doc Ron's home and office. John knew it because of the sign in the front yard and the fact both he and George had worked for the man for half a day back last April.

"George, won't he hear us prowling around in his back yard in the middle of the night?" he asked, already regretting the decisions that brought him to this place and time.

Consortium of Acquaintances

"Doc Ron is a good man, but he is known to partake in sleepi powders to calm his mind. He wanted me to do the same for the sar reason," he answered, peeking in the side window.

"Why are we here?"

"Yous' remember that pulley and rope we used," he answered.

"You mean, last April? Maybe, what about it?" he asked even thou he didn't remember the rope.

"We need the rope because I know you don't have the money for new one," answered George, wiping a near-frozen booger from his nos

Tallying yet another one of George's nasty personal habits. "How you know he has it?"

"Because I..." he answered, seeming to slow as his brain began rattle the logic around for a minute.

"George, can we just find the rope?"

"I reckon it is in here," he answered, moving off into the small sh that wasn't much more than a lean-to before returning with the rope.

"Good, where to next?"

"We need to take a trip over to the mill and find some planks," said, taking longer steps than average, stomping the fresh snow under h worn boots.

***

Two hours later, it started to snow just as the faint light of Yakin City came close enough to make out the silhouette of the individu buildings. Lucky thought it was ironic that on a night without th slightest sliver of the moon to show the way, Binky would send the back to town. "Say, fellas, when do you figure the full moon would l overhead again," he asked, pulling to the left on the reins to avoid sticker bush.

"It's up now just hiding behind the cloud and fog, but won't be fu for a week," answered Kelly, following Lucky around the bush.

"We should have waited until then," said Joseph pushing through the bush, and was rewarded by the horse nearly throwing him to the snowy ground.

"This business can't wait a week," demanded Lucky, snickering at the horse clatter from the rear.

"What business is this that brings us here so late in the evening on a Saturday night, besides drink'n?" asked Sebastian, handling his horse with the confidence of a child.

"We aim to kill a man," answered Lucky, quietly, without a bit of remorse in his tone as they passed the darkened mill.

"You mean Mr. Binky sent us to town to kill a man," announced Joseph loud enough to rattle every last nerve in the group of outlaws.

"Shut your food hole, you're no longer allowed to speak until we get to the Lucy," shouted Lucky watching Joseph for any sign of aggression. It might be said his life was in the balance even if he wasn't smart enough to understand it.

It began to snow again. This time, nickel size flakes fell on the men and their horses with only their hats and coats for protection.

***

A few minutes later, John and George sat behind a woodpile at the mill. They had heard riders on the trail coming into town.

George had covered John's mouth.

John pulled at the older man's hand, not because he wanted to make noise. It was because it was George's hand, and he had not seen the man clean himself to a standard that he wanted the man touching his face. He was surprised at the older man's strength.

As the men passed, they spoke loudly about killing a man tonight.

"Did you hear what he just told us?"

John didn't answer because of the before-mentioned hand. The best he got out was a muffled noise that sounded like a mating call of a bird.

"My apologies, that was Binky's gang," said George, wiping his hand in the snow and then drying it on his trousers.

Consortium of Acquaintances

"Did they say they meant to kill a man?" he asked, taking a dee breath of fresh air and noticing the 3 inches of snow was cold an somewhat uncomfortable.

"He did," answered George, picking Two planks and handing the to John.

"Why are we taking boards?" he asked, wondering just how man items George borrowed in a week.

"Well, it's because we are going to need them to cross the mudflat c the other side of the river tomorrow," he answered, and as quickly a those words left George's mouth, he found respect again for the man.

"So, where is the last place we are going to this late at night?" aske John taking care not to fall into the wagon ruts left by the many travele to the mission.

"Well, I thought we could stop by the Lucy for a quick pull," h answered, stumbling towards town.

'And there is the George I know,' he thought, luckily he had onl thought it. "We took a man's rope and took two boards from the mill, an you want to what set them on the front stoop of the Saloon and wha hope no one trips on the evidence?" said John, lifting the boards onto h shoulder.

"Well, not when you say it like that," said George pausing a momer to let the younger man catch up.

"Well, maybe if you help me back to your tent, we could drop th inside, and then I could stay and poke at the fire while you head t Sheriff Miller's place and tell him what we heard," said John startin again for the tent city on the other side of town.

"What we hear?" asked George getting in step behind the younge man, almost putting his board through the seamstress' shop window.

"About the men planning on murdering someone," he answered raising his voice and moving closer to George.

"Oh yeah, we should tell someone about," he uttered, looking aroun to see if they were being followed or watched.

"Yes, maybe you should try to do it, so no one knows it is you," he suggested, stopping and turning, spinning the ill-gotten spoils held on his shoulder.

"How should I do that, call up to his window and hide behind a bush," said George, counting at least three ways he could lose his life over that plan.

"How about you knock on the door of Sheriff Miller's house and leave a note," suggested John, turning back to face the direction to the tent.

"Nope, won't work. I can't do what you demand of me," answered George, ducking in time, so the planks didn't knock him out.

"I didn't really demand. Why George?" he asked, slowing and only turning slightly this time.

"Why, what?"

"You know, talking to you is like pulling teeth. Once you begin, it is awfully painful," declared John a little too bluntly.

"I don't know my letters, so I can't leave a note by my hand," answered George rather glumly. Of course, he was lying, and if the light had been brighter, he was sure John would have known. He had his reasons, and they would have only complicated the matter.

"My apologies, I can write the note," he said, moving the boards to the other shoulder.

"It's fine. I headed off to war with a drum in my hand before I picked up a rifle for my land," continued the older man in a sing-song kind of voice.

"You know a great many Battle Hymns from both sides, why is that?" asked John, more than interested in the man's past. He believed if he could get a straight answer or two from the man, he could start adding things up. However, at this point, it wasn't hopeful he would ever really know George until the man was ready to tell him.

"Good music is catchy even if a man is wearing grey," he said, trying to remember who had told him that the first time. He thought of Ulysses Grant for a moment and decided he wouldn't have said that to him.

Consortium of Acquaintances

"How long were you in the army?" asked John, wondering how t[ ] man's story ended him up out here in the middle of nowhere.

"Twelve years in the Union Army, serving in one capacity another," replied George.

"So did you know anyone that ran off and joined the Confederates?"

"Once again, you don't see the forest for the trees," answer[ ] George, sounding as lucent as he had in all the time John had known t[ ] man. "I may have grown up in the south, but not every southern foug[ ] for the Confederacy. As not every Northerner fought for the Union. [ ] man just made up his mind and chose a side. I had been in the army f[ ] six years before the Confederate States Army attacked Fort Sumter. I h[ ] the same commander all through the war. I was there at the beginni[ ] and there at the very end," answered George as his eyes turned down the edges, and he looked like a man that had seen things that haunt[ ] him.

"That leaves a couple of years after the war," said John, with [ ] questioning look on his face.

"Followed along on the coattails of the man I served during the war[ ]

"Amazing you lived through so much. I can write it down for y[ ] sometime," said John, looking back over his shoulder.

"Thank you, but a man's experience can't be summed up by wor[ ] alone. Unless you experience something near the same."

They stood on the boardwalk not far from the Lucy Saloon. "I shou[ ] have thanked you for everything you have done along with all the he[ ] you have given me. How many men did you kill?"

"Ah, John, that is something you should never ask a man that serve[ ] It's between him and his God." His shoulders slumped a momen[ ] contemplating his response. "I will answer, because I am proud a[ ] ashamed of my answer of none, at least not intentionally," whispere[ ] George with the kind of remorse that comes with age and neglect.

He looked at the veteran and was confused at his answers an[ ] somehow understood the older man a little better. "Thank you agai[ ] George."

"No, I owe you a debt I am aiming to repay," said George, picking up the pace and attempting to end the conversation on the matter.

Struggling to keep up with the older man on the verge of a coughing fit. "I'm sure you have covered any debt you owed me."

"Trust me, John," said George, stumbling a little before regaining his footing.

"I trust you because my little girl told me too," he said, smiling awkwardly at how he sounded.

George looked up, seeming a little confused as to what John had just told him. After a second or two, he nodded and continued their walk back to the tent.

***

Sixty minutes later, Lucky held his amber swill high in the air, above the table tucked in the back corner of the Lucy Saloon.

"We should go check out the Emporium," suggested Sebastian, quickly concurred by Kelly, "What I'm trying to say is he might be over there. If we sit here all night, we might miss him."

Joseph groaned.

"I told you not to drink it so quick. That stuff will make you go blind," declared Kelly, who looked over at Joseph, who had not so much as muttered anything for the last 45 minutes.

"I needed to steady my nerves. I never murdered a man before," whispered Joseph into the crook of his arm.

"You still have not broken that commandment, fella," said Lucky, swallowing his shot in one gulp and taking a deep breath as it burned its way to his stomach.

"What are we going to do if he doesn't show up?" asked Kelly, pouring more whiskey into Lucky's glass and touching his own up.

"Kelly, take Seb over to the Emporium, just make sure you keep it in your trousers. Take a quick look around and see if you notice him, then come back here before I finish my next drink."

"Awe, Lucky, you knowed' I wanted to."

Consortium of Acquaintances

"Kelly, you can keep it held up one more hour until our business done," said Lucky, watching the two boys already heading for the on brothel for 100 miles; he watched as the younger men passed by t window out front. He could see the snow was coming down even hard than when they rode in earlier.

"You know they are going to run, don't you," muttered Joseph, n looking up because the room was spinning.

"Yet they will be not back any sooner," whispered Lucky, taking t shot of alcohol, raising it to have a look at it before pouring it into h mouth and swallowing.

"Why do you do that?" asked Joseph.

"Long story. Let us just say it is for luck," said Lucky, whisperir with a certain sadness in his eye.

"I would give them an extra 5 or 10 minutes," muttered Josep glancing up to look at Lucky.

"I was just reckonin' we should wait at least that long," laugh Lucky, watching a couple of the sheriff's deputies as they poste themselves up by the front door.

Chapter 20
December 20th, 1873
Yakima City, Washington Territory

Sheriff Irvine Miller sat behind his desk, cleaning his Peacemaker given to him by the good people of Yakima City. He gave far more to his town than the town offered to him. In the western towns he worked in, his experience as a lawman and his large frame helped him stay alive. He liked to believe he could handle most problems without resorting to violence.

His deputy, Don Barber, was an average man of average intelligence. He excelled at nothing and seemed to struggle with the most common of tasks.

For instance, Sheriff Miller suggested finding some candidates to fill in for him on his days off each week. When he returned, he had offered four men his job. Unfortunately, they all accepted and showed up at the same time.

"Don, I asked you to find another deputy so you could time off each week. How many days off are you planning on taking?" asked Sheriff Miller, picking up his Peacemaker and running his fingers down the barrel and spinning the cylinder before holstering his weapon. He waited for the less experienced deputy to speak.

"Just the two," answered Don, looking to the men standing just inside the door.

Consortium of Acquaintances

"Well, I quit my job for this," declared Linnie, slipping his han into his pockets and managing to pull his shoulders closer. Maybe as effort to show he wouldn't take up much room.

"Well, if it's just the same, I can go to the feed store because th told me I had a job there if I wanted it," suggested a short, overweig man already walking out the door.

"Well, I bet they do since that was my job. I quit working there wh your deputy convinced me there was a much better paying job rig here," complained Linnie, now showing his disappointment by turni around and glaring at Deputy Don.

"Mama is going to tan your hide, Donny," admonished Matt Barb who was, in fact, Don's little brother. Little being of age and not a other aspects of the man's description.

"Quit," said Don, looking sternly towards his brother. Who may ha been his little brother but wasn't in size.

"Who might you two be?" asked Sheriff Miller, turning to one of t men that was partially hiding behind Matt Barber.

"I'm Wally Dutkow, and this is..." he answered but was elbowed the other man. He turned to his friend slightly.

"Linnie Smit, I'm...well, we are from up north and been here in tow since the fires in August. We are trying to earn money to purchase ranch here or up north," he said, looking back to Wally to see if there w anything he wanted to add on his own accord.

"Ranching is an honest profession, so I take it no one here has a law enforcement experience?" asked Sheriff Miller, adjusting his weig in his chair leaning it back against the wall. His eyes wandered over t applicants and stopped on Deputy Don. He briefly wondered if Depu Don and understood his implication.

"No, but we wanted to learn," answered Wally, taking a step forwar and hitting his thigh on the desk.

"I want to learn as well," declared Matt, deciding Wally's answ was a good one, looking from the sheriff to Don, his brother.

"Well, here is the thing of the thing. I only need one extra man, and experience really isn't needed, but it would have been helpful," he said, stopping and looking at Deputy Don.

Don lowered his head, "I apologize."

Sheriff Miller brought both hands down on the table with a loud report. He watched as Matt Barber nearly jumped outside. The other two were as cold as ice. He wasn't sure it was a good sign or not. "I will give it a try for the week. I want two men on at all times for the next few days. The city will cover your wages. If I can swing it, two of you will have a job by the end of the week," said Sheriff Miller, pushing off the wall and dropping the legs of the chair back onto the floor. Pushing off with each hand on the desk, he stood. He reached into his drawer and pulled three deputy badges used for posses.

"They are cheaply made but gets the job done," stated Deputy Don, repeating a speech the sheriff had given posses more than a few times.

"Yes, they are, and they will work just fine for the week. Now, take the new deputies on a tour of Yakima City, point out troublemakers and places where trouble usually happens," ordered Sheriff Miller, waving them away with several swipes of his hand.

"Yes, sheriff," said Deputy Don, already motioning for them to follow him.

"Sheriff, I wasn't planning on walking around tonight. Now don't get me wrong, I am willing to do it. The trouble is I don't have a gun," said Deputy Matt, after taking three turns down blind streets to convey his meaning.

"Well, Deputy, you shouldn't need one tonight. Come see me in the morning if you have nothing useful at home to strap to your hip," he replied, leaning forward and preparing to leave.

After they said their farewells, he watched the four younger men leave and turn to the right once they reached the boardwalk.

In the distance, he heard a few shots. He knew Don would look into it if there were something to investigate. "Now to head home for the night and gets some sleep," he said, turning the light down and locking the door behind him.

Consortium of Acquaintances

He brought his coat together at the top and tipped his hat low. It w cold, maybe 30 degrees, and snowing. He judged there to be about thr inches now. He looked up, trying to evaluate the clouds, but it w impossible to tell due to the fog and snow falling the size of acorns.

"Evening Sheriff," said a younger man, passing him on the stre with a four-seater buggy.

"Evening Henry, would you be passing my place?" asked Sheri Miller, already deciding if it would be easier to move the bundles goods or just sit in the back.

"Sure would, would you like a ride?" asked Henry, placing his hai on his items picked up from the feed store and nodding for the sheriff ride in the back. "We will just need to move them back when I drop yc off."

"That would be nice of you. I wasn't looking forward to walkir across town on a night such as this," he answered, climbing in tl backseat. "I see the misses had you out buying food for your chickens the feed store?"

"Oh this," he answered but was interrupted by Mayor Daniels.

"No, Irvine, it was my little bribe to get Henry here to give us a ric so we can talk."

"Well, Mayor, I'd thought you would have been out home in yov slippers by now."

"I might have been in bed by now if not for a little birdie. I was c my way home when someone told me that you hired four men th evening. I am here to see what has become of your senses," he said, onl stopping when they went by the Lucy. He noticed Lucky and several the new fellas taking up space.

Sheriff Miller started to follow his gaze when the mayor touched h shoulder and caused him to look back at the large man. By the time h took a quick look, he had missed whoever caught the mayor's eye.

"Why are you ramping up the amount of lawman. When you hav only needed one for the last four years?" asked Mayor Daniels, wit what seemed to be a genuine concern.

"There is no good reason I can share with you at this here moment. If you like, foreknow them as a forecast of the future," answered Sheriff Miller, which was strictly speaking the truth. If he told the mayor how Deputy Barber had asked four men to come in for a part-time job, the mayor was likely to fire the deputy.

"Well, we have secrets between us now. You know there isn't anything that upsets the apple cart more than secrets," he said, mixing metaphors.

"Who will it upset to have an extra deputy or two, and what do apples have to do with it?" asked Sheriff Miller, trying a little levity since logic seemed to fail.

"Oh, shut up, you know what I mean," answered Mayor Daniels as Henry started to snicker in the front seat. "Henry, there is no need to encourage the Sheriff."

"Mayor, this town is full of secrets, and the more I look into them, the more I've become concerned that you're leading our town down a dark path. You have only been here for a few years but have risen to how an office that is normally held by someone that is elected," said Sheriff Miller, stepping off the carriage when Henry stopped to let a group of men walk across the street.

"Well, unless you plan to pay for those new deputies out of your pocket, you will reduce their size tonight."

"Fine, I will let one go as soon as I find him," he said, figuring the man that left for the new job at the feed store was the fourth man, but the mayor didn't need to know that.

"Thank you for your understanding, but even three new hires will need to be thinned unless you don't wish to become just a memory like the last mayor. If I were you, I would fall back in line," said Mayor Daniels, which was the first time he had directly threatened him.

"Mayor, I will need a little time to figure out who are the better men to have. Deputy Don is good with people but not so good with his gun."

"Well, make your decision quickly," he said and motioned for Henry to continue. "These minor inconveniences are beginning to add up to a reckoning." His voice faded as the wagon pulled away. He was alon again in more ways than one.

He had never been talked to that way in as many years as he cou remember. The hairs on the back of his neck rose when a wagon full men wandered by. It was mostly the way they looked at him. Halfwa home, it occurred to him the wagon had been following them. They ha even stopped when he got out of the carriage and waited for him to finis their conversation.

He stopped at his front door and looked at the notes that had bee pinned to the door. He slipped them into his pocket and headed off find his deputies. He had business in town and would need the ne deputies to at least look like they could back his play. Which wa whatever he decided to do in the next few minutes.

Chapter 21
December 21st, 1873
Yakima City, Washington Territory

Some mornings you wake up with the smell of breakfast and your mother singing in what stands for a kitchen. Then there are the mornings you're unfortunate to have a traumatized child sleeping twelve feet away. Screaming in into the darkened cabin as if it were her job to wake the people around her.

This morning, if one could call it morning since the sun had yet to make its appearance, was peaceful until Annie let out a scream that undoubtedly was heard by the wildlife for miles. Elizabeth thought of wildlife running away and then thought how easy it would be to follow them.

"I'm coming, baby girl," declared Elizabeth, as she pulled at her covers and reached for her stockings. She was telling herself that she was getting used to the night terrors and the wet sheets. 'No one alive could get used to a young girl's wretched screams in the middle of the night.' she thought, glancing up into the loft.

"They're getting in," screamed Annie.

"Who dear?" asked Elizabeth, squinting through foggy eyes to find a match to light the lamp.

Annie let out a second scream.

"Oh, please come back to me, John," whispered Elizabeth as she climbed the little ladder into the loft where Annie slept when she got a chance to rest. The nightmares plagued her dreams and spoiled a chance for anyone in the cabin to relax.

Just two days, they had been alone, knowing, no hoping, that J was safe in the settlement and would be starting for home soon. Th what took a few hours to travel to town could take a week or longer return. She had no idea how many variables to consider, from weather to the wildlife that wanted to eat him.

Everything affects travel out here in the middle of nowhere. A m comes to your door in the dead of night, and you have no one to call help. She glanced at the door, the bolt, and the handle before turning her ward.

"Annie, Annie!" she said lovingly, pulling her sweat-covered bo free of the quilts. It suddenly occurred to her that the work was nev done, and she would need to wash her daughter's bedding once aga She briefly thought of the Blue Wave saloon and cleaning the rooms Sunday morning. She decided that life wasn't so hard compared to t work accomplished there in a day and night.

"The Drake was here, and he turned into a wolf and scratched at th door and threw his body against it and came to the window and looked and watched as we hid behind the beds," said Annie behind tear-soake eyes and a snot covered upper lip.

"Yes, little one, you are safe," she spoke calmly and deliberately. Sh then glanced at the door and decided to leave the beam in place unles they went out.

"I know, it's when they are digging at the roof until dirt begins to fa on the bed, I started to, you know," Annie muttered through pouting lip She tucked her head against her new mother's bosom.

"We saved you months ago, and I chased Drake off," said Elizabeth patting her back. She decided that her nightgown would need a goo washing.

Even on trying nights such as these, Elizabeth had decided that it wa fine because Annie would always come first. She just wondered if eve she would come first. She held her daughter as if she were her own Hiding her eyes, she began to cry into Annie's shoulder.

"It's alright to cry," said Annie plainly and patting her new mommy on the back.

After a few minutes, she straightened her nightgown. "Let us get you cleaned up, and you can rest awhile in my bed," she said as she began to pull her nightshirt off, stopping herself. "Wait here." She slipped down the ladder and walked quickly to the water bucket, where she pulled a red piece of cloth from the wood slat basket that John had made. She poured a little water into a large washbasin and started back to the loft.

She stopped near the table and set the bowl down. Then calmly walked back to the window to make sure they were alone. She could see that it was still snowing, and it looked like they had nine, maybe ten inches out there in her yard, and the drifts were even more foreboding. She wished she knew the temperature only if it was so she could record it in her journal. She had put a thermometer on the list. However, what was essential to her wasn't always vital to John. She hoped he would bring one back but wouldn't fret about it. She only wished he would hurry back.

When she was satisfied that no one was watching, she turned and picked up the washbasin returning to Annie's loft.

"Did you see him?" asked Annie, lifting her arms as Elizabeth washed her from top to bottom.

"No, I did not," she answered, already in the planning stages for curtains for the window. It was true that she was out of usable material, although that didn't include that ugly pattern that her husband bought to keep the window panes safe from the bumpy trail that led them to their meadow.

Soon she was clean and redressed in one of John's shirts. It didn't take her long to fall asleep from pure exhaustion. Quietly, Elizabeth moved off the bed. She covered her with a blanket and kissed her forehead before returning to Annie's loft to retrieve the soiled bedding.

The cabin was like a cave. Even though most of the drafts are plugged with moss and grass, it was still drafty. Stopping the drafts gives the cabin warmth from just being free of the effects of the cold winds of

winter. She understood now why John had covered the roof with a th
layer of thatch that insulated their home.

She gathered the bedding and started for the kitchen side of
cabin. It was where the washing would take place due to the snowsto
last night. She passed Annie, who was snuggled with Mister Nickels, l
dolly. She could feel a slight draft that she had not noticed before com
from under their bed.

Leaning down, she noticed a little door behind the bed. "Now, w
on earth did John put a hatch into the back of the cabin. Didn't he kn
that all that was back there was dirt," she said, pondering the reasc
why he would do so.

She made up her mind that the air leak would need to be plugg
with some insulation made from the cloth she wanted to use to ma
curtains. She wished she had a better color of the material. She had us
all the fabric supplies when they met Annie. All those months ago, wh
they found her, the child had nothing. In a matter of a few days, she h
made the poor girl three dresses, and John even provided a church sh
so Annie could have a nightshirt that fell to her ankles.

She smiled at the thought of her husband's caring heart; as she set t
bedding on the table, she said quietly, "Morning, husband."

She knew her love couldn't hear her. However, it felt good to say
anyway. She walked to the fireplace to stir the coals and added small
pieces of wood.

She watched the little pieces of wood take the flame and added larg
pieces to the fire as it grew higher. "You said I would never get used to
hearth fireplace. Well, John, I'm used to it, and now, I want a stove," sh
said to no one but thought she would practice for when she talked to hi
again.

One day soon, she would tell him that they needed a stove fc
cooking, and until that opportunity arose, she would practice what sh
was going to say on the fireplace.

She didn't like asking her husband for things all the time.
reminded her of St. Louis. She didn't miss the days she spent working a
the Blue Wave. She felt guilty and dirty as it crossed her mind. Mayb

hat's why she loved living out here in the middle of nowhere. It gave her place to believe that being alone felt normal.

She warmed the wash water in the large kettle and left it near the fire on the right side. It was tricky to cook on the hearth without getting burnt. She had a few months of trial and error to figure out what worked and failed to different degrees.

The fireplace was built quickly without really a complete understanding of the needs of cooking. For instance, the fireplace was constructed of pillow basalt collected from the hills east of the cabin. Elizabeth remembered carrying each piece to the wagon and then carrying the blocks from the wagon to the cabin's future home. If they had bought brackets and metal arms to hang the pots, she wouldn't need to blacken one side of the pan only to stir them and twist it around to heat the other side.

She filled the second-largest pot with potatoes and the last of the deer meat from last night's dinner. Then seasoned the pot with salt and dried peppers from the farm. Rations were running out, and they only had the potatoes and carrots left in the field under the snow. If she had to, she would take the shovel out and dig for her dinner.

John's green thumb seemed to grow potatoes and carrots and not much else. It was strange how they planted all the seeds Harry had given them, but nothing grew except for the potatoes and a few carrots. She didn't mind; he had won her heart, risked his life for her freedom, then he brought her out to this paradise, and she loved every minute of it.

She glanced at the door once more and made sure the beam was in place. Her eyes wandered to the windows, and she imagined that odd pattern hung in front of them. The image of the patterned material in the window half talked her out of the curtains. However, it occurred to her that she undressed in front of those windows last night.

***

There was a time not so long ago when Elizabeth was known by another name. Now, her given name was legally known to be Elizabeth

Tate. It would be explained that there was no need or use for last name or even Christian names at the Blue Wave. They only needed to recall her name upon her death, which drew a nervous chuckle from several ladies of various nationalities and ages.

It wasn't long before she would figure out why the talk of death drew nervous chuckles. It was the day she witnessed real cruelty and learned to laugh nervously as a coping mechanism.

When she applied for work at the Blue Wave, the man behind the bar, thin and middle-aged, spoke in a European accent of an unknown nation of origin. His face was like a ferret, and his whiskers were as rough to look at as they were to feel. When questioned about where he was from, he was like the rest of the people that sought work at the Blue Wave Saloon. He changed his story to fit his mood or the lunar cycle, whichever made the man more money.

When Eliza met John Springer, she wished she could say it was under better circumstances, being the first time she met him, he had walked into the Blue Wave Saloon. She felt like a sausage in her new blue dress that was a size or two too small. She had bought the dress that way, and every evening she stuffed herself into it by sucking in her gut and with a bit of help with her buttons.

A portly woman with large breasts, Mags would sit on Eliza and pull that dress tight, buttoning each button from her lower back to her shoulders. Then Eliza would return the favor by doing the same for Mags. Only most of Mags' dresses had straps, which made the job a little easier. However, it was harder to get out of it by herself. After all, the point of her employment was getting out of dresses for the patrons that frequented the establishment.

Officially, she was paid as a seamstress even though she didn't sew anything other than her buttons, which seemed to pop off several times a night for some unambiguous reason. The weekend crowds always caused rips in exquisite fabrics. Mags would always say, "Don't look at the rip as an offense, but an opportunity to improve one's sewing skills."

Now, no one wakes up one day and says, "Hey, I want to work at the Blue Wave Saloon and sell my private wares to nasty old men and nexperienced young drifters." You're led like a lamb into the life by the imple desire to fulfill a need in your life. For instance, Mags had a ninor addiction that required four doses of Laudanum for pains in her nead and her mommy parts, as she called them.

Marybeth, the oldest in the gaggle of women, claimed she got into he business after her husband died in the first battle of the War Between he States, even though she could never name the engagement and had a nard time pinning down the name of her husband.

Jenny's only desire was to live where she didn't feel fear every minute of the day. It was true that she missed the plot when she chose to work at the Blue Wave; however, she would remind the others that there were always far worse places to live and work. Places to live, where the cruelty flows freely from the tap, and she was forced to lap it up like a dog.

Eliza's addiction was that of food: she desired to be fed a couple of times a day, and a roof over her head was an added bonus. However, when Elizabeth was questioned about why she had come to work at the Blue Wave Saloon, she would say Laudanum while complaining of various pains. She had made a game of it, never giving the same body part twice.

Then John came into her life. He took one look at her, and Eliza's eyes locked onto his like a predatory animal. She smiled shyly and moved close enough that John could smell her French perfume. It was the love he shared with her in those first moments.

It was the kind of love where a man would ignore every reason not to love a woman and only see the beauty within and the softness of what must be inside.

She would always regret what she had said to him the first time they met, asking him, "Do you want to read my book, and maybe I could eat your sandwich." Except, it wasn't to read a book and the Blue Wave Saloon served no food.

Yes, the before-mentioned softness was indeed buried deep inside.

John was there with friends and wholly mortified at what had come out of her mouth. He had fallen in love as soon as he had seen her next to

the bar. He had married her in his mind as she floated over to his side a
froze when she had questioned him about going with her upstairs.

He wished that he had said something the first time they met,
snappy comeback like "yes," or "no," or "maybe later." Instead, his bo
had chosen to lose all reason and the use of his vocal cords.

He froze for a minute or an hour, he wasn't sure because when
looked around, she was gone, and his friends sat with silly grins at a tab
with half a glass of ale down their gullets.

"Fellas, I'm going to marry that woman," said John, after his voc
cords came back from wherever they had retreated.

The three other young men let out bellows of laughter; even th
would not deter his love for her.

Chapter 22
December 21st, 1873
Yakima City, Washington Territory

Sheriff Miller stopped at the end of the street. He glanced at the note one more time and folded it, placing it in the breast pocket of his wool jacket. The message read, Binky's Boys are in town to murder one of the fine citizens of Yakima City. You have been warned.

He always had an understanding with the Mayor and Binky that their lawbreaking would refrain from entering the city limits, and no murdering of anyone would be allowed anywhere in the region.

He walked up the street, turned at the Emporium, and bumped into two younger men who seemed intent on entering the town brothel. "Excuse us, sheriff, Lucky only gave us 20 minutes," said the younger of the two.

"By all means, gentlemen have a free feel on me," he said, letting them pass down the boardwalk. He wondered in the morning if he would be getting a bill from the Emporium. He laughed and thought. 'If I do, I will pay for it. It's only fair. After all, at this point, Lucky is short a couple of men.'

"Where the heck are They?" said Sheriff Miller aloud, looking up the block as he started across the street, primarily due to the fact the snowdrifts were half as large on that side. He needed to find his deputies that were supposed to be walking the streets this evening. He hadn't expected them to stay out all night, but it wasn't even midnight.

Consortium of Acquaintances

Passing Johnston's Boarding House, he slowed and looked up th alley. He was in darkness as he moved, half feeling his way, pausin when he heard someone moving in his direction. The footsteps sounde like the cracking of ice.

"Well, hello, Sheriff Miller," said Deputy Don, walking from th alley. "I just showed them the Winston and the Labor Camp."

The sheriff quickly counted three deputies. "Where is the big fella?"

The two new deputies began to laugh, but a stern look from th sheriff quieted them down.

"He was crossing the street down that away, and he slipped an landed in what looked to be a shallow frozen puddle," said Deputy Do even he was fighting back the laughter. "It turned out to be neither froze nor shallow."

"That's not the worse of it?" said Deputy Durkow, losing the battl with the humorous nature of their conversation.

"When he stood up, he continued down the block with us, being th trooper, he is known far and wide to be," said Deputy Don, trying t bring a little dignity to his brother's plight.

"He started yipping and hollering my little soldier is going to freez off," said Deputy Smit before getting a look by Deputy Don that told hir to be quiet.

"We looked down, and his trousers are frozen solid,"

"Where is he?"

"We left him around the corner in the hotel to warm his littl soldier," said Deputy Don, finally giving in and laughing at the whol matter.

The sheriff chuckled for a few seconds, then told them to keep i down, mainly using gestures with his hands. "Alright, you had your fun We need to find your brother and put a shotgun in his hands and hav him meet us in front of the Lucy. You two head down in front of the Lucy but try to stay hidden. I will take the alley and get my double from th gun-rack in the office. We need to hurry. A couple of his men are in th Emporium. They said Lucky is expecting them back in I would say abou quarter-hour."

"What are we arresting him for?"

"They are suspected to be planning a murder. I have a letter from a reliable source that says as much. If we act fast, we can save lives, maybe our own," answered Sheriff Miller, starting for the sheriff's office. The truth was, after the talk with the mayor, what worried him the most was if the latter was talking about himself. "If those charges don't work out, then we will get them for being drunk and disorderly."

Don headed around the corner and into the hotel to find his brother. He came out almost as quickly with his brother without his pants figuring his long-johns would have to do.

Within five minutes, they stood in front of the Lucy. Sheriff Miller stood aside and waited for Deputy Don to call him out.

He walked out with his hand on his gun, and his hat leached up around his neck. "Evening Sheriff," he said, now noticing the two shotguns and three revolvers already pointed in his direction.

"Lucky, it's my understanding that you are here in town to kill a man. I'm here to tell you that it is not going to happen. To make sure the peace is assured you're going to spend night in the jail or until I decide otherwise," said Sheriff Miller, motioning from him to raise his hands.

"I am just here to enjoy a night drinking with my friends. But if you want to feed me for a few days. I can wait until someone informs the mayor. I'm sure he will want to hear about it." he shouted over his shoulder back into the Lucy.

"I'm sure someone will run and let him know in a few minutes. You can count on the townsfolk and their gossip," said Deputy Don, taking Lucky's revolver and his boot-knife.

He looked over at one of the deputies who was without trousers. "We better hurry and get over to the jail before this one has his pecker froze off."

They all laughed at his prodding, somehow releasing the tension. Lucky thought it odd they laughed, but who was he to ask questions. He glanced over and saw Kelly and Sebastian about to draw down on the deputies and shook his head. They were liable to get him shot in the crossfire.

Consortium of Acquaintances

"What you want us to do with the other one in the Lucy?" ask Deputy Don, still aiming his revolver in Lucky's direction.

"I reckon we should bring him over to the office, and we will let h sober up over there. We can decide what to do with him tomorrow."

A few minutes later, the street was empty, the jail was full, and lamp was lit over at the mayor's house.

In the fresh snow, there could be seen three different sets of tracks. set of tracks led from the Lucy to the mayor's house, one trail led over the livery, and a couple sets headed back to the Emporium.

After all, they couldn't be expected to ride out and tell Binky in t middle of the night. It was hard enough to find their way into town.

Chapter 23
December 21st, 1873
A few west of Yakima City, Washington Territory

The campfire popped, sending embers into the sky as well as at the feet of Binky and his men. Kelly and Sebastian had stayed in Yakima City after Lucky's arrest. They were both new to the area, having been to town a couple of times, so they had little options afforded to them as to where they could spend their night.

"Whores, you spent the night with whores at the Emporium. Where were you when Sheriff Miller took Lucky?" asked Binky, spitting his words at the two younger men in the hot seat. He was mad but hadn't decided who to direct his fury, these numb-skulls or whoever approved his Lieutenant's arrest.

"Lucky told us to head over to the Emporium and go see if the man was over enjoying the skills of the ladies. We came back pretty quick," answered Sebastian, sounding altogether too friendly.

Binky noticed Sebastian was worried. He got face to face with him and commanded, "Stop talking."

Sebastian thought Binky looked like a devil spitting steam from his mouth. He often had trouble daydreaming about people he both knew and watched from afar. He often mused internally about a person's past or at least the history he made up for them.

"We just spent the night in the parlor of the Emporium. We didn't have the money for the works," answered Kelly, looking back and forth between Binky and Lomax, who was becoming more involved in th discussion as it progressed.

Sebastian nodded in agreement with Kelly's explanations of th events as they transpired before returning to his thoughts of Binky an the gang. The truth was he could have told Binky every detail that ha happened today. But, he could not have explained how and the question left unanswered would bring unwanted attention in his direction. H looked at Kelly and admired him for the way he carried himself. Kell was just as young as himself and seemed to be the most genuine. He ha made a measure of the men around him, and at least in his eyes, ther wasn't anyone else that had told the truth about where they came fror and how they ended up here.

"Joseph, where the heck is that idiot?" asked Binky, seemingl satisfied with what Kelly had to say. He looked at Sebastian.

Binky had noticed Sebastian had been unusually quiet, watchin clouds of breath vapor escape when everyone spoke. He hadn't made u his mind about the young man, should he keep him in the gang or sen him to drive wagons in town.

Sebastian noticed Lomax had raised an eyebrow and moved withi reaching distance of both of them. "He was lying face down on a tabl until they took Lucky over to the holding cells in the Sheriff's Office, he answered, finding it hard to speak with such a large man so near, man that had been known to have thrown someone through a wall.

"Was he killed?" asked Lomax, leaning closer as if he could loo more menacing. He had brought Joseph in from The Dalles last mont and acted as if he owed him. At least that was the rumor.

"No," answered Kelly, looking at Lomax, waiting for the big man t knock Sebastian or him on their butt. When Lomax refrained fron beating them, he added, "I'm sure he is fine. He was drunk."

"No, sir, he was asleep," said Sebastian, looking over to Kelly Binky, and Lomax. He decided he might be inebriated also but though he would keep that fact to himself.

"Asleep, drunk!" exclaimed Binky, looking over at Lomax, offering im two fingers indicating wherever Joseph was, he had two strikes gainst him. A third, and he would need to find a new job.

"He kinda fell asleep after he took a few shots when we got to the ـucy. He told us he was nervous and needed to calm himself," answered ぐelly, looking back to Sebastian for support.

"Well, because of you fellas losing Lucky and Joseph, I will need to ᑈead back into town and take care of Frank's problem as well as bust ـucky out of jail. I might even eat a steak while you fellas are freezing ⁄our clams off," announced Binky, grabbing for his rifle and sliding it nto the scabbard attached to Tuffy's saddle.

"Where do you want us to be while you're in town?" asked Lomax, ;ounding a little disappointed, walking through four inches of snow to :he tent and slipping inside.

"I know you want to go look into Joseph's whereabouts. It is ⁢mportant to me, as well. You need to understand we need to keep a low ⁣profile and slither around on our bellies a bit. I will see where he is and then send word. How about you have the men break camp and move over ⁣closer to town, maybe Wide Hollow," he answered, giving the orders mostly to keep them busy so they wouldn't repeat last June and go riding through town shooting up the place.

"I like the campsite. It gets more sunlight during the day and less wind at night. The cabin is a tight fit, but then the stove keeps the men warm. It is an added benefit a man can even see someone coming for 1000 yards or better," said Lewis Hawking, the older brother of Tommy and Petey, the younger two who had been in the gang as long as Sebastien.

"Would you apologize for us to Lucky when you see him?" asked Sebastian, honestly trying not to get killed upon his return. He always felt nervous talking to people, whether it was his employer or the one he loved. He would reach for the words that would inspire, but they would not come.

Binky noticed his body language that held something else other than an apologetic disposition. "You are going to need to work it out with

Lucky when he gets back," he said, looking from Sebastian to Ke
before nodding at Lewis, who seemed determined to speak with h
before he headed to town. In the back of his mind, he was deciding
the better of two choices. "Kelly, grab your bedding. We are heading ir
town."

Kelly nodded, looking disappointed, and wandered off to pack.

Sebastian was also disappointed but had pressing matters of his ow
He slipped away to seek out a bush to relieve himself. He was particu
about the bush and was known to need his privacy.

"I'm thinking it's getting mighty cold, and the mountains are alrea
topped with snow. I reckon my brothers and I need to head back to o
family's ranch up north," said Lewis looking down and pushing sno
around with his foot.

"You reckon you could stick around until Lucky gets back? I am
the mind when he gets back, we will all ride out for warmer climates
replied Binky, slipping Tuffy's bit into his mouth and pulling reins ov
his head.

"What's got you spooked? I mean besides Lucky's arrest?" aske
Lewis, turning to watch the others.

"I'm worried about those two," he said, looking over at Kelly an
wondering where Sebastian had disappeared to as he pulled at Tuffy
belly strap.

"What do you want me to do if I stick around? I mean with Sebastia
while you're gone," asked Lewis, taking that moment to yawn an
stretch.

"We will need to play that by ear. As the facts are found out, I will b
making a decision or two concerning those two," answered Binky
noticing Sebastian returning from the bushes only to sit by the campfir
and look disappointed in his direction for some reason.

Chapter 24
December 21st, 1873
Few mile south of the Union Gap

When John's journey began, the river was not much more than that of a stream. A tributary to a nameless river that eventually flows into the Yakima. In turn, the Yakima River in 80 or so miles will make its way into the Columbia. Here, south of town, through the gap in the hills, the river widens, and fortunately for John, the snags and brush go unchecked.

"Are we sure the raft couldn't have landed closer to Yakima City," he said, hacking at the weeds with his father's Bowie knife.

He stirred from his thoughts as the older man took a break in their struggle through the brambles. "No, if that raft ran aground anywhere, it would be hereabouts," answered George. He stumbled over a few stones and pushed his way into the brush that seemed to guard the snowy banks of the Yakima River.

"You know your river," said John with a rather broad smile on his face as he noticed the mountain to the southwest. They were white with snow. It was nice to see the contrast between his mountains and the hills around Yakima City.

The scenery changed dramatically, the river widened, and rocks made the water seem lumpy in places as the current pushed the water over them.

John was about to give up when he spotted the broken raft caught in the snags, just as George had predicted. The river had pooled about

halfway out, and it looked as if a family of beavers had built a rather nic
dam along with the largest beaver lodge he had ever seen.

"Well, lookie over der, who be your best friend now?" asked Georg
as he slapped at his knees and performed a little dance that resembled a
Irish jig but just in a passing way.

"You are my friend," replied John, gleefully pulling him into a one
armed hug, and he also started to dance the jig.

"What are you going to do?"

"Now, the hard part is figuring how to bring it back to shore,
answered John.

"No, now it's time to make a fire," said George, walking away fror
the river in search of bits of wood to start the fire.

"How is that going to get my cargo to shore?" he asked, watching th
old man walk away with long strides as if someone was giving chase.

"It isn't, although, as you mention before, it's freezing, and thes
beans won't finish cooking without a good fire," answered George as hi
voice trailed off back the way they had come.

John pulled the borrowed rope and pulley from the bag, stretched
out, and prepared it by tying the pulley to a small tree with white bark
He didn't recognize the type of tree. It seemed older than the rest of th
trees that lined the river bank.

He fed it through the pulley and prepared to walk out onto the beave
dam to secure the broken half of the sunken raft with the rope.

"I'm going to walk out on the beaver dam. It should be fine; I'n
going to tie myself off." He noticed the smoke coming from about 3
feet away over a small natural berm.

"Yes, it will be fine," answered George, who sounded a bi
distracted.

"If I fall in would you be kind enough to pull me back in and bury
me somewhere nice-n-warm, like Texas?" asked John, saying what migh
be his final words. He tied the rope off to his waist and walked out onto
the dam.

***

Over by the fire, George stood over his beans, blocking the wind. "Yes. I got you," answered George, who went about keeping his fire going and preparing his dried beans. George had a trick to making beans. He figured the sack of beans he had had more than a few bean-sized rocks in each bag. He would use his gold pan to wiggle and shake the beans until the heavier bits would separate.

"Ya, all right," he shouted before realizing the younger man hadn't said anything.

Setting the pot over the fire using tree branches lashed together to make a tripod, he tied the wire handle at just the right height with a piece of string.

"Now to go find out what John is up to," said George to himself as he walked back into the brush.

Coming back to the river, he noticed his partner halfway out and struggling with his balance as he asked, "Say, are you doing all right?"

"Yes, I have the rope tied off to the raft, just having trouble getting back," he answered, reaching out with both hands in different directions for balance.

"How is the gold?" he asked, snickering under his beard.

"George, for Pete's sake, I told you there is no gold," he answered, practically screaming and almost slipping in the water, losing his balance to face the shore.

"So we lost the gold?" he asked, grinning ear to ear. He didn't know why he liked to rile up his new friend, but he knew it was fun to watch his reactions.

"Yes, George, we lost all the gold when the raft turned over. We just have the frames to help with the supplies," he answered, obviously trying a different strategy.

"That's too bad. Ah, John?" he asked, trying to sound as confused as possible.

"George?" answered John, almost back to shore, pausing to hold a tree branch for support and turning to the old man on the bank of the river.

181

"I thought you said there wasn't any gold, like a half dozen times? he asked, again snickering under his beard.

"Old man, are you fooling with me?"

"Maybe a little," he answered with a silly grin reaching out to hel John off the beaver dam and back onto the river bank.

"Are you ready to pull, old man?" he asked as he leaned hard into th last few tugs.

"I'm pulling, I'm pulling," complained George, sounding as if he ha not worked his old bones for a few years.

John had noticed the older man's wrinkled hands were that of bookkeeper's and as nimble as an artist. "There, I can see it, we almo\$ have it," struggling to hold his excitement in place.

"Yous' better hurry. The current is wanting to pull the raft away, admonished George, struggling to hold onto the rope.

"Do not let go. It will fall in and break up in the current," warne John, riding an emotional seesaw, pleading as he started to remove hi boots.

George dug his feet into the mud and settled down to take all of th pressure that was about to be applied to his arms. "Be careful. Th current is still swift even in the shallows, and remember..." He stopped a he watched the younger man take the first step.

"Oh my lord, it is so cold," yelled John, struggling to sound manly he took a second step.

"Ya, yous' didn't remember, did you," laughed George as he watche the younger man take a second step.

"Yes, I did," he acknowledged just as he took another step letting th water come up to his knees.

Just then, the rope slipped, causing John to grab the rope as the olde man attempted to regain his grip. "My apologies, it slipped," saic George.

"If I don't untie the crates and lift them onto the bank, all will be fo not," said John, reaching for the first crate and began pulling at the knots The water climbed up his legs and reached for his groin. "My heavens, didn't reckon it could get any worse."

"I see the Yakima has found your man parts," he laughed, almost letting go of the rope, letting it slide through his weakened fingers once again, causing John to grab hold of the rope once again and wait for George to steady himself.

"Oops," he said, pouting at his momentary mistake.

"George! Hold the rope tight," exclaimed John, with more than a hint of desperation in each spoken word.

"I got it, I got it," he yammered, pulling with a renewed strength and managing to pull the raft a little closer.

"Thank you, George," he said, nodding his head mechanically.

"You will thank me when we are eating beans and getting warm by that fire I took time to build, yes you will," he said, laughing, lowering his head, and struggling with the rope.

"Yes, George, you are a man of many talents," he declared as he set the first crate onto the river bank.

"You mind tell'n a few people in town. I gets the feel'n they don't take me seriously," he stated, sounding solemn as an undertaker.

"If we get these crates into town, I will tell anyone that will listen," he answered as he worked at the knots holding the first crate to what remained of the raft.

"You reckon we can still have that steak and potato dinner you mentioned last night?" asked George, sounding a little tired.

"Yes," he answered as he carried the freed crate back to the bank, setting it a few feet from the tired older man.

"I thought they would be bigger, the crates. I didn't mean anything else," laughed George.

"The frames are in pieces. Even the crates are made of the carved wood," said John walking back to retrieve the last crate.

"In pieces! Are they all broken up? Oh, the ravenous Yakima has taken so much, first the gold and now the crates," he exclaimed, holding the rope tight and sinking into the muddy bank.

"No, there isn't any glue back at the farm. So I brought them down unfinished. I was hoping to finish them in the hotel and sell them the next day," stated John, freeing the last crate and lifting it from the wate and back onto the bank near where he had set the other.

"Let me cut the rope free so that we can return it," he said, reachin down with his knife and starting to cut the raft's rope.

"Say, why didn't you just cut the crates free?" asked George, startin to shiver from the water.

"Because," he answered as he cut the raft free. With just one cut, th raft seemed to separate as it was caught by the current, explaining, "W would have lost it all."

"So even your crates can be made into frames?" asked George, as h saw the crates were erected from the same slats as the contents.

"Yes," answered John.

Picking up the first crate, he started for the warmth of the fire he ha made for them. "That's ingenious. You ready for beans and meat?"

"Yes, I would love to have some beans, and maybe you can tell m what animal ended up in your culinary concoction," he answerec shaking some of the water loose.

"Maybe later, let us, say, a warm day in mid-spring."

"That's perfectly fine," he acknowledged, although he was left t wondering why he should need to wait five months to be told the recipe however, like all of George's stories, it was best to wait for the truth tha rush into a lie.

Chapter 25
December 21st, 1873
Yakima City, Washington Territory

Binky sat in the saddle, feeling every bump as his horse Tuffy did all of the work. They had ridden from West Camp, a bend on the Ahtanum Creek halfway from the mission to Yakima City.

"You know there was a time the only destination in this valley was the Mission," said Binky to Kelly, who was trailing with his horse at a short distance behind him.

"There wasn't a great number of white folk in these parts, I take it," stated Kelly, making a clicking noise with his lips and tapping his horse with his heels to keep up.

"When the Yakima Indian War ended, it opened up most of the Scablands to settlement. Then again, I do not know for sure. I was in New York when it started. I didn't get here until around 12 months ago," said Binky, looking up into the sky, admiring the view.

"Wait, I heard you killed a dozen men. That's quite an accomplishment in such a short time," declared Kelly, stopping to look up at the sky.

"Who told you that?" asked Binky, turning his horse and coming uncomfortably close to the younger man.

"Lucky might of mentioned something, and your wanted poster filled in the details," answered Kelly, as his horse chose to move back to widen the gap.

"Well, I will have a talk with Frank and get that straightened out," h answered, pausing to think about it.

"Is it true, or not?" asked Kelly, waiting for a response.

"Not exactly. Killing a man for any reason is not an accomplishmen nor worth bragging about, to a boy. You have a long way to go befoi anyone will say any different, so for now, change the subject or ride i silence," he answered, egging Tuffy on a little to create a gap betwee them while remaining vigil on his young man's weapons. He had bee told that same lecture by a freed black man named Coyote-Jack.

"You're not in any hurry to get to Yakima City, are you?" aske Kelly coming alongside his boss at a gallop.

"No!" said Binky. He was starting to understand Lucky's opinio concerning Kelly, Joseph, and Sebastian.

"Why?"

"Just ride and enjoy the view."

"What view?" asked Kelly, looking around at the brown hills an clouded sky.

"The clouds are beautiful and would be amazing to paint if one ha the time to do so. Look at the pulchritude of the structure of the clouds unlike a woman's body."

Kelly stopped to watch the clouds and looked back towards the trail He had to ride hard to catch up to his employer. He was quieter now mostly from wondering what his boss just told him because when h looked up, he saw no woman, not even a bunny rabbit.

He brought Kelly with him as a lookout. He was young and neede(more experience. The boy showed signs that he would be a good man t(have around someday. Binky just hoped he would be around to see it.

Coming past the mill, they could see that the town was quiet, whicl Binky had hoped. He knew if he had come to town before the Sunday service, he would have bumped into people like Kelly, that thought h(killed twelve men.

"Look at the footprints in the snow," said Kelly, breaking the silence.

"Yup," answered Binky, tipping his hat down to hide his face from the freezing temperature and prying eyes.

"Where is everybody?"

"Where do you reckon they have gone," replied Binky, answering Kelly with a question.

"I read a Penny Dreadful once, that this Persian prince had the ability to raise the dead and let them walkabout," answered Kelly, sounding as if he was nervous.

He stopped his horse and pulled a cigar out, half-smoked days ago, and slid it between his lips, keeping a close eye on the window curtains making sure people minded their own business.

Kelly rode up close to his employer, watching him light the cigar, waiting for him to respond.

"Hmm, let me ask you again," said Binky, taking the smoke into his lungs in two long drags. "You see a bunch of prints on the ground heading in the same direction at around, let us say, eleven in the morning on a Sunday. And, you being a great reader, have come to the conclusion there are living dead walking the boardwalks of this here town," said Binky, knocking the cherry off the cigar and tucking it away.

"Suppose they could be at church," answered Kelly, watching the older man move off towards the main street.

"Either way, it's best to be ready," said Binky, reaching back and throwing the hammer back on his Peacemaker and pulling the flap off the scabbard that held his Winchester Yellowboy.

"Where do we head from here?" asked Kelly, setting his scattergun across his lap.

"I go pay my respects to our fine mayor and get him to tell me what the heck happened to Lucky last night."

"You reckon he knows?" asked Kelly, turning towards him.

"That man knows everything that happens in this town," he responded, turning up a street one block over from Main and slowly heading up the snow-covered back streets to Frank's house before saying under his hat, "and everything that has happened."

"What was that?" asked Kelly, speeding up his horse to a trot to catch up with him again.

Consortium of Acquaintances

"Nothing of consequence," he responded, looking at the young man bouncing in his saddle next to him.

"You reckon he will be home?" asked Kelly.

"Not many people are, I would imagine," he answered, slowing the horse at the intersection and watching for a minute for movement on the street ahead.

Kelly smartly paused at the same time and listened. "What we wait fer'?" asked Kelly, blowing warm air from his lungs into his balled-up fist.

"Skeletons and ghosts," he replied at a near whisper, clicking his cheek and letting the lead vibrate down Tuffy's neck. His horse liked long walks in the snow as much as he did, although he would do it when the need arose.

Kelly sat hunched over the saddle horn in the spot, watching his boss move off. He wondered if Binky was fooling with him, then thought against that notion. "The man has no sense of humor, so there must be a crumb or two of truth in that statement," he muttered this as a child would talk behind their mother's apron, low and out of earshot of the father.

"Kelly?" asked Binky.

"Yes, sir," answered Kelly, just then catching up with him.

"When we get there, I want you to take Tuffy over to the stable and get the horses fed and brushed out. Be there when I need you."

"Can I go find something to eat?" asked Kelly.

"Yes, feed the horses first, then feed yourself. We may need to head out in a hurry, and they will be no good to us if we don't treat them right. Make sure you can see both sides of the street, so if you see me, you come running."

Another block, and they stopped in front of a two-story white and yellow house with a steep roof. "Doesn't look like he is home," said Kelly, turning his horse around.

"You never mind, he will be along soon enough," said Binky, pulling his leg over Tuffy's back and standing for the first time in a few hours

He groaned as he grabbed his rifle from the scabbard and handed the reins to Kelly.

"I will be on the lookout."

"Stay out of trouble, or else," admonished Binky, watching him disappear down the street before heading around Frank's home and into the back door.

Usually, he wouldn't have cared what the neighbors thought about him entering into the man's front door like regular folk. He saw himself as a man that could kick in another man's door, knock the man out and then finish the man's dinner. The way he figured it, if Frank saw a set of footprints leading up to his door, he might not come home.

***

Kelly rode slowly into town. It was normal to see people walking around even on a cold morning like today. When he passed the Lucy, he had hoped to see that it remained open. He understood the proprietor, even if he wasn't a godly man, would shudder his doors until at least church let out.

He stopped at the livery and slipped off his horse. 'Jackson Livery,' he read the large sign painted on the side of the red barn.

The snow crunched like fresh crackers under his boots as he walked around to the front of his horse. It was below freezing, and there were at least three or four inches of snow on the ground.

He rubbed between his horse's eyes from his forehead to his muzzle. He felt terrible because he didn't know the horse's name. The horse was a product of thieving the pony from a settler up north named Olmstead. He referred to him as everyone else had "whats-his-face" or some derivative of that name.

"Hello," he called out as he opened the large door leading into the main barn.

He stuck his head inside, looking around the barn for anyone that may be inside. The horses nudged him from behind.

"Hello," he called out again, noticing the warm air pushing past hi
and into the street.

"Well, I better get you inside and close the door," he said aloud as
noticed both horses already edging their way closer to the door.

"So you're smarter than I was giving you credit fer," he said aloud
the horses as he guided them into the receiving hall of the livery.

"Horses are smart animals, more than likely, they just felt the warm
temperature inside," said Gilbert, coming into the receiving hall from tl
back door.

"I hope you don't mind me bringing the horses inside?"

"Just shows you care about your horses. Some folk would sit here t
my fire and leave their animals outside until we come up with some so
of arrangement. Speaking of which?" asked Gilbert, who now that Kel
could see him better, was a clean-shaven man dressed in dark brow
trousers and a clean shirt.

"Did you shave for the church service?" asked Kelly, only noticin
because beards seem to be the facial choice in this town.

"No, I keep a clean face. My woman likes it that way."

"I was just noticing because it doesn't seem like this town will eve
get a new barber," stated Kelly.

"Oh, one will open a shop, as long as no one shoots the next one
maybe, he might even stay a while," said Gilbert.

"How much do you reckon you need to let them hold up for th
day?" asked Kelly, holding both horses at tether.

"I figure, I need a dollar for the day, one fifty for overnight,
answered Gilbert.

"Each?" asked Kelly.

Gilbert nodded.

"What if I dried them off and brushed them out myself?"

"Short on coin?" asked Gilbert, looking over at his forge.

Kelly nodded this time.

"How much do you have?" asked Gilbert.

"Enough for a horse and something to eat," answered Kelly lookin
down at the loose hay littering the floor.

"Well, if you clean up around here some, I can ask the wife to seat ou for lunch," offered Gilbert.

"I would love that. That's kind-hearted of you. I do need to stay close o the livery. I'm waiting for my employer to fetch me."

"Well, we will just need to eat here. Can I make it a picnic?" asked Addle Jackson.

Kelly spun in the voice's direction, and Addle Jackson came in the front door letting a cold wind inside and making the horses complain. "That's how you knew I had come in," said Kelly.

Gilbert nodded and removed his hat, "Do you mind?"

Kelly's eyes went from Addle to Gilbert before settling on a scar across the top of his head.

"Bring my husband some lunch to feed a man he has yet to introduce? This I shall surely need to ponder and mull over in an endless internal struggle," she said so dramatically that not even the horses were worried about Kelly being fed. He noticed that she seemed a little older than John and beautiful. She walked over with the grace of a dancer.

"Hint taken, my dear, and you have my apologies. I didn't get your name, and it seems to be a condition of our agreement?" asked Gilbert in a runabout way, kissing Addle on the cheek before putting his hat back on his head.

"Phillip Kelly, I go by just Kelly. I'm told I'm Irish, and I was born back east. My parents were raised and educated in Boston. However, we moved around when I was a child," answered Kelly, talking too much because he was nervous.

"Well, you seem to be a well mannered young man. We would love to have you for lunch," she said as she walked to the back door.

Kelly watched her walk through the open door, and, honestly, he was nervous about her last comment.

"Yes, she is older and a bit wiser than me, and she does know how to treat a man," said Gilbert, referring to lunch and not at all what Kelly was thinking at the moment.

"Where did you meet a woman like her?" asked Kelly, feeling a little warm all of a sudden.

"Right here, walked in looking for work. When her husband pass
away a couple of months later, I moved into the role," responded Gilbe
pulling the saddle off Tuffy and sitting it on a stand in front of an emp
stall.

"We need to get these guys dried off and rubbed down," declar
Gilbert, holding out a cloth and brush.

"How much will I owe you for the horses?"

"Help me while they're here today. I will feed you and the horse
You can keep the coin. Overnight, and it's a dollar.

"Sounds fair," replied Kelly.

"Of course it does. You might want to hurry. Addle put something o
the stove before she left for church this morning. It won't be long befo
it's ready to eat."

Chapter 26
December 21st, 1873
Not far from the Springer Ranch, Washington Territory

He was known as just Drake because he had never warmed up to his Christian name. He was a man liked by few and loved by less.

He had been visiting the Springers for four months. His boss had a vested interest in the Springers. He was first told they were squatting. Then even the likes of Drake knew that there were several problems with that story. 'First, you don't pay a man once a month to walk thirty plus miles into the Cascades and not visit them. You would mention the squatters to the sheriff. He would make his way up here and evict them from the land at gunpoint.'

"No, I'm not the fool my boss reckons I am. I'm no one's fool," he said, opening his eyes and looking around his lean-to cabin. It looked less like a cabin and more like a pile of twigs and brush. The snowfall had started his roof troubles about two hours before the first light.

He had used 17 limbs about 2 inches in size lashed to a 3-inch limb that ran perpendicular from the rest. He had made improvements to his shelter for a few months, but no temporary lean-to could stand up to 12 inches of snow. Today would be his last day due to the crazy woman in the cabin and the threat of more snow. He was still mad at his partner for leaving a couple of days ago with the saw. They had built the raft together, but he couldn't even fall a tree without a decent ax. He wondered if he used his ax if the Springer lady would sneak up on him and shoot him through the neck. "Who says that?" he asked out loud.

Consortium of Acquaintances

The snow fell in large flakes making a noise somewhere betwee falling rain and silence. Drake paused to listen, hoping the girl would n jump on him again.

"I know shooting a man in the chest and shooting a man in the hea Why the neck? It seems mighty detailed like she had done it. But the wa she said it. She wasn't proud of it either," he said, rambling because F had spent the last four months alone.

He had been told to motivate them off the land. His first attempt wa to kill their burro. Then the second was to eliminate their chickens. H didn't mean to knock over the lantern that burnt the Springer's bar down.

They thought his mission was finished, and they headed back t Yakima City. They waited after a few weeks when no word was hear from the Springers. They were once again told to make their way to th middle of nowhere.

They had made it up a few days before the man of the house finishe a raft and set out for Yakima City, leaving his helpless wife and daughte His partner took some supplies and headed back to town as soon as h saw the raft.

"She is cute," he said in a fatherly sort of way.

Drake learned that the wife was as mean as a rattlesnake, had kille as many men as he had. After getting the drop on him, he ran off, makin his way back to his makeshift shelter.

"Damn, it's cold up here," he said, tossing wood on the fire. He ha picked this spot because it was far enough away from the Springers, s not even that nosey little girl could find it. He jerked his head around a if he had seen her out of the corner of his eye. He wanted off thi mountain. He was half-Inuk and grew up believing there wasn't anyon that could sneak up on him until he met Annie.

He grabbed a long limb about an inch at most on one end and pulle it down, tying it to the other end. This created the shape he needed. Witl the outer frame tied together, the project looked more and more like a snowshoe.

"Now to make the webbing and a place for my feet to tie to the shoe, 1en they will be ready to take me down the mountain," he stated as part f the roof of his shelter gave way. He pulled his pack out and finished is shoes taking about a half-hour for each.

"Well, I wonder what Binky and the fellas are up to," he said as he hrew his pack on his head and started down the hill.

He started down the trail that would lead him to Flint's ranch. He ould always talk his way into a meal from the older man.

He loved the winter months of the northwest. When he would tell riends that would stop and say, you're Eskimo, of course, you would ove the snow. "It's impossible to teach a man that reckons he knows verything. I am half French and haven't been that far north since I was hat little girl's age."

He stopped when he heard a voice that wasn't an echo of his own. The trail that had led to the meadow was rarely used in the winter. So he did as his father had taught him, and he hid behind a tree. However, as the voice grew louder, he thought of heading back up the trail. When he turned, he realized they would follow his footprints in the snow.

It was not in his nature to face an enemy head-on. He thought of himself as the kind of man that would sneak up on a fellow. He slipped his knife free of its sheathed and pressed against the tree.

They were practically on top of him when he realized he knew the men and had spent hours playing cards at the Winston. He called out, making a passable raven call even though there was some argument about his ability.

They stopped a few dozen yards from where Drake had hidden. "Hello," called out Kentucky-Bob, putting his hand up to keep the other man from speaking.

"It's just a crow," whispered Dirty-Nick.

"Who is there? Come out," shouted Kentucky-Bob, moving slowly, ready for almost anything.

"It is just a bird," said Dirty-Nick, starting around the large man.

"Good morning," said Drake, stepping from behind his tree. He had thought they were closer and worried if he could hit them.

"Drake, we were told you had fallen ill. Why else would you ha
failed to bring the woman and child with you," said Kentucky-B
moving sideways to get a better look at Drake's position?

"Where are the women?" asked Dirty-Nick, moving closer.

"The crazy woman and her child are back in their cabin."

"Why haven't you burned them out and brought them down
town?" asked Kentucky-Bob, moving closer only to keep Dirty-Ni
from spoiling his line of sight if it came to that.

"I tried, but the old man talked me out of that. Said the cabin w
worth keeping even if it was used as a trapper's cabin.

"Why didn't you just kick the door in and introducing yourself?"

"I about got my headshot off," he answered, rubbing his neck.

"Well, we are here to finish the job. Why don't you head down t
trail and let us introduce ourselves?"

As they passed, Dirty-Nick asked, "Are they at least pretty?"

He continued down the trail for another twenty minutes. He recall
when he first met Annie. He had been standing behind an outcropping
pillow Basalt and wondering where the little girl was when she pulled c
his pocket and about gave him a stroke.

He laughed at that, letting his mind drift. Soon his thoughts dwelle
on his wife and child. He hadn't seen his child since she was a year ol
"She must be Annie's age by now," he said aloud as he edged his wa
towards a decision that would change the course of the rest of his life.

He stopped mid-stride to ponder his thoughts. He began to rock bac
and forth. It bothered him how Dirty-Nick wouldn't talk of Annie as
child. It was then he decided to do something that he had never don
before. He dropped his pack on the trail and pulled his rifle from it
sheath. He turned and headed back towards the cabin.

Chapter 27
December 21st, 1873
Yakima City, Washington Territory

Mayor Daniels ambled along with his wife on their way home. They had walked this same route for three years, only missing one Sunday all the time they had been in their new house.

She was in her early 50s and a few years younger than her husband. She had become a widower a few months after the town had an influx of bad seeds. He came along and swept her off her feet. She was old fashioned for most, choosing to wear formal clothing for all occasions. He always tried to match her dress with a blouse of the same color or a pocket square with a hint of her dress's color.

"The snow makes this time of year more special somehow. Christmas is just around the corner," she said, taking his hand.

"Well, here we are," he said, helping her up each step.

"Thank you, dear," she said, stopping at the front door, waiting for him to clean his boots and let her in.

When the door opened, with a wave of his hand, she entered, "After you, my dear."

"Oh, dear me, it's still warm in here," she declared with a surprised look on her face, walking to the closet to remove her coat.

"Yes, it is," he acknowledged as he helped her with her coat.

"Well, it is nice to walk into a warm house," she declared as she closed the door, kissing his cheek.

Consortium of Acquaintances

"Dear, could you go get my slippers? I believe I left them upstairs," he asked, giving a sad look. When she headed upstairs, he walked into the sitting room and caught the scent of a cigar. "Who is there?" he asked, moving towards his study.

"It is I, the ghost of Christmas past," whispered Binky, turning the mayor's high-backed chair around and surprising the mayor.

"Oh hell, you gave me such a fright," declared the older man while he held his chest.

"I apologize for dropping in on you today. I had trouble deciding t either come unannounced or bump into you at church, which would yo have preferred?" asked Binky, leaning back in the chair.

"No, I see your point, and thank you for stoking my stove," h answered, moving to the door to open it, so that he could slam it.

"Who is there, dear?" asked his wife from the stairway.

"Just a man from town who needs a word," he answered, waving hi hand in Binky's direction.

"Would the gentleman like some coffee?" she asked.

He started to say no, until Binky placed his gun on Frank's desk, thu winning the argument. "Yes, dear, that would be fine."

"Benjamin, put that away; you're known for not having a sense o humor, so don't start now, before I need to explain why you have a gu on my desk," he warned, sitting in his guest chair.

"I'm known to have killed a dozen or so men more if you coun Indians," he said brassily, "What happened to Lucky last night?"

"It seems the sheriff got word a murder was about to take place, an Lucky was in town to do the deed."

"Go on," said Binky picking up his pistol and dropping it into hi lap. Then he acted as if he had placed it back into his holster.

"He hires three new deputies and went over to the Lucy to arres him. Once courthouse opens tomorrow, I'm sure we can take care of th whole matter."

"Here we go," declared his wife, coming into the room and setting the little tray with three cups on the desk.

"My apologies, my love. This rancher needs to talk about some rouble he is having with his wife," said Mayor Daniels.

"Oh, I see," she said, pouring a cup and heading for her kitchen.

"Frank, you have known me a long time, and you know my wife lied," said Lucky, attempting to keep his anger in check.

"Oh, my apologies. I had not considered your past. I was envisioning how I would get my wife out of the room."

"Just make my wife out as a saint and put the blame on me."

"Why would I need to do that?" asked Mayor Daniels.

"Frank, you have the gift to lie to a child to get their candy, leaving them grateful to having given it to you, so when, not if, you tell your wife about my problems, you make me be the fool, not my wife real or otherwise."

"Yes, I will apologize if it will help, either way, I mean it," he said, pouring a cup for Binky and one for himself.

"So what happened then?" asked Binky, leaning toward his cup.

"Sheriff Miller walked over with his scatter-gun to arrest Lucky and your other fellow. He had four deputies with him backing his play. I was told that one of the deputies didn't have trousers on."

"How did they know he was in town?" asked Binky, taking a sip of his coffee, finding it tasted excellent compared to the sagebrush blend he was used to drinking. He laughed thinking, 'This is my steak.'

"I don't know, but I can find out tomorrow. I'm sure Sheriff Miller had to turn in a report to the court. Understand, I can't look until Monday, I'm afraid, at the earliest.

"How the heck would anyone have known about what they were coming to town for?" asked Binky, now taking more interest in the older man; he seemed tired and worn out.

"I only told your men yesterday morning. How many men did you have with him last night?" asked Mayor Daniels, leaning forward, hitting his knees on the desk, forgetting he was sitting on the wrong side.

"Two others came into town, and by the sounds of it, they didn't have time to tell anyone. We drank until late, and no one left my camp last night to tell anyone about our business."

Consortium of Acquaintances

"Well, I will find out tomorrow and let you know," said May Daniels, sipping at his coffee like it was fine wine.

"I will need to get Lucky out before there is trouble," he warne pouring coffee into his cup and drinking half its contents before looki up at his father.

"Leave that to me. If the judge doesn't help, I can get him a k around four pm on my way out. Now, about my problem. I still see hi walking around, and we can't have that," said Mayor Daniels, standi up and motioning for him to leave out the back.

"He won't be for long," said Binky, setting the gun on the desk, "a you can tell the director of our little drama that if anything goes wron Lucky knows where most of the bodies are buried."

"He better keep his trap shut, because if he talks, we are all finishe ruined, understand me?" asked Mayor Daniels.

"Yes, as long as nothing happens to him. All parties should bewa that I know where all the bodies are buried, including yours. How mar bodies did you leave in Boston?"

"Ben, there is no need to sink to the level of threats," replied Maye Daniels, sounding unusually distressed. He rose to his feet.

"I will start with truths of what happened to your wife's fir..." sai Binky, standing up to keep a better eye on the mayor.

"Shh," hushed Mayor Daniels as his wife came back into the roon He looked frightened, a look that showed his true feelings for his wife.

Chapter 28
December 21st, 1873
Not far from the Springer Ranch, Washington Territory

Drake's breath was a fog of frozen crystals as he stopped near the cutoff to his shelter. He had figured they would have followed his footprints. "Okay, they are going to take a while getting to the cabin if they even know where it is."

He headed up the trail towards the cabin but was weary as he passed the path to his shelter. He felt the cold as the Cascades winds again bit him through the seams of his clothing.

What bothered him the most was what Dirty-Nick was saying. "The women? No, you hedge-creeper, it's a woman and a child." He picked up speed as the terrain steepened, letting the snowshoes flop against his heels.

He worried about Annie and even the crazy woman who had threatened to shoot him in the neck.

Drake left his wife and child up north with her family. He had no way to contact them, but he would like to imagine if they were in trouble, someone would take the time to help them. Drake had no idea what to do when he found them, but he felt he would know what to do when he did.

He stopped and held his breath as the trail bottlenecked due to the terrain. The basalt narrowed here, and just through the gap in the rocks was the cabin. It was just through the tree cover. He took a slow breath and listened as something moved closer from somewhere above him in the trees.

His heart stopped when he realized it was the largest wolf he ha
ever seen, and the fact that he has lived his whole life to this point in th
wilderness should give a measure of how massive the wolf was befor
him.

The wolf's eyes were like stars in the night sky, silver as the wolf
back.

"Are you going to kill me, Mister Wolf?" he asked, expecting a
answer. He let his rifle fall to his feet, and he removed his bearskin coat.

It had not even crossed his mind to fight the alpha wolf. The on
thing he had always known the pack was never far from their alpha.
was a fight he could not win.

"I am trying to do something right. I've never done anything right i
my life. But I can't let this happen to the child," he said, pointing t
where he believed Kentucky-Bob and Dirty-Nick were preparing t
attack the cabin.

The Alpha wolf looked in the direction he was pointing and back a
Drake.

"I can't let it happen."

The alpha turned and ran away.

He let out a breath of air and relaxed, closing his eyes. He listened t
the world around him. It was then he heard the pack move. They wer
like phantoms moving as quietly as a leaf on the wind.

He picked up his jacket and slipped it on, and shivered as th
coolness of the inside touched his skin. Lifting the rifle, he cleaned it o
what little snow had collected on it.

Drake had figured he was about to die, and when a man is about t
die, all his worldly possessions become nothing to him. He continued u
the rise and through a narrow gap. He found his way over to the tree lin
closest to the cabin, where he waited for a few minutes.

He expected to hear Dirty-Nick chattering away as they move
towards the cabin. Then it crossed his mind that maybe they had set u
camp for the night at his shelter.

"Where the heck are those hedge-creepers?" he asked himself as h
stood up and stretched. He decided to wander over and find them.

"Just take your time and stay quiet," he said to himself as he lifted his foot and set it down and paused a moment before lifting the other. He moved closer and saw that his shelter was empty. They had passed his camp and headed directly towards the cabin. He picked up speed when he reached the meadow.

About halfway to the cabin, he spotted what remained of Dirty-Nick. His limbs were pulled from his torso, and his head was missing. The gruesome scene made Drake sick to his stomach. The only reason he knew it was Dirty-Nick was the torso was wearing the man's clothes.

He wasn't known as a tracker by trade but had knowledge and skill that he rarely shared with anyone. He followed the tracks made by the wolves but stopped when he noticed a cougar had walked along with the pack.

"Impossible," said Drake to himself. However, there before him was the oddest of evidence. There were places where the cougar had stepped on wolf tracks, and the wolves had stepped upon cougar tracks.

North, of his shelter, he picked up Kentucky-Bob's trail. He was a mountain man in every sense of the word. Some men would boast about being a mountain man, but Kentucky-Bob was well known around these parts for his skills. That said, Drake followed the trail a spell until he spotted the man halfway up the ridge heading for the Naches River Valley on the other side.

Drake wondered if he would make it. "If anyone can, Kentucky-Bob can," he said as he felt he was no longer alone.

The alpha wolf walked up beside him on his right side, and another of almost the same height walked up on the other side. He could smell their wet fur. It smelled of blood from their fresh kill.

They watched Kentucky-Bob moving higher up the ridge with each step. They waited for just a moment and then raced after him.

If his eyes hadn't been open, he might not have even noticed them, for they were like phantoms.

He watched as the wolves started to climb. What happened next would make him envision Barbie Hanover. The wolves from this distance no longer looked like wolves. They looked as though they were mountain goats. He thought of Barbie and how the Mayor had him murdered fc just talking about the wolves that were up here.

Halfway back, he stopped and built an igloo. When he was finishe he stood back and had to admit it was too large for one person. He pulle pine tree boughs into the shelter for bedding that was almost two fee thick. The snow and wind picked up as the sun disappeared over th ridgeline.

He lay on his back and wondered if Kentucky-Bob was still out ther running for his life. He wasn't sure what he would tell people about wha happened up here. If he was confident of one thing, that was he wouldn be mentioning the wolves.

He made a decision after today's events. He was going to do thing differently from now on. He would find his wife and child and beg ther to take him back because that was the right thing for him to do.

Chapter 29
December 21st, 1873
Yakima City, Washington Territory

South of Yakima City along a dirt road paved with rock and good intentions. John and George stood on its edge, glancing towards the river, taking a moment to regain their strength. The terrain had only appeared to be easy going. It had been only an illusion, for the trail had been nonexistent, worse yet, blocked by endless snags. Great knots of brambled trees and brush had stood as barricades baring them from a direct exodus from the river's edge.

"I don't know what was worse, climbing up out of there or working our way through the mud. How you fairing?" asked John, stretching to one side, then the other.

"I must admit it's been a while since my legs have hurt this bad," replied George, coughing to clear his lungs.

"So, George..."

"No."

"George?"

"We are not even," he answered, kneeling to slide the board through the ropes to make carrying the load easier.

"By what gauge do you gander to come to that conclusion?" asked John, holding his end of the plank as his friend wandered towards the other.

"That of guilt, John, that of guilt. When I stop feeling guilty abou wut I done did, we shall be even," mumbled George, picking up his en of the plank.

"Will you tell me then what you have done to render this sel punishment."

"I am not hopeful," he whispered, sounding as though he were stuc in a well.

"Alright, George," said John, stretching to relieve pain.

George adjusted the load on his right shoulder and glanced bac towards the fork. "Young feller, do you see what I see?"

"The gap, the river, the fog, the snow, What would you have m notice?" he asked the older man, taking the lead and lifting the other en of the plank.

Between the men, there were two crates lashed to the plank with th borrowed rope from Doc Ron's place. It was unusually quiet. The fou inches of snow between the Gap seemed to be the reason for the silenc The only noise was from the men's footfalls as they managed the load o their shoulders and struggled to keep upright.

"No, gander the other way," directed George, laughing at th strangeness of this morning's activities. "There is a wagon coming."

"Oh," he said as he turned around. He managed to see the snov cloud behind them and a faint sound of horses.

Five minutes later, they heard horses and a wagon coming down th road behind them.

"Hello," called out George, slowing his pace and about pulling Joh off his feet.

Stopping altogether, twisting around, holding onto his end of th plank and cargo, "Can you hear the wagon?"

"Good afternoon," said the man upon the wagon.

"Would you happen to be in the mood for some company thi morning, Mister?" asked George, waiting for a response.

"Mr. Harrison of Kansas City," announced John as the wagon passe them.

"Thought you told me you don't know anyone in these parts?" George asked John, glaring at his partner.

"I know only a few," answered John, hoping the man would remember.

The wagon slowed to a halt, and the man turned and asked, "Who might you be?"

"Springer by way of Walla Walla last April," he replied, hoping he would remember.

"Yes, I met a John last spring as I recall, he had a pretty wife, are you the man I gave a ride to?" asked Mr. Harrison, glancing back at him.

"Yes, sir, that was Elizabeth, she is still my wife, and she is still pretty," answered John, grinning as his mind wandered to that of his wife.

"Well, hop on and tell me what happened to you folks," he said, pulling what looked to be his lunch closer to him.

"We are mighty grateful, Mr. Harrison," he said, helping George load the crates and the plank into the back of the wagon. George climbed on the back, and John jumped up beside Mr. Harrison.

They started towards town. "Well, did you make it to Seattle?" he asked, turning back to see where George had settled himself.

"We did not make it to Seattle, we were offered a land deal that seemed too good to be true, and for most people that would have been the case," he explained, glancing back and noticing George had moved closer.

"Well, be careful. You would be surprised to know some of the stories I've heard about people struggling to keep hold of their land," he warned as they passed the first house coming into Yakima City.

"Thank you for the ride. It was better than carrying those crates for a mile," said John, tipping his hat at a woman who was sweeping her sidewalk in front of her house.

"Where are you fellas hankering to be dropped off?" asked Mr. Harrison, nodding to the same woman.

Consortium of Acquaintances

"At the Northwest Mercantile, over on the left," answered John turning towards George, suddenly reminded of how his wife had ridde into town eight months ago.

They stopped across the street from the mercantile and unloaded th plank and the cargo. John decided it wouldn't affect his mood that it wa snowing again.

"Well, thank you again, Mr. Harrison," said John, pushing his han toward the man still sitting up on the wagon.

"It is my pleasure to transport you anytime we are heading in th same direction," stated Mr. Harrison, slapping his hand into John's an pulling him close. He struggled as the man pulled him into a handshak and looked him straight in the eyes. "Watch your back. If I had know you were foolish enough to take the deal, I would have never brougl you into the Yakima Valley."

John stepped back onto the boardwalk and pondered what he ha been told and looked back at George, who complained to himself h needed to make up for something.

"Good luck to you, Mr. Springer," declared Mr. Harrison, pullin away from the boardwalk.

He looked at his hand before glancing up the street to see the wago: blend into the commercial traffic. George walked over to stand with hir before grabbing John's elbow, pointing to the mercantile. "You, sir, hav about 3 minutes to get the glue and the wire you need to finish you frames before the man closes up for the night."

John slapped his pockets as he headed for the mercantile, dodgin, the wagons that always seem to run up and down Main Street. Halfwa: across the street, he found the bulge of his wallet and looked up just as horse team almost ran him down if not for George, grabbing him an pulling him to the other side.

"It closes in two minutes," warned George, pointing towards th Northwest Mercantile. He started back over to the other side of the street

"Yeah, yeah," he said, pulling away and reaching for the door managing to pick up the supplies and even some food for the next day o two. It was ten minutes after five when he walked out of the Northwest Mercantile. The street seemed noticeably quieter.

He walked back across the street where the older man was sitting on a turned-up crate.

"You notice something?" asked John.

George looked up and down the street and back at John to answer, "Nope."

"There aren't any wagons running up and down the street," said John, waving his hand about to emphasize what he was saying.

George picked his end up, answering, "Of course, it's after 5 o'clock. They are probably halfway home by now."

"Well, of course," said John, looking at the back of George's head, wondering if he was insane or if his best friend was, he was banking on the old man.

The tent was warm there hours later, the slates were dry, and they were full of beans and potatoes. George moved around the tent. His eyes couldn't believe how detailed each piece was carved. "They are all beautiful," he said, looking at John in a new light. "You really are a talented whittler."

"Thank you. I have been practicing for years. My father thought it was important too, as you say whittle than to go to school," said John, crossing his arms in front of him because thinking of his father always made him feel defensive.

"You reckon they will be ready to sell tomorrow?" asked George, lifting a frame that had a carving of a bear chasing a woman riding on a cargo wagon.

"They are ready now," he answered, swinging his arm around as if he was presenting them. "We use these inserts to increase the size of the edges to accommodate larger paintings.

"I just don't see the gold anywheres," he said, watching the younger man spin around.

"George," John snapped, patting the air to avoid another round of the 'someone said they found gold' game. He waited for someone from another tent to start their banter. He wasn't disappointed when no or spoke up.

"Just joking with you, no need to get your feathers ruffled," sai George as a genuine smile flashed across his face that seemed to rela the younger man.

They weren't sure how much the frames would bring. What Georg did know was John's family wasn't going to starve if he had anything t say about it. He would climb into the mountains and bring them foo himself, if it were necessary.

"You going out?" asked John, not wanting to go out, just makin conversation.

"Naw, it's late, it's snowing, and the temperature will surely dip int the 20s," he replied, not realizing John was already asleep.

Chapter 30
December 21st, 1873
Jackson Livery, Yakima City

Most towns in the west seemed to undergo a metamorphosis at around five each day. The town transforms from a bustling community raring to enter the 20th century, becoming a settlement more akin to a village of the middle ages. Yakima city was not an exception; it was rather a prime example.

The crowded boardwalks dwindle to only a few people. The streets of the fast-paced community are empty by half-past five. Doorways are lit only by the oil lamp hung out for the occasional late-night strolls, but even those are out of oil by midnight.

Kelly had spent most of the day taking care of the livery and had grown to enjoy the experience of a good day's work. He had been on the lookout for Binky for the last few hours. Kelly even readied the horse when the sun rushed over the western horizon. Just as he decided to pull the saddles off the horses and find a place to sleep for the night, he spotted his boss making his way up the street.

"Mr. Jackson, I will be taking my leave," declared Kelly, moving the horses towards the door. He opened the small door, and the wind took it out of his hand, and it slapped the wall on the outside.

"Kelly, you can call me Gilbert. Mr. Jackson was Addle's first husband," he said, following the horses towards the door and patting Tuffy's backside to let him know he was passing him on the right. He knew the horse was almost blind and appreciated the notice.

"Gilbert, you have a restful night," he said, leaving through tl smaller door one horse at a time.

"I'm sure I will. You done completed all my work for the day ar most of the evening chores," laughed Gilbert, guiding Tuffy out of tl barn and putting a carrot from his pocket to give him a snack. When l noticed who was crossing the street, he found something to do inside tl barn.

Outside, Binky was crossing the street, doing his best to keep his h. turned low. The wind coming from the west was as cold as ice. "Are tl horses ready?" he asked, hugging Tuffy around his muzzle befo looking towards Kelly.

"Been ready for hours. I almost put them back in the stalls, and the I saw you sneak up the street," whispered Kelly wondering where Gilbe had disappeared even the door had been closed.

"It's not sneaking. It is more of a skulking maneuver when you'r planning on breaking the law," mused Binky winking a bit.

"Any luck on finding the man?" asked Kelly a little too loudly.

Binky's eyes went wide, and he patted the air with his gloved hand i front of him. "Remember, if that rumor gets around, our prey may go t ground, and we may not find him," admonished Binky, throwing a le over Tuffy and waiting for Kelly to join him in the street.

"I checked the Emporium a few minutes ago, and Abby told me sl hadn't seen him in there. I then stopped by the Winston, and Billy tol me he saw him there the other night. He wasn't sure what is keeping hir away. So that leaves the Lucy."

"Well, I guess we go to the Lucy," said Kelly, smacking his lips as i he hadn't had a drink of anything for a few days.

"No, I reckon you need to slip inside the Lucy and have a loo around. I will lurk around back and, if you see him lollygaggin' th evening away, we will wait outside for him. If not, I have found a plac that overlooks the jail. We can keep an eye out in case a mob tries t hang Lucky.

"You believe that is a possibility?" asked Kelly.

"Yes, that's the only reason I'm worried," answered Binky.

"I'm gettin' a drink while I'm in there," whispered Kelly.

"Just don't linger in there too long. It is mighty cold out here."

Kelly rode his horse towards the Lucy. Binky went back a block and down what passed for an alley stopping at the rear of the Lucy Saloon. He wondered if Kelly was joking about stopping for a drink. After 15 minutes, he had his answer.

Meanwhile, Kelly had stepped into the saloon half expecting the music to stop when he came through the doors, but as it was, no one raised so much as an eyebrow in his direction. He figured he was much less menacing than Lucky, having killed no one of consequence within 50 miles from here. Regardless of his less than exciting entrance, he stepped up to the bar and ordered a shot of whiskey.

Kelly swallowed it before the bottle was capped and indicated his wish for another, pointing at his glass. This time, he turned and took note of each of the patrons before returning to his shot of whiskey and the barkeep who wanted his payment. Kelly nodded at the barman, dropped his coins, and dropped the whiskey into his mouth; he let it slide down his gullet before the barkeep could retrieve the payment.

"Have a nice night. This place is too quiet for me," he said as he slipped his hat down to his ears and headed out the door. The truth was he could not have paid for another shot due to the lack of funds.

"Did you see him?" asked Binky of Kelly as he approached.

"He wasn't in there," answered Kelly, letting out a belch.

"So you had a drink," said Binky.

"Yup, had two in quick order," answered Kelly.

"Do I have any change from the livery?" asked Binky, slowly riding a block down the alley before stopping.

"Yes, the barkeep took it," answered Kelly, falling in behind Binky.

"You spent my money to buy yourself a shot," said Binky, not expecting an answer.

"No, I spent your money to buy myself two shots," laughed Kelly, holding up two fingers on his right hand.

Binky chuckled before saying, "We will consider it an advance."

"Wouldn't have it any other way," answered Kelly. *hic*

Consortium of Acquaintances

"Tomorrow morning, I want you to walk over here, so take note of where you are at the moment. But for right now, I want you to ride out of town and then circle back over by the mill. Ride for a while and come back into town from the south. Stop back at the livery and put the horse up for the night. Gilbert will let you stay in one of the cleaner stalls."

"Where will you be?" asked Kelly.

"Oh, don't worry about me. I have a place in mind that I can stay for the night. It's just best if we let people believe we are riding out for the night."

"I understand," said Kelly. *hic*

"That's what you get for drinking rotgut too fast."

"Night boss," said Kelly fading off into the darkness. *hic*

Binky waited for him to disappear around the corner before he took a single step. He had a hideout over the bakery that he stayed in when he was in town. No one in the gang knew about it, and he wasn't about to let Kelly in on the hideout. Mainly because the young man seemed to talk continuously, and he was afraid of being discovered.

Chapter 31
December 22nd, 1873
Yakima City, Washington Territory

There is no colder place to wake up than a tent when the weather was as it was in Yakima City. The snowfall never seemed to halt completely. It only slowed a bit until the next storm made its appearance. The trouble starts when a person settles in for the night; unless they make an effort every few hours to throw some wood in the stove, the fire goes out. When this happens, the temperature will drop to what seemed more like an icehouse than a home. Then the wind leaked in from under, over, and around the seams, making it even colder for the occupants.

"Thank you, George, for letting me stay here and sharing your food. I would also like to thank you for the extra blankets," said John, rising to stretch on the cot tucked in the corner of the one-roomed tent.

"I'm happy to share my tent and half my blankets with you," answered George. Usually, he had no less than ten blankets on top of him on a night like this. However, he shared half of them with John, who had left him with six to keep warm. It was as if math wasn't his strongest subject in school, especially when it came to sharing his blankets.

"Mind if I throw some wood in the stove and warm the place up?" asked John, standing with his arms raised over his head.

Usually, touching a man's stove was akin to touching his wallet. George wasn't into that much formality when the temperature was near freezing inside his tent. He nodded his agreement in John's direction before he settled back into his cot, pulling the blankets up to his chin.

"Why are you helping me out so much? I know we knew each oth[er] back last April, but you are really going out of your way to make sure[I] get back on my feet," asked John, sitting back down as he raised h[is] second pair of socks to his nose to give each a sniff before adding the[m] to his cold feet.

"I just want yous' and your wife to be back on your feet. It 'bo[ut] broke me when I heard that yous' died. I knowd it was my advice th[at] made yous' buy that property so far from town, and I feel bad," answere[d] George, tearing up a little. He chose to hide his face under his blanket.

John stood up and wrapped the patchwork blanket over h[is] shoulders, and squatted next to the stove. "How much does a stove lik[e] this cost? If I were to purchase one in town," he asked as he pitched th[e] wood into the fire and locked the little door.

"You need to make a query at the Northwest Mercantile. You order and wait for someone to head to Portland and get supplies."

"Does your wife like to cook on an open hearth?" asked Georg[e] peeking from his pile of blankets.

"I don't know," answered John, leaning up against the warm stove.

"Do you reckon she likes it?" he asked again, this time with hi[s] blanket pulled down.

"She doesn't complain about it much anymore," answered Joh[n] moving away from the stove that was putting out more heat than h[e] thought it would.

"I'm betting she just wants something nicer that doesn't burn he[r] every time she uses it," said George, putting his feet on the cold floor an[d] tapping them to get some feeling into his toes.

"I bet it is more money than I have right now, especially since m[y] barn burnt. I need to replace the supplies that I lost before I buy a stove."

"What about taking a note out on your land?" asked George. "No[t] everyone in this town is up to no good."

"I won't do it without a way to pay for it. It all depends on these her[e] frames," he answered, looking at the two canvas bags with the frame[s] ready for market.

While John finished getting dressed, he sat on the cot and pondered s options. "What about a sled and donkey?" asked John, standing and utting his backside close to the stove and facing George, who was tting wrapped up like a burrito.

"It would be impossible to bring it up by donkey. At least, while here is this much snow on the ground. Unless there is a clear trail," nswered George, waving his hand around as if they were in an open eld.

"There wasn't more than an inch of snow out there the last time I hecked," said John in disbelief, opening the flap.

"No, we got two or three inches last night," declared George, pulling he blankets tightly against him because of the draft from the open flap hat was quickly turning into a sail in the wind.

"How would you know, you haven't been up?" he asked, stopping in nid-sentence when he stuck his head out and noted the much deeper now around the tent.

"As you mentioned more than once, my tent walls are thin, and I heard Abraham complaining about the snow a couple of hours ago on his vay to take his morning constitution."

"My lord, how will I get back to my wife and child?" asked John almost silently. He wore the expression of a broken man.

"John, don't worry about how deep the snow is until you're ready to leave. Even then, you won't need to worry about it if you have a good pair of snowshoes and maybe a small sled. I pays' my debts. You just wait and see," replied George, moving from his blankets, putting his hand on John's shoulder.

Just as John was starting to think George was being kind, he was yanked from the open tent flap, and George tied it closed.

"Gee George, I was starting to believe you were consoling me," muttered John humorously.

"John, you don't need cuddlin', you need to sell your frames and buy your supplies. Ideally, you'd need to be on the trail tomorrow morning before sunrise," stated George, plainly and to the point.

"George, you have a way of simplifying situations. Has anyone e told you that?" asked John, putting his boots on and tying them tight.

"Is that your way of telling me I'm simple?" asked George, rais his bushy white eyebrow.

"No, I was just..." answered John once again, tripping over his wc and wondering where he would be sleeping tonight.

"I'm a simple man in a complicated world. I have known that fo while now," said George, letting John off the proverbial hook.

John let out a breath he was holding and continued. "The wa understand it, there are three establishments in which my frames wo bring a decent profit. The hotel, Northwest Territory Mercantile, a Maggi's Emporium," he said, naming in the order that he thought wo give the highest to lowest profit.

George had a different opinion, and John needed just a li convincing. "John, you need to hear me: Maggi's is the place you need go first," said George, as he trimmed his beard and gave his cheeks a neck a close shave.

"Hmm, why are you choosing this morning to groom yourself asked John, watching the old man wrap a towel around his neck and fac

"You don't go into Maggi's looking like you're fresh off the tra You will end up paying extra or will be told to go take a bath," repli George, acting out each step, including the bath.

"Hello, excuse me?" he asked, holding his arms above him, trying get the old man's attention.

"Yes, John," he answered, stopping and looking a little confused.

"What sort of proprietary business does Maggi conduct?" he aske slowly lowering his hands, watching George's eyes drop to his own.

"First off, there isn't really a Maggi. Well, there once was until sł ran off with our last mayor, then again that fact really isn't important t your question," explained George as he started to comb his grey ha back with his fingers with limited success.

"And?" he asked, slowly losing his patience.

"And? Oh, well, they dance, and they drink, not like the saloon, min you, it really is a classy place full of oh-be-ons," he uttered as h removed his shirt and began looking through his things for a shirt that had been laundered in the last month.

"What are you getting all gussied up for?" asked John, laughing at his effort, having to move as George moved around the small tent looking for a comb to run through his hair.

"Women, Miss Abby has women," declared George, taking a shirt and snapping it in the air a couple of times to remove the excess wrinkles. It was an act of fertility, but he repeated the process anyway.

"Are you sure Miss Abby would be interested in my frames, or are you just hankering to take advantage of the situation?" asked John, knowing his friend and based on his past experiences with the man.

"Young man, I'm hurt at the thought that you think I would take advantage of you," replied George, as he put his hand on his heart.

"Well, ya better not be," warned John, finding himself nodding with each word and imagining his father doing the same to him not long ago.

"You, sir, are right, you need to take a shave and be dressed for the occasion, so when them women come over to your table hanging off you as you know they like to do in a place such as Maggi's, you can thank me for letting you go all alone. I will see you when you get back," George said, letting his words sink in a bit, although he made no effort to remove the clean shirt.

"You are smarter than anyone I know or maybe just more conniving. I haven't made up my mind yet," John replied, looking into the mirror and combing his hair. His mind drifted to the Blue Wave Saloon and what went on most nights.

"So you see my point in me needing to attend your negotiation?" asked George, his face at this point looking like a cat that caught the widow's yellow bird.

"Just remember, if you bed any of Maggi's ladies, it comes out of your share," declared John, tucking his shirt in and making sure he was ready.

"Well, there isn't a Maggi, at least not anymore. She done run off with the first mayor. I'm sure we talked about this before," he said, turning his head away as if he was talking to himself for a few momen before righting himself.

"George, my statement holds water," he said, turning to look Georg directly in the eyes.

"Can we go, big man?" he asked, bursting with impatience, lookir like a new man.

"Right this way," John answered, opening the tent flap and wavir his hand ushering him forth.

"Thank you, my good man. Please lock the door and come along said George, sounding three or more rungs higher on the social ladd than he did only seconds ago.

Chapter 32
December 22nd, 1873
Springer Ranch, Washington Territory

Elizabeth and Annie walked towards the river taking high steps and pushing the deep snow flat. The flakes continued to fall, adding to the already 14 inches they got overnight. It was the first snowfall of the year, and it seemed that it was here to stay.

"Little one, what do you hear?" asked Elizabeth with a great big smile on her face.

"I don't hear nuffin', mommy," she answered, looking around as if something was stalking them.

"Nothing, you hear nothing, and that is just my point. It is so quiet," Elizabeth said, picking her up and spinning in place.

She giggled and wiggled in her mother's arms. "Again, again."

Twice more around, and her arms started to give out. She didn't know how John could lift Annie and spin her for what seemed hours, only to do it again. 'Hope he is doing well,' she thought, letting a look of worry cross her face.

"What is the matter, mommy? Do you want to talk about it?" asked Annie, looking up ever so kindly.

This made her laugh openly, breaking her train of thought and reminding her of how many times she had asked her the same thing. "Well, no, it's nothing," answered Elizabeth, turning to brush a tear off her cheek as she started for the cabin.

"What's wrong, mommy. You can tell me anything," she sa
holding on to her mother's apron from behind.

She turned to meet her daughter's quizzical stare. "I will make yo
deal if you share with me something of yourself."

"Do you wanna know about the night?" asked Annie, now looki
glumly at the snow-covered ground.

"I want to know about your life, Annie. What it was like before y
came to live here with us?" asked Elizabeth, now kneeling in front of l
child, looking back up into her sad eyes.

"That's fine, you go first," replied Annie, looking from the ground
her mother and back to the ground.

"I'm worried about John. I'm worried about not knowing if he ma
it to Yakima City. I'm worried about everything."

"I'm worried too, about daddy John, about food. I'm sad about wh
happened," she whispered, "I'm most afraid of losing what my mama
face looked like." She began to cry into Elizabeth's sleeve.

"That is just it, little one. If you talk about life before that night,
will help you remember all the wonderful things that happened."

"We came from Minnesoka' territory with a wagon train. It was n
family and four others. It wasn't until Scotsbuff that we met up wi
many, many more families heading to Oregon."

"Where was your family heading?" asked Elizabeth, looking up ar
deciding if the weather was going to get worse.

"We were supposed to meet my daddy, a ways back, but we took tł
wrong trail. I looked at the map, and it didn't look right, but no or
would believe me," answered Annie. She was distracted while trying 1
decide if a particular cloud looked like a puppy or a bunny.

"How were they supposed to know? How did you know?" aske
Elizabeth with a bewildered look eclipsing her face.

"I have dreams that show me possibilities, kinda like a daydream'ı
sometimes I just see the right answer," she replied.

"You have family here. Annie, we asked you if you knew any famil
around here we could contact," said Elizabeth just as the snowflake
became larger, catching on their bonnets.

"Yes, but I don't know where he is," stated Annie, sticking her tongue out as if she was fishing for snowflakes.

"So you were going to homestead land your family bought?" asked Elizabeth, trying to draw some more memories from the child's traumatized mind.

"Yes, but something went wrong," Annie answered as she began shutting down, letting the sadness seep in.

"Hey, little one. Have you ever seen a snow angel?" her mom asked, giving her a smile she was famous for back in St. Louis.

"No, what's that?" she asked, returning the smile.

She didn't respond as she fell back into the snow and started making the first snow angel ever made at the Springer Ranch. It was an easy claim because she imagined that her's was the first snow angel ever dared to be completed this high up in the Cascades. She laughed, imagining the trapper from last fall, dropping his furs and jumping into a snowbank to make a snow angel.

"What's so funny?" asked Annie.

"It's fun," laughed Elizabeth.

"Oh! I wanna make one too," she said, falling into the snow.

They lay there for a couple of minutes, staring up into the sky.

"Mommy?" asked Annie, leaning up to a sitting position. "I wonder what happened to Mr. Hanover?"

"I was just thinking about him, and I don't know. Trappers are a dying breed if you believe what is told in books," she answered, letting her breathing slow as she calmed down.

"I don't think we will ever see him again. I think you're right," acknowledged Annie, as she let out a remorseful sigh as she padded the snow around her. She remembered that Mr. Drake had Mr. Hanover's coat on the last time she saw him. A tear formed in her eye, maybe the only one that would be shed for the old trapper.

"You never know," Elizabeth said brightly.

"I know," she said as the world fell upon her shoulders.

Annie's tone changed as she struggled with something unspoken. "Mommy, can I ask you something?"

"Yes, Annie," she answered, turning towards her daughter.

"Can we go back? I'm getting cold?" declared Annie.

"Me too," said Elizabeth, looking into her child's green eyes.

"We should go in and maybe eat some of that stew you have bee cooking," she answered, smiling just a little.

"Yes, it would be nice to warm ourselves by the fire, eating son deer stew. I mixed some potatoes, beans, and carrots in it also." Sh wondered if the girl's smile was as fake as her own.

"Now, I'm cold and hungry," declared Annie as she stood and helpe her mother up.

They walked inside and stopped in front of the fireplace for a fe minutes to warm themselves. Annie started for the box next to her be She pulled her clean clothes out and started to redress. "Do you thin daddy will bring me some warmer clothes to wear?"

"That's what he told us he would do," answered Elizabeth, alread pulling a thick shirt of her husband's over Annie's shoulders.

Just as Annie returned to the fireplace, a single wolf let out lonesome call that sent shivers down both their backs.

"He sounded like he was close, mommy. Are we going to die?" sh asked, already running back to her mommy's side.

"We should lock the door and maybe make sure the rifle is loaded, she replied as she calmly walked to the entryway and placed the larg plank across the oak door her husband had made using wood from th little wagon. "It looks like it's loaded," said Elizabeth, carrying the rifl over to the fireplace and leaning it against the wall.

"Can I sleep with you tonight?" she asked, giving her mother her sa eyes that could stop an ice wagon in July.

"Sure little one," she responded. "We just need to clean up and stok the fireplace and sit down to some of that stew."

Chapter 33
December 22nd, 1873
Boardwalks of Yakima City

"George, won't you slow down. I am about to sweat through my shirt, and I haven't another to put on. Why are you rushing?" asked John, struggling to keep up.

"My apologies, sir, it has been a while since I had business at the Emporium," he said, stopping and letting the younger man catch up.

"If we show up like we stole these frames, they are liable to call for a lawman," said John, breathing hard.

"You sure don't walk fast, John."

"George, you call that walking? I can tell even you are almost out of breath. What is going on? Why do you insist on moving from place to place as if you are being chased?"

"John, it is just my way. I don't like milling about on the streets."

John knew questioning George further would mean endless turns down the rabbit hole, so he decided to table the discussion for another time when he could tie the man down and beat him like a rug to get the answers he wanted. John had looked down, and George was off again. He decided to catch up with the man at the Emporium.

"What a beautiful day," he declared to a woman that swept the walk in front of her business. Laughing, he looked up and saw a spool of thread and thought of the back door into the Blue Wave.

A block away, he could see the Emporium, a two-and-a-half-story building. It seemed as though the owner wanted to make it seem like a hotel of sorts, with the balcony only usable over the front door. H considered that it was used to lure young men just as the Blue Wave ha done to him two years before. "Has it been two years already," he near exclaimed but settled for a near whisper.

He stopped at the steps leading up to the front door. Part of hi wondered if there was a basement. The other part hoped he would nev find out.

The Blue Wave had a basement and what it was used for w criminal. Men were put in chains and sold off as mariners, never to se their loved ones again. They would fall asleep in the arms of the kinde of women and wake up weeks later in the middle of the Gulf of Mexic heading to Ports of call so far away; they hardly stood a chance to retui to America, let alone St. Louis.

"John!" he yelled, walking back down the stairs.

"Yes, what is it," he replied, looking faint.

"Yous' went somewheres," he insisted, tugging at his coat.

"I'm fine, George."

"You're not a little nervous to walk into a business such as this' asked George, winking and poking about the younger man's ribs.

"No, I'm not nervous at all. Now, let us go inside and sell som wood to these women," he answered the older man while grabbing th door handle and pulling it open.

"It's just my opinion, but you might want to rephrase your words bit, maybe a little less innuendo, or we might be thrown out a window, said George, falling upon deaf ears.

John walked up to what passed for a regulator for the establishmer and asked, "Can you please tell whoever is in charge that I need a fev minutes of their time? It is fine to make me wait. My time is of littl consequence. May I wait over in the corner."

The bouncer looked at the little man who spoke directly to the poir with absolute respect for him and the management. He was at a complet loss as to what to say other than nod and point at the very spot that th little man had wished to wait.

George smiled and waved to several of the ladies while John walked) the table and sat down.

After a few minutes, a black-haired woman in her early thirties valked towards the table and introduced herself. "Hello, my name is Miss. Abby and this is my place."

"Thank you for seeing us on such short notice. My name is John Springer, and I'm here to sell you some wood."

The older man's mouth dropped, and his eyes almost bugged out of his head, first staring at John then back to Miss. Abby, who he wondered f she would signal her man at the door.

"Excuse me, we rent rooms here for that purpose, and the men pay upfront," she said, waiting for John to explain.

George's eyes ran around his nose, and he watched and waited for his friend's reply.

"I noticed when I came in that someone had made their mark on this place. It is beautiful," he said, staring at Miss. Abby's eyes not lowering his gaze to her bosom as most men did.

George looked at her, then her bosom. He was having trouble not glaring at the lady. He looked back to his friend, then back to her when she spoke. It occurred to him the younger man's eyes never left hers.

"Please go on," she asked, mischievously noticing he wasn't there for a free look.

"I noticed that except for one omission, this place has the ambiance of a fine restaurant," said John, softly waving his hand around; however, he refrained from looking away from her eyes.

George's eyes glanced at her well-presented bosom before remembering she had eyes.

As for John, he waited for her to look away and around the sitting room. He waited until she stopped at a painting.

"You see it, don't you," he said, almost hinting at what he had under the table and what Addy needed to perfect the interior of the establishment.

He then reached into the bag and laid the frame in front of h
"Imagine this around the border of that painting. That painting over the
doesn't even have a frame."

"Where on earth did you get this frame, and do you have more?"

They sold nearly half the frames and for almost thirty dollars. Ad
made him promise that when he came back to town that he would bri
his wares to her first.

George managed to get his eyes under control and worked a deal
install the frames for a payment on account.

"John, you were amazing. You could have sold that woman sno
How was it you were so comfortable talking to her?" asked Georg
patting the younger man on his shoulder. "You even got Billy to go g
her without even offering him any money."

"It was easy, I guess. They are people, and we are people. First, ?
respectful and show them what they need and then offer them what the
now want," he answered, glancing at the check and towards the bu
boardwalk. He let a small family pass before adding himself and Geor;
to the foot traffic.

"You could have sold her anything. When you told her you wanted
sell her wood, I about fell from my stool," said George, holding h
hands up to show the different sizes of steaks to emphasize what I
envisioned in his mind.

"Where can we cash this check?" asked John, holding the slip
paper up to look at it. He reckoned it was enough to feed his family fc
several months.

"Well, that would be the bank, but we will need to stop by my te
and several others to enlist help installing frames at the hotel."

"George, I believe there are some frames that need to be delivered t
the Emporium," said John, finding himself sounding a little stuffy as h
struggled to keep a straight face.

"Oh, John, please don't you dare mention that fact to John Albrecl
and his friends. I won't get anyone to help install frames in the hote
Besides, I was planning to take care of them myself."

Chapter 34
December 22nd, 1873
Jackson Livery, Yakima City

Yakima City was advertised as being the hub of all agriculture and a gateway to Seattle. In fact, it was a cluster of buildings that serviced around 450 people that made up around ten percent of the population of the newly formed county.

With that appeal came the lawbreakers and law enforcers and the townspeople caught in between. Whichever side you were on, you ended up needing the services of the local livery.

Kelly stretched his back, wishing he had laid more hay in the stall where he slept last night. He had left Binky and brought the horses back. When he woke, he had a word with Gilbert and made sure he handed over two dollars. When Gilbert had asked him to clean the stalls for breakfast, he agreed.

"You're doing a great job working with the horses. If you ever want full-time employment, we can sure use a man like you," said Gilbert, walking into the receiving hall of the livery and looking around.

"Thank you. I do like working with horses. I would love to work for you if I weren't happy with my present employer," answered Kelly, leaning on his broom for a minute.

"Well, who knows, a person's station changes around here like the shuffling of a new deck. If you are ever tired of the excitement of outlawing, you have a place here," said Gilbert placing a basket on the table and turning back to Kelly, now pointing his revolver at Gilbert chest.

"What do you know about it?" asked Kelly with a murderous look his eyes.

"Wait, wait, easy now. It is good, don't shoot," responded Gilber raising his hands and stepping back a foot from the table.

"Start talking," demanded Kelly, pulling the hammer back on h Smith and Wesson, Model 3 Revolver.

"Easy now, I saw who you were with last night," said Gilber reaching up and removing his hat.

"And who was that?" asked Kelly, with gritted teeth.

"You would know him as Binky. He is the man that gave me this answered Gilbert, pointing at his forehead as Kelly lowered his gun an slowly lowered the hammer.

"Why did he shoot you in the head?" asked Kelly.

"Well, let us just say, I came down on the wrong side of a certai exchange and ended up losing. Just so the man that calls himself Bink could make a point, but in the end, I moved up the ladder, and now work here," he answered.

"You saying we all work for the same boss?" asked Kelly as he hear a noise and looked back into the darkened barn.

"It's fine. I understand why you are jumpy. I was much the sam way. If you calm down, we can have a real talk about life and grav covered biscuits," he answered, pointing to the basket.

"They do smell good," said Kelly, softening his grip on his revolve and glancing at the basket.

"They are good, and if you holster your 44, we can eat some lunch, he said, sitting down as Kelly dropped his revolver into his holster.

"What do you do for Binky?" asked Gilbert, pulling a bowl out fo each of them.

"Not much of anything, just odd jobs that need doin'," replied Kelly pulling the bowl closer and taking a cloth napkin from Gilbert.

"Well, that's how it starts: he has you do odd jobs until he can gaug your worth."

"Gauge my worth?" asked Kelly, holding out his bowl as Gilbert dropped a biscuit and poured a few ladles of gravy over the top. Then dropped some stewed beef over the whole thing.

"He needs to know how reliable you are, are you made of stone, or will you fall apart like clay," he answered as he poured the gravy onto his biscuit and dropped some meat into the bowl.

"So everything is a test," said Kelly, opening his mouth and spooning the food from the bowl.

"Yes, if he asks you to do something that seems more like a challenge, do it because it means your final test has begun, and if you want to stay in the gang, you better pass.

"Can I take Binky a bowl?" asked Kelly.

"Sure, is he in town?" asked Gilbert, pulling the third bowl from the basket.

"Yes, I can be back in just a few minutes," stated Kelly, finishing his portion and contemplating licking the bowl.

"What happens if you don't pass his final test?"

"You end up working a livery for the rest of your life," answered Gilbert, holding the bowl for Binky out for Kelly to grab.

"It's no hurry," said Gilbert, "take all the time you need."

"I like working here, so I will be back as soon as I can," said Kelly, heading out the service door in the receiving hall.

Gilbert stood and gathered the plates and lifted the basket. "Did you hear all that?" he asked, turning to meet his wife coming through the back door.

"I did, although wouldn't it have been better if you would have asked him where he was," answered Addle, reaching into the basket and pushing her finger into the gravy bowl.

"You know he nearly shot me," he declared as he handed her the basket.

"I had you covered from the window over there," she said with a wink.

"Yeah, but I would have been dead," he said.

"But thoroughly avenged, I assure you," she laughed, sniffing tl gravy on her finger and licking it off.

"Hello, how are you?" asked Kelly from outside.

Both Gilbert and Addle's hearts skipped a beat. The shock showed both their expressions.

"I would have to ask inside. How many days are you needing? asked Kelly.

"That was quick," said Gilbert.

"He must be close," whispered Addle.

The door swung open. "Hey, there is a man out here with buckboard with a bad hub band, and three spokes need replacing. H wants it repaired by morning and board his horses while you do th work?" asked Kelly tilting his hat politely, looking over to Addle.

"Well, it's a hay-day," answered Gilbert.

"Is that a yes?" asked Kelly, looking at Gilbert's hands.

"Yes, is it still snowing outside?"

"Yeah, pretty hard now, there are six, maybe seven, inches out ther on the ground," answered Kelly, pulling the table from the middle of th room.

"Well, we better bring the wagon inside then," said Gilbert, walkin over to the stove to stoke it with arm-sized pieces of wood.

Chapter 35
December 22nd, 1873
Yakima City, Washington Territory

The boardwalk was congested with morning shoppers who made the simple act of walking slippery with packed snow that turned to ice overnight.

Not far from the livery, John followed George in close formation. He carried a large canvas bag with half his frames. He had left the rest drying in George's tent. "How you are doing, George?" he asked, readjusting the frames hoping his friend would slow down.

"I'm fine. Would you like me to take your wares for you?"

John thought about it, taking a minute to decide if only to give himself some rest and maybe delay their arrival at the hotel. He had been calm going into the brothel yesterday.

"John, are you alright? You are starting to sweat a little and look like you passed gas in church," he asked, wagging his mustache.

"I'm stressed, I think," he answered, stepping off the boardwalk into at least half a foot of snow.

"Well, even if they don't buy any, we can inquire at the Northwest Mercantile, Mr. Dumas trades for goods, and if he doesn't want them, we can go door to door."

"Thank you."

"It's nothing, just next time if you use gold inlays, the frames are sure to sell faster," he mused, sounding as if he had a cold.

John shook his head and then thought about it and said, "Your log is sound, only if I had the gold."

George paused in front of the hotel's entrance turning back with smile across his lips. "If you had the gold, then you wouldn't need to se the frames," he said, giving him a wink and turning back towards th entrance.

Now, there was some argument as to who had thrown the snowba that impacted the back of the man's neck. Some say it was serendipit others being, George would claim it was revenge, but whatever th cause, John laughed, and George spent the next hour with th uncomfortable feeling of a moist neck and back.

"Is it cold, George?" he mused as they waited on a lovely sofa in th lobby of the hotel.

"I knows yous' did it," he answered, throwing his shoulders back an arching as the ice began to melt under his collar and the cold wate dripped down his back.

"George, you have to believe I had no part in the assault you suffere in front of this here establishment," said John, trying to keep fror erupting in laughter again.

"You just wait, I will have me some revenge when you least expec it," declared George.

John looked as though he was going to fall to the floor in a fit. H would be lucky if someone wouldn't try to hold him down and make hir bite down on one of his frames.

"Excuse me," said the hotel manager, who was a ferret of a man. " was told you wanted me to see some frames."

"Would you like to see them here?"

"Here is as good as any place, just be quick about it," replied th human polecat. George would claim later to have wondered if the mar was at least partially a ferret.

He slipped one out of the bag. The carving was of the trip on th mountain boat up the Missouri River. It felt like ten years had passec since then. The manager accepted it without looking up, asking, "Hov many do you have, and are they all carved the same?"

"They all depict different points of my travel to the Northwest."

"And, how many?" he asked impatiently.

"Fourteen."

"How much would you want for them?"

"Five dollars each."

The weasel, as he was referred to at this point and forever known, at least in George's company, thought for a moment and saying just one word, "Half."

John nodded in agreement. George about fell over, wondering why didn't he dicker with the man.

"Would you be willing to install?" asked the weasel.

"Yes, for 50 cents, each," demanded George.

"Excuse me, why are you speaking?" asked the manager, not even turning towards George's direction.

"This man is my installer," John managed to blurt out.

"Fine, a quarter of a dollar per painting," countered the weasel, choosing to turn and at least face the older man.

"Forty cents each, and you get one of your boys to bring your paintings to a room where we can work in peace," stated George.

John was starting to wonder who his friend really was. He was smart at times, other moments crafty, but always played the fool.

"Thirty-five cents, one room for the night, you take the paintings down from all the public places, hallways and such. I will bring you the rest when you are done with those."

John almost blurted out his loud and clear approval. However, the old man spoke first, "Now, I counted three paintings here in the lobby, two at the ends of the hallways upstairs. Three in the stairway, so I will need to be walkin' up and down the stairs all day long. So how about three nights stay, and we agree to your terms," demanded George as John's eyes went from the ferret to his friend and back.

"Two-bits per frame and I agree to your terms," replied the ferret-faced man who seemed to joy the art of the haggle. He was willing to pay far more.

Consortium of Acquaintances

"Make it 35 cents each, and that can be paid by vouchers for liqu and the three nights stay," said George before adding a threat of goi places neither of them had talked about going. "Or we take the frames the Winston and the Lucy."

John struggled to keep up with the exchange before setting on tl hotel's manager.

"Fine!" exclaimed the weasel as he ran off to help an impatie guest. His face showed anger, but the bounce in his step showed he w. satisfied with the outcome.

"Wait, so, no actual payment will be exchanged?" asked Joh looking towards the hotel desk, where the manager was standing.

"Yes, although I did get us three nights to stay warm and cozy. Tl alcohol I bartered for was for the three carpenters I know that will l willing to install the frames," answered George. He seemed to relax as l told John of his plan.

"I see the way you act around people, but you seem to be in yor element among people in charge. I just got to know who the heck are yo really?" asked John, leaning towards George, hoping the simple gestu would give him the opportunity to come clean.

"I'm who I am, and I can't change that," answered George, suddenl looking a little sad for some untold reason.

"Well, thank you, my friend. We are even," said John, slapping th older man's knee.

"Not by a long shot, mister, I still owe you. Plus, a little interest i the form of a snowball," laughed George, slapping his knee.

John chuckled at the comment and stopped when he noticed th manager was waving them over. He started to get up.

"I didn't do anything more than what you did yesterday at th Emporium. You were an amazing negotiator when you were talking t Abby. How is it, an upstanding man, such as you are, is mor comfortable in a brothel than in a hotel?" asked George.

He leaned close to the older man. "I will explain, just as soon as yo explain why you sounded well educated just now," replied John.

Chapter 36
December 22nd, 1873
Near the city jail, Yakima City

Binky sat by a window upstairs of the bakery across from Sheriff Miller's office. He knew that it wouldn't be long until Frank gave the cell key to Lucky. He sat, waiting for him to free himself.

He picked up the bowl, stabbing the biscuit with the fork, and bit it into two pieces swallowing without slowing to taste it. He hadn't eaten since breakfast, and that wasn't as nearly as good. He watched as one of the deputies came from his right, walking across the street, and headed towards the Sheriff's Office.

"Where you been, and why are you in such a hurry?" he asked, taking another bite of the stewed meat and letting it sit in his mouth. "So three inside, the one that entered, and Sheriff Miller makes five," he said, thinking aloud. "They must be waiting for me. How did they know, and more importantly, who is the informer?"

***

Mayor Daniels sat behind his desk, looking out at the crowded streets. "Mable, why are so many people out on a cold day like this?" he asked, scooting closer to the window. "It's snowing out there."

"It will be Christmas in a few days. Maybe people want to visit and buy gifts for the holiday," answered Mable cheerfully.

"I don't recall the town looking so busy last year. Can you?" asked the mayor, tapping his fingers in a rhythmic matter on the desk.

"There weren't as many people living in these parts," answel Mable, shutting her desk drawer.

"Mable, I am going out," he said, looking up at the poster of the pl Jeanie Deans signed by the cast. "We are the sums of our decisions of t past."

"When can I say you will be back?" asked Mable.

"No one has come in all day. If I'm not back by 4:30 pm, please fe free to lock up, and I will see you in the morning," he answered as shut the door and walked down the narrow flight of stairs that wou drop him onto the boardwalk less than a block from the bank.

The mayor walked across the street and passed the bank. Despite t crowds, he felt alone. He turned into an alley and walked a few blocl He saw the lack of footprints in the seven or so inches of snow. When came to the five-foot fence near the alley's end, he stopped and reach over, unlatching the lock. The gate opened with a squeak, and he walke up to the back door. The footprints were leading from the back door to side gate.

He knocked lightly, and the door opened a crack coming to rest t more than an inch from the jam. "Excuse me, we should talk," he sai trying to muster as much pleasantness as he could.

"I told you to stay away, and I would send for you."

"Have you seen how many people are milling around in tow tonight?" asked Mayor Daniels, leaning closer to the door.

"Yes, so what of it?"

"What if someone gets hurt? Should not our plans be placed on hol for a few days," answered Mayor Daniels, glaring at the crack.

"Are you out of your mind!"

"Did you not hear me?" asked Mayor Daniels, stepping in place t push the snow down and maybe warm himself up a little.

"The play has been written, the scene has been practiced, and th audience has arrived."

"There are far too many people around," said Mayor Daniels with touch of anger in his voice.

"I want them to see what happens when you cross us."

"I practically raised Benjamin," said Mayor Daniels, stomping his feet, waiting for a response.

"He was like a son to me also, or have you forgot, but he hasn't been ight for months. He took Harry and Robert without asking you for your pinion. They will never step back into these parts until Benjamin is finished. Not to mention if he puts the facts together, we might be next. Sheriff Miller has also been sending inquiries back east about friends of urs. I have stopped at least three letters from reaching their lestinations."

"What if he wins?" asked Mayor Daniels.

"Then he will have to make a reckoning with Mr. Jason' Hangman' Luther. He will be here to deal with both of them."

"Why would you bring that man back to town? He is crazy; he loves o hurt people," said Mayor Daniels, leaning closer.

"He is a strong leader and will bring men in to take care of anyone that gets in our way."

"He should be locked up," said Mayor Daniels, leaning away and looking at the foggy sky and watching the tiny snowflakes fall.

"If Sheriff Miller wins, then the Hangman will be paying him a visit. He is finished as Sheriff."

"There are too many unfavorable outcomes, and too many people can get hurt," stated Mayor Daniels, blowing his nose into his monogrammed handkerchief.

"Would you like me to send Mr. Luther to your house?"

"No, no, I'm sure he will be far too busy hurting people to see me," answered Mayor Daniels, recognizing the threat.

"Go, and do as I have asked and meet with Lucky, then go tell Benjamin that you couldn't help. Tell him to wait until after Christmas."

"Oh, will you call the Hangman off then?" asked Mayor Daniels, putting his handkerchief back into his pocket.

"Benjamin will not walk away. He will go forth and wreak havoc upon our town to get his lieutenant freed from jail."

"Why would you have me tell him to stop?"

"For your conscience, my dear," answered the voice behind the d with a cruel laugh.

"You have it all figured out then?" asked Mayor Daniels.

"I had this figured out for a few months."

"I just hope you are right and all the pieces will fall into place," answered as the door shut.

***

Back above the bakery, Binky stretched his back as he yawn "Where are you?" he asked no one in particular. He was about to ya again when he heard a noise behind him.

"Good afternoon, Benjamin," said Sheriff Miller.

When Binky turned around, he had his hand already on his revolv "How did you find me?" he asked, figuring he would catch him off gua if he needed to make his escape.

"Don saw you perched up in that there window and came by t office to tell me. So I snuck out the judge's window, in case you we watching the courtroom doors," said Sheriff Miller, stepping out fro behind a few crates stacked upon one another.

"So you here to arrest me?" he said, lifting his hand from h revolver. The truth was he could draw just as fast if his hand were on h gun or not.

"Heck Benjamin, I'm not even sure if it is loaded," said Sheri Miller, turning the revolver as if to see if bullets were clogging th cylinders. He put the pistol into his holster and moved a little closer.

Binky moved back and let him look out the window.

"You know when I first come to town, there was nothing but tents, he said, motioning for Binky to sit down for a spell.

Binky reached for his bowl of stew and motioned for the Sheriff t have a seat where Kelly had sat almost an hour ago.

He leaned back and sat down on the offered crate. "Oh, that was long time ago. No, I have back problems and get stuck in the outhous for what seems like an hour.

"How did you hurt your back?" asked Binky, looking towards the Sheriff's office, mostly out of habit at this point.

"I have been a lawman for years and have been in more fights than I care to remember. But until recently, I have been able to recover after a day or two," he said, glancing towards his office if only to make sure it was there.

"Why are you telling me this?" asked Binky, wondering if the man had a point to make.

"I'm slower than I was last year. I've been slowing down for a few years now," he said, turning back to Binky.

"Maybe you should retire, maybe build a cabin near the river and spend your time fishing instead of chasing the likes of me," said Binky, noticing the Sheriff was staring at him now.

"Late last night, I received two notes posted on my door," he said, reaching into his vest and producing the first note. "It says that the Hangman is coming to town, hired by the council. His first job is to kill me and find you for the same reason," he said, then handed Binky the note. The second said Lucky and half the gang was at the Lucy desiring to murder someone in town."

Binky handed him back the note and waved off the second figuring it was from one of his gang, and he would have no clue who wrote it, but it was accurate.

"Who wrote the other note?" asked Binky leaning back.

"No idea."

"What you reckoning you want to do about it?" asked Binky, wondering who wanted him dead.

"The way I see it, the Hangman will take his time killing me. He never had respect for the law," he whispered for no other reason than he was tired of talking. "That's why I arrested Lucky, he doesn't need to be killing anyone, and I figured you would rush into town."

"So we could have this here little chat?" asked Binky, watching someone enter the Sheriff's office only to be rushed away.

"I want you to kill me. I know you can make it fast, and so I won't feel it coming," said the Sheriff, blurting it out.

Consortium of Acquaintances

"Run," said Binky letting his mind find other possibilities.

"I'm too old to run. Besides, I don't do so well in the cold," said t[] seasoned lawman, rubbing his knuckles on his right hand. "Just dor shoot the deputies. If you can manage it."

"You don't know me. You have no idea about me," whispered Bink not wanting anyone to know the truth but the man before him. "How c you know you can trust me?"

"I saw what you did with Robert Hinkle and Harold Jackson. Whe you came back to town last May, you just ran them out of town," he sai hearing someone walk out of the bakery and into the alley. "Besides, I' not doing you any favors."

"So you know I'm not as bad as my father has made me out to be said Binky as a look of surprise splashed on the Sheriff's face.

"He is your father? I thought for certain he was the one that he hired the Hangman."

"No, there is a council for those kinds of decisions," whispere Binky, letting secrets go like birds at a wedding.

"We have no city council," said Sheriff Miller.

"They live here and control your city. If you decided to vote a ci[] council into office, they would stuff the ballot-boxes with nothing b[] puppets," whispered Binky, not wanting to be overheard.

"Well, I wish them well because I expect to be dead soon," he stoo and shook the younger man's hand.

"I haven't decided to do the deed," said Binky, releasing the man hand and leading him to the door.

"Benjamin, when you come for Lucky and Joseph, I will be ther with my shotgun. If you don't kill me, I will do my best to kill yo[] There is just no other way around it," said Sheriff Miller.

242

Chapter 37
December 22nd, 1873
Hummel Hotel, Yakima City

In Yakima City, there was just one place that a man could hang his hat and get a good night's sleep for a dollar. The Hummel Hotel, where they served anyone with the ability to pay the room rent and did it with a smile.

George had found out more than once the hotel staff had no patience for anyone that could not pay for the room or just wanted to sneak in for a quiet nap in the formal lobby. On more than one occasion, he had found himself pitched across the back alley into the mud that seemed to gather there in rainstorm or drought. He always wondered why but was never brave enough to explore the plumbing of the back alleys of Yakima City.

Today was different concerning how he exited the hotel. George had smartly negotiated with the hotel manager to throw in the room for three nights. He had wondered what it was like to leave through the front door. "John, how about that steak now?" he asked as they left the hotel's entrance and were suddenly assaulted by the temperature in the lower 20s. They stood on the boardwalk, making passersby change their course slightly to avoid bumping into them as they adjusted to the weather.

"That is an excellent idea," he answered, glancing up the street for somewhere as yet revealed by his friend. The town wasn't as crowded as the night before, but there seemed to be a lot of foot traffic. He observed another heavy wagon roll past that was having trouble finding the ruts.

"If you's looking for a great place, there are two that I know of th
are heavenly. One serves a steak that is better than good. The other serv
a steak that is not as good, but they make it up in quantity. I am serious,
could serve a small family," he said, rambling on about the restaurants
town that offered the exact fare for a bargain.

"George?" asked John, waving his hand about and snapping h
fingers to get the older man's attention, which seemed to get mo:
challenging as the day progressed.

"I'm telling you it is the biggest steak around. I don't know how the
cut that steak from one cow," said George, watching John draw attentic
from their conversation by foolishly waving his hand.

"George?"

"Ah, yes, John?" he answered with a questioning look magnified b
raising one of his bushy eyebrows.

"We still need to cash the checks before we can pay for those tasi
meals you mentioned," replied John, still looking for the bank and wa
more than a little curious about the last place he mentioned with steak
that need to be carried out by more than one person.

"Why didn't you say so. We should get a move on before our steak
get cold," stated George as he lost thirty years of age and broke out into
near sprint disappearing into the fog.

He followed the older man as if he were a bloodhound for wha
seemed longer than it was due to ice-covered boardwalks. "How com
they put it so far away from the hotel?" he asked as he caught up with hi
quick friend, who had paused for a moment to catch his breath.

"It is because they decided that it wasn't a great idea to have th
bank so close to the Emporium," replied George, losing himself i
thought as a wagon rumbled by them with a cargo of some sort.

"Why would the distance matter to anyone?" asked John, touchin
his arm slightly to keep the older man's attention. He was far from losin,
patience with him because if he hadn't found him, helped him, and give:
him a place to stay. He would have been on his way home with beans an
little show for his effort.

"Too many people, mainly men, were coming out of the Winston
ranting their life-savings just to lose it in the saloon at the poker table or
or some more time at the Emporium if yous' knows' what I mean," he
answered, elbowing the younger man who showed little reaction. They
both stepped off the boardwalk and crossed the street simultaneously,
although George took the lead once more.

He watched the older man manipulate his body in a sense, making
himself narrower as if it were a learned trait. He remembered people
back in St. Louis that had come from even larger cities. They had walked
the same way.

George zigged and zagged through the crowd that seemed to be
milling around on boardwalks on both sides of the street. John presumed
his ballet of shoppers had some purpose for being out so late in the
afternoon. He had no idea that they would be hip deep in the middle of
why so many people were braving the snow and wind to be present.
George stopped suddenly without warning, and John slammed into his
back, and someone else bumped into John from behind. After the cursory
examination of the situation, he noticed that George had stopped in front
of the Yakima City Bank.

Breathing hard, as he reached for the door, he asked, "Why were we
rushing to get here?"

"The bank closes at 4:30, have your transaction ready, so we can
quickly help everyone in line," called out the bank manager.

"That's why," whispered George as if he had just entered a church
meeting a little late.

A tall man talked to a shorter woman wearing a white top and long
blue skirt as John nearly bumped into them coming in from the cold. "It's
about seven inches out there, I'm guessing, and we could have more by
morning if this weather keeps a-going the way it is going."

"I was hoping for a white Christmas, and it seems we are getting a
blizzard out there this afternoon," replied the woman.

He turned slightly to face George, asking, "How deep does the snow
get around here?"

"I have seen 10-inches just a few miles west of town," offered man.

"I heard that we were supposed to get that much snow this yea replied George.

John looked closer and couldn't make out the bank manager's nai tag. He even so much as leaned a little closer.

"What in tarnation are yous' doing?" he asked, with the oddest lo on his face.

"I'm trying to read the manager's name tag, and I'm having no lu even with the leaning," he answered as it occurred to him that everyo else in line was watching him like he was a circus act.

"Young man, either stops your leaning over or let me put out collection hat," whispered George.

"Old man, you don't have a hat," he said, pointing at his expos bald spot.

"Now, where did that hat go?" he asked, giving the room a qui once over, and then he touched his head one more time as if it wou have suddenly appeared.

"Well, didn't crawl off and hide in the corner," answered John, no standing straight and trying to ease everyone's mind concerning h mental state.

"Next," called out the bank clerk. Like lemmings, they all took a ha step and readjusted the line each time the young lady behind the tell cage called out.

"Did I have it before I took my bath? Did you see me in the ba with my hat on?" asked George, a little too loud because everyone wa staring at them.

"I have no idea what you're talking about," answered John, adjustin his footing, so his body faced the other side of the room only to find o there were just as many people staring from that direction.

"Yous' knows' when yous' stood there talking to me while I took m bath," he said again with that same pitched wheeze he had in the hote and the bathhouse.

"I didn't see it on you when we left the hotel or the bathhouse," he aid, looking at George like a hawk that was about to spoil a field ouse's day.

"Must have left it somewhere," interjected a younger man of his arly twenties, that neither John nor George recognized.

"Where did we drink last night? The whole night seems a bit fuzzy to ne." asked George. "Let me think." He raised his hand and acted as hough he would start listing the evening libation stations. They stood here waiting for him to start even though he was having difficulty naming the first, let alone any of the stops.

"You were at the Lucy's after midnight," replied a younger man who ooked to be a blacksmith.

"Lucy's," said George and lifted one finger slowly.

"I reckon Mr. Hicks' was saying something about the fact that you were over there most of the night," answered a woman that John couldn't see from his vantage point.

"Next!"

George stepped sideways and raised the second finger on his hand, and said, "Winston's. Thank you, Mrs. Violet."

John couldn't believe just how nosey everyone was being, so he decided to make it a point not to talk in public again. His silence lasted all about a minute. "You didn't go out drinking for the last couple of nights, and you had the hat on coming into town on Mr. Harrison's wagon; that means you lost it in the tent, the hotel, or wherever you disappeared to for your constitutional walk last night."

George noticed him leaning again, trying to make out the name on the badge. "It says Yakima County Bank in bold letters and the word Manager underneath."

"How does a man of your years see across the room so clearly, but can't seem to read the difference between cod liver oil and whiskey?" he asked, looking up into the cloudy eyes of his friend.

"Well, you see that name tag has a history of sorts. It has belonged to seven managers before, and with such a large turnover rate, it became a symbol like, like a..." George responded, stumbling on his words.

"Next," called out the clerk. He noticed each time she called out, t bank hushed, waiting for the person in front to move forward.

"Like a lawman's badge," said Ellen, a lady of 60 years and abc four feet nothing.

"Thank you, Ellen," said George, turning back to John.

"Well, that's good to know. Still, it doesn't help me in the fact tha still don't know the man's name."

"Oh, it is written above the date just inside the door," said Georg pointing to the black slate chalkboard.

"Harold Hicks," said John, reading the board out loud. He took moment to notice the date, and he suddenly felt guilty for not being (the trail heading home.

"Next," called out the clerk. They moved a little closer, and tl people in front of them seemed to stay quiet as if they could make tl transactions go faster.

John looked up and could see by the rafters of the building that was quickly built. Like most of the buildings, it looked new on tl outside and disappointing on the inside. He laughed as he extrapolate the concept to include the townsfolk he had just met.

Chapter 38
December 23rd, 1873
Springer Ranch, Washington Territory

Elizabeth walked out of the cabin and onto the porch stopping in her tracks. The sun was out, and the sky was blue. The sun felt warm on her face. She couldn't tell how much new snow they had received, but it was a lot for one night. The drifts made it almost impossible to tell. "Annie come and see how beautiful the sky looks," she said, pushing the snow off the porch that had invaded from the west disguised as a snowdrift. The shovel was made for digging, so the chore took longer than she wanted to spend outside.

Annie walked out and smiled at how beautiful the snow-capped trees were. "It's peaceful," she said, moving over to the bench.

She remembered seeing daddy-John load his raft before he left them. She promised she would be strong, so she stifled back a tear and braced herself.

Elizabeth could see the worry and wasn't sure what she should do. She was finished cleaning the porch. She looked up at the tower that stood out away from the cabin. It had a small ladder leading to a door that was supposed to hold enough meat to last until John would return. "Should we clear a path out there?" she asked, really hoping Annie would give her a reason not to spend the time.

"Are you sure there isn't any meat in the locker?"

"Yes, I'm sure, we cooked the last of it yesterday," she sa
wondering if someone had been taking the meat at night, then let t
falling snow and the snowdrifts cover their tracks.

"The time and energy should be spent clearing the way to t
firewood. If we lose the fire, we lose our way to melt snow and ke
warm," answered Annie, looking in the direction of the meat locker.

"You're right, and the fact the outhouse is over by the woodpile is
bonus," said Elizabeth, ruffling Annie's bonnet with her left hand whi
moving to start the path to the woodpile.

"I don't reckon he wouldn't take from us."

"How much time did you spend with him?"

"Not really all that long. I mostly watched Drake. Until the Big-O
told me to go home."

She started towards the woodpile, and a minute later, somethir
occurred to her. "Annie?"

"Yes, I'm awake," she answered, lifting her head from her knees.

"The Big One?" she asked, realizing asking her daughter question
was like dancing through a briar patch. Sooner or later, someone wa
going to get hurt.

"Opposed to the Small One."

"Oh," she said, letting Annie's answer sink in a little. She shook he
head as if to reset herself and asked, "Who or what is the Big One?"

"The Biggest Indian across the river," said Annie, lowering her hea
to the bent knees once again.

Elizabeth felt faint. Her hands tightened on the shovel. "Annie, di
you go over to their side of the river?"

"No," she answered, not offering any detail.

She released a breath and shoveled some more snow from the path t
the woodpile.

"He found me when I was spying on Mr. Drake."

Elizabeth stopped and felt as though she would faint. She felt lik
she didn't even know the child on the porch. She tried not to overreact
knowing Annie would close down. "When was this?"

"He found me over that way just into the trees. He spoke funny and pointed towards the cabin. He was telling me to go home."

"How do you know that if he was speaking Indian to you?" asked Elizabeth, more interested than anything else.

"I'm a kid, and when an adult tells you to stop and go home, you know it. I could see it in his eyes and his face. He was worried."

"Annie?"

"Yes, em."

"Add encounters with the local tribes to that list of events you are supposed to tell me. In fact, any encounter with human or wildlife larger than a rabbit, and you come tell me."

"Yes, ma' ma," she said with a slight smirk.

"Speaking of rabbits, there is one buried in the snow," she said, looking down at the grey rabbit with what looked like a singed tail.

"Annie, bring me the pot."

"It can't be any good," she said, opening the door and walking back with a small pot.

"Must have died the night of the fire," said Elizabeth, taking a stick and working at the ice.

"That was a long time ago," she turned up her nose and gave Elizabeth the oddest of looks.

"It has been under the snow frozen. It might be alright to eat.

She finished the path, and they slipped inside to get warm. She poured warm water onto the rabbit and washed her hands. "When you were with Mr. Drake, what did you talk about?"

"The weather mostly," she answered.

"Really?"

"He wasn't much of a talker. He talked to himself more than me. That's why I spied on him."

"Did he ever try to hurt you?" asked Elizabeth.

"He tried to scare me," she answered.

"What happened?"

"When he charged at me, snarling, I giggled and told him he was funny. So he stopped. Then he told me to go home."

"You giggled at him?" she asked, letting a smile slip onto her fa
before bringing her lips under control.

"I looked at him without blinking. I have seen scary men that liked
eat children and pile their clothing as evidence. I could tell he wanted
be good. He just needed a little push," she said, sounding sullen.

"What he say to that?" asked Elizabeth even though she wanted
know what happened to the evil men.

"He asked me what became of the scary men, and I told him,
watched them die," she answered, looking sad.

"Is that what you dream about that terrifies you late at night?"

"I dream of many things."

"So, what did he say to your bravery?"

"He looked at me and seemed to size me up. Then he told me to g
tend my potatoes."

"You are leading an exciting life. Who was the Small One?" sl
asked, realizing they were names that she had given the men from tl
tribe across the river.

"Is that what it's called? How's the rabbit?" she asked, obvious
changing the subject. Her nose wrinkled at the sight of the rabbit.

Elizabeth lifted the rabbit and gave it a sniff. She began to retch a
she headed out the door with the pot held out before her.

"I told you it was bad," said Annie, following her out onto the porc
where the pot had been dropped into the snow.

Elizabeth sat on the bench and fought back the tears that welled up i
her eyes. Speaking to her husband as if he could hear her, "John, I don
know what we are to do. We can't fish the pond because it's frozen eve
though the book says we can ice fish but doesn't say how. What are w
going to do?"

"We eat potatoes until daddy-John comes home," answered Annie
staring at her with the same look she gave Drake. Her expression showe
hardened nerves.

Elizabeth was starting to believe her hard life was nothing compare
to what was going on inside her daughter's mind.

Chapter 39

As with most Yakima City storefronts, LaVerne's Bakery was freshly painted and looked like it had just been built. It was inviting to people walking down the street to come in and have a look around.

In the rear, like most businesses, it told a different story. The building was unpainted, and the stairway leading up to the gabled entrance to the attic was threatening to collapse as Binky came down, taking two steps at a time.

When he reached the ground, he turned the corner bumping into Kelly. "Hey boss, why are you running?" he asked, reaching out and steadying Binky.

"Frank left work and is heading this way. He was supposed to give Lucky a key, but he signaled he didn't have a chance to do it," answered Binky, squaring his stance and pushing away from Kelly's grasp and continuing down the alley.

"Have you seen that man you are after because I did," he said, watching him turn on his heels as he changed his direction and came running back.

"You better not be messing with me, I'm not in the mood."

"Boss, I wouldn't mess with you about anything, not after I saw you beat Gabriel half to death for jumping out at you last month. Now, don't get me wrong when I say it was funny at first. However, he just doesn't talk right anymore."

"Just tell me where he is," demanded Binky.

"My apologies, boss, he and another fellow went into the bank just moment ago," said Kelly flushing red in his cheeks.

"Keep an eye out on the bank and follow him if you need to. Ju make sure you don't lose him."

"I will, boss, where will you be?"

"I'm going to get Lucky out and then come take care of the matter the bank."

"Boss, Frank just walked by on the boardwalk," said Kelly, movir closer.

"Just watch the fella, and I will come to the bank after I get Luck freed from the jail," said Binky, spinning back on his heels and turnir right at the end of the alley in the direction of Mayor Daniels.

"I will watch them from over there," responded Kelly, pointir towards the hat shop.

He could see Frank two businesses down, walking at a leisurely pac like he was a king, and the people around were his subjects. He walke behind him, and with each step, he got all that much closer. In the nez block, he got close enough to call his name, "Frank," he called ou practically whispering.

Frank noticed Binky and headed down the alley.

Binky followed the man at a reasonable pace. "Frank, what the he happened?" he asked, coming alongside.

"When I tried to visit with Lucky, Sheriff Miller told me to leave fe my protection. It seems that they know you are about to try to brea Lucky out."

"And how would they know that, I wonder?" asked Binky, movin close enough to Frank that he felt the need to move back. "Frank, you ai the inside man. You tell me that you will handle the town and its people Over and over, you tell me this. So tell me what is going on?"

"I really have been left out of the plans on the trap they have set fe you," answered Mayor Daniels, now looking as though he would swee through his shirt.

"What do you mean a trap?" he asked, waiting to see if he would te him of the Hangman.

"They have three deputies in the jail. He deputized three men that come in from out of town a few days ago," answered Mayor Daniels, unbuttoning his top button.

"Go on. What are they doing in there?"

"He is at his desk, and one is behind the door on a chair, two more are sitting in chairs near the cells. If you go in and draw, the man behind the door will shoot you in the ear," said Mayor Daniels, relaxing as Binky stepped back a little.

"So what is the man behind the door holding?" asked Binky.

"He has a double-barreled shotgun, and the two down the hall have pistols. I didn't ask them what they had buried in their holsters," he answered, trying a little levity.

"Does Sheriff Miller have a scattergun or sidearm?" asked Binky, moving and turning away to check if they had an audience.

"His revolver is close, and the shotgun is leaning up against the corner of the room near his desk."

"Oh, one last question: the deputy behind the door - is his shotgun a long-gun or is it sawed-off?" asked Binky, feeling more confident.

"Long-gun, double-barreled, long stock," answered Mayor Daniels.

"That is fine. I'm going to get Lucky."

"Ben, don't do it! If you kill anyone, you will get federal troops in town from Fort Walla Walla, then no one will be making money," admonished Mayor Daniels.

"We wouldn't want that," he said.

"They have a bad man coming to take care of a short list of people. They are going to start with the head lawman and the head outlaw," said Mayor Daniels as if he was giving a revelation.

"Well, Frank, Mr. Luther will just need to wait his turn. I have some business to finish. If I do their business, maybe they will let me stay on as head outlaw or at least the Hangman's valet," he said, walking away and back toward the Sheriff's office.

"Good luck, Ben," said Mayor Daniels, heading down the alley and toward the direction of his home.

Frank had known Ben longer than he had known his present wif having met her shortly after losing her husband when he ran off wi Maggie, the owner from the Emporium. He was the one that invite Benjamin to come out to the Yakima Valley to make good money. H father even suggested Ben bring his family and make a life out here. F intended to get him into the family business to teach him how to ga wealth through alternative means.

Benjamin had always looked up to Frank. He had practically raise him when his adopted father suddenly died of a stomach ache, or th was at least how he remembered it.

Frank felt as if he were losing someone dear to him. Maybe it woul be better if he were gunned down. "You made your choices, my son said Mayor Daniels, walking into his little yard and looking up at th large house, then glancing down at the tree that overshadowed h indiscretions.

***

Binky ambled, following the crowd as they did their last-minu shopping. Once five o'clock came, the town would slow, and the peopl would disperse, heading for home and warm meals with their familie: Binky missed both meals and the happier times with his family; howeve he would never admit the weakness he felt every time he saw a famil walking down the boardwalk enjoying the holiday weather.

He neared the Sheriff's office and could see Kelly near the bank. H nodded his head, and Kelly did the same. His eyes shifted to the bank and Kelly indicated that they were still inside. He nodded at Kelly on more time and stopped just before the large door to steady his nerves "Get the horses," said Binky in Kelly's direction.

In turn, Kelly tipped his had and disappeared down the boardwalk t obtain their horses for their get-away.

Binky pulled his Peacemaker from his holster, letting his hand slid down to his side, so the pistol was pointing down and hiding in th creases of his trousers.

Binky opened the heavy door and stepped back with a smooth motion, then kicked it with all of his might.

The opened door swiftly hit the man sitting behind it, who had been pointing the shotgun in the direction of the entrance.

He raised his Peacemaker and fired twice, taking time to aim; he caught Sheriff Miller in his right shoulder and the left forearm before he could put a weapon into his grip. He wasn't known for speed as much as he was known never to miss.

He heard Coyote-Jack's voice, the man that taught him how to use a revolver, telling him never let anyone see how fast you are or you might not see the man that is trying to kill you until it's too late.

The shotgun behind the door went off. Fortunately, by then, it was pointing down the hallway catching the two deputies off guard and causing them to fall to the floor for cover. Pulling the door closed, he aimed his Peacemaker at the head of the man holding his nose in one hand and a smoking side-by-side in the other.

"Are you livin' or dy'n?" he asked, tipping his barrel and motioning for him to drop his sidearm.

He handed the double-barrel over to Binky and reached for his buckle, and dropped his belt to his feet as he stepped away.

Binky moved behind him and pushed him toward the two men on the floor, who were by now reaching for their revolvers.

"You fellas can walk out of here tonight, or you can be carried out. Make your move," he said in a graveyard, calm voice that sent chills down the backs of the toughest of men.

"I'm not dying," declared the deputy closest to Lucky's cell.

"Then hand me your revolver," said Lucky, whistling for his attention.

Both men didn't respond, just slid their gun belts towards Lucky's awaiting hands.

"You fellas made a good choice," said Binky, moving closer to Sheriff Miller and picking up the twin of his Peacemaker off the desk and slipping it into his holster.

He then checked on their boss, who was hunched over and groani
"How you are doing, Sheriff?" he asked, watching him grab his shoul
wound tightly.

He let out a louder groan as if to answer Binky.

"You should get Doc Ron here as soon as I leave. We wouldn't w
to lose Sheriff Miller here. The truth was he didn't like the Calvary h
either. That much Frank had been right about; no one would ma
money, including himself and his cast of highwaymen.

"Lucky, you lock our guests up, and I will meet you outside. I hav
problem I need to deal with," said Binky, hearing the deputy let Luc
out. He could rely on his best man to get the job done.

"Yes, boss," answered Lucky, already motioning for all th
deputies to step into the cell, and he was in the process of telling Jose
he could come out as he shut the cell door.

Chapter 40

Late at night in the mountains, miles from anywhere that could be called civilization, there is a kind of loneliness that can be felt. There is a lack of sound that can't be explained to someone that must endure the constant noises associated with living in a city.

A squeak is heard from the direction of the door. Annie's eyes opened, letting her eyes adjust to the pale light. She tries to say something, but Elizabeth has her hand on Annie's mouth.

"Stay quiet. I hear someone outside," said Elizabeth pulling her hand free and rolling over towards the door.

"Daddy-John?" asked Annie quietly, looking over Elizabeth's shoulder and the door that seemed closer than before.

Their eyes widened when someone pounded on the cabin's door.

Elizabeth's reaction was swift. She reached for John's rifle, raised her legs straight into the air, and spun at the waist, causing her to roll over Annie and land on the other side of the bed.

Annie started to scream when she felt her mother's claw-like hand pull her to the floor with a thump.

The noises grew in intensity as the latch gave way, and the oak beam that laid across the entrance began absorbing the impacts from the attacker.

Annie struggled with the blankets to free herself. She could hear her mother's breath, and in the pale light, she could see her fear.

Consortium of Acquaintances

The pounding stopped, and Annie slowly turned from her mother could see the table and the window with a man silhouetted against moonlight peering inside.

She screamed as she felt the discharge of the rifle. Sounds w replaced with a buzzing that only she could hear.

Elizabeth lifted Annie to her feet, more bright flashes of light as pulled the trigger and racked the Spenser only to repeat the action bef the spent shell had stopped bouncing on the floor.

At the table, she stood where her daddy-John had eaten dinner. S looked up as her mother lifted the other end of the table. Bright flashes light, impacts felt from stray bullet strikes all around, a silence or interrupted by a buzzing within their ears.

Together, they lifted the table to cover the window and added chairs to brace it from moving.

More silence, less light; Elizabeth pulled her by the elbow from barricaded window to the back of the cabin. They knelt behind the be and her mother helped by loading the rifle of Elizebeth.

"They plugged the chimney," Annie screamed as smoke bellow from the fireplace.

Elizabeth started for the hearth but stopped near the end of the bed someone began to dig through the ceiling, dropping debris in thr different places inside the cabin.

Muffled reports of her father's rifle returned fire. Half in shock, s sees the bed slide away from the wall. A small door ignored by everyo most days comes into view.

"Annie, you need to hide," yelled Elizabeth pulling her by the elbo to the small door.

Inside, it was cramped because her mother had stuffed the beddi through the door.

She heard the bed slam against the wall, more gunshots, but soc they slowed and stopped.

Taking a breath, she could smell the smoke finding its way inside h hiding spot. She could hear someone arguing and someone searching th cabin.

Chapter 41

The man known as Benjamin to some and Binky to others opened the doors to the awaiting crowd outside of the Yakima City Jail. Some shouted while others stayed silent, but the one thing they all had in common was the look of surprise they shared. They had believed he had died when he faced Sheriff Miller and the three deputies.

The townsfolk hushed when the door to the Sheriff's office opened. Benjamin "Binky" Keys walked out and closed the door behind him. It seemed every farmer, shopkeeper, and woman married or otherwise stood between him and the doors of the bank. The only sound that could be heard was the snow falling from the sky. If one could call it noise, some would say it was deafening. He ambled to the edge of the boardwalk, and the mob parted like the Red Sea.

He took his first steps from the boardwalk into the street, drawing the borrowed revolver, pausing briefly to take notice of his audience. He felt like singing at the moment, as if he were on a stage. Then the notion passed almost as quickly because, after all, who would have taken him seriously after witnessing a grown man walking across the street singing a show tune.

Binky swept the revolvers wide, pointing at no one in particular as he came to the middle of the street. The crowd on the other side slowly sidestepped away, clearing a path almost in unison. He chuckled at the sight as he continued to move the revolvers sweeping the crowd.

He stopped his approach when a single man stood up for the town in front of the bank. He had black hair and held a pistol at his side. 'His

mistake,' he thought already with his Peacemakers leveled at the ma
chest. "Well, what do you want?"

"What?" asked the man.

"What's your name?" Binky asked through gritted teeth.

"Jerome Mayford of Virginia," answered the man who was starti
to shake.

"Well, Jerome Mayford of Virginia, what do you want?" he asked
guard from a side attack from some coward in the crowd.

"I don't quite understand what you mean, mister," answered Jero
Mayford of Virginia, looking as though he was about to relieve hims
in a most unmanly way.

"Jerome, what do you want on your tombstone, because I will ma
sure that your name is spelled right and your epitaph is correct? I me
once you start to raise that pistol."

Jerome Mayford started to do just that when the townsfolk began
shout. "Don't do it, you fool."

"He is going to kill you."

"Shut up," yelled Binky, sweeping one gun away from Mayford a
then the other, never leaving the man uncovered by at least one of t
Peacemakers. "Let the man make his decision if he lives, or he dies." I
stopped the sweeping of his revolvers and pointed both pistols at t
man's chest less than fifteen feet away.

"I don't want to die," declared the man as his hand began to shak
He chose to lower his revolver and let it drop into the snow. He the
moved away from the gun and into the arms of his wife. The crowd too
a collective breath that they didn't know they were holding.

"Now, if there are no takers, I need to see a man in the bank," he sa
as he continued the sweeping of the pistols and walked across the stree
He stopped and turned around as he stepped onto the boardwalk in fro
of the bank. He scanned the crowd and saw Kelly on top of his hors
Whats-his-name, and he held Tuffy's tether for a fast getaway.

"When I come out, there better not be anyone hankering to be a her
I won't be in the mood to write down your epitaphs," he said and steppe
up to the door.

***

Over in the bank, everyone jumped at the sound of gunplay across the street. Several customers slipped outside to join the growing crowd.

"Next," said the bank teller as the manager motioned for Ellen to move ahead.

"Now, I know I heard some shoot'n out there," stated George, moving over to the window and peeking out. Surprised at how many people had lined the boardwalks.

"What do you see?" asked John, holding his place in line.

"There is a crowd forming. Does anyone know if there was a parade scheduled this evening?" asked George, turning towards John and then back to the commotion outside.

"If there were, I would have known about it," said Ellen, picking up her dollar from the teller and moving towards the exit.

"And?" asked the bank manager, heading to the same window.

"Something is going on over at the Sheriff's office. Oh, the door is opening. It's Binky, and he looks all riled up. He just stepped towards the bank," replied George, looking away from the window.

"Mr. Manager, do you have a back door?" asked John, stepping from the line.

How calm and collected he appeared caught George off-guard. Here the bank was supposedly being robbed, and he just didn't seem phased. It seemed more like John was in his element. Not unlike he was at the Emporium yesterday.

"No, sir, that would just be another way for the thieves to get in," answered the bank manager as though John was a simpleton.

"Well, sir, if you saw fit, we could have just put the money in the safe, turned the lamps out and unbolted the back door, and made our way to safety. Since no exit exists, we will need to make our way out the front door before we get caught up in whatever is coming this way," he said, walking to the door with George right behind him.

Consortium of Acquaintances

"Miss Jenkins, lock up the cash. We are leaving with everyone el said the manager, bumping into several patrons as he hurried to the s He slammed the door and spun the dial.

Miss Clifton pulled her Jacket from the hanger and started for door.

John reached for the door just as another man was coming inside bank.

Ellen saw the man on the other side of the door and gasped.

Epilogue

The town of Yakima City was somewhat of a ghost town last August. John and his family were busy working on their farm and making a new life for themselves.

The summer's heat and the dry winds were a lousy mixture when small compact thunderheads moved through the skies over the Yakima Valley. Early in the morning, a fire was spotted on the ridge.

Every healthy man and woman was pressed into service, fighting the fire that raged on Ahtanum Ridge.

In the aftermath, they found out that the Yakama tribe had fought the fire on the reservation, which was the ridge's south side. At the same time, the townsfolk fought on the north side. It was the first time both groups had worked together for a common goal without someone from the town trying to take advantage of the situation as far as anyone knew.

The only business that remained open was the Lucy, and even it was subject to the lack of clientele. The only customer for the last hour was the mayor, and even he was waiting for someone.

"Here is what you have been waiting for all week. Mr. Harrison just dropped it off," said Darius, walking in from the boardwalk with a small crate in one hand and a broom in the other. He pulled at the bindings and slipped the bottle free of the shipping crate setting it in front of Mayor Daniels.

"How is he doing?" he asked, speaking of the deliveryman.

"He said his freight delivery seems to be picking up," answered Darius, examining the bottle's fancy French label.

Consortium of Acquaintances

"Having him travel Yakima City to Walla Walla sure has been go for us and the town," said Mayor Daniels, reading the side of the bot wishing the bottle's contents were what was written on the label.

"You need to have him start running a stage," said Darius, pushi the bottle closer for the mayor to examine.

"It's in the works, I assure you. We just need to buy a Stage fro Portland, and we will have service from Walla Walla to Yakima City."

"Why not to The Dalles?"

"We don't want people to leave, my friend, and if they do, they c head back to where they started. So this is the special stock I've heard much about."

"It's used in Portland to procure sailors for the ships heading to t far east. We bought it from Smithy at the Bulkhead Inn," answer Darius.

"How well does it work?" he asked, looking from the bottle to t barman.

"One shot of this the man catches a case of the hiccups and le likely to remember. The second makes them talkative until they pass o for several hours, depending on their size."

"What about taking a third shot?" asked Mayor Daniels, taking kerchief from his pocket and blowing his nose. The smoke in the air th had collected in his nose was now deposited in the white kerchief.

"It wouldn't be recommended, another shot and the man will forg to breathe. Dying that way isn't pretty," answered Darius, leaning dow to pick up a bottle from the lower shelf that belonged on the second.

"Dying anyway isn't pretty," said the mayor, pushing the bottle awa to around the middle of the bar top.

Darius nodded and picked the bottle up with both hands. "Wh would you like me to do with it?"

"Put it in my cupboard and lock it up. Wait, pour some in this flask said Mayor Daniels, reaching into his pocket and producing a tin flas wrapped in cowhide.

"Don't be forgetting what is in this flask. The amount that it takes to ill a man has a lot to do with the health of the man drinking it," whispered Darius looking towards the door.

"That's fine, fill it up and return it to me. Lock up the rest. Just remember when I ask of my special stock, you pull from that bottle."

"I know my job," said Darius, cleaning a shot glass with a twist of a dirty rag.

"Don't worry about the man. I will have someone here too, to remove him," he said, laughing a little at the underhandedness.

"What will we tell people?" asked Darius, looking a little nervous.

"The new ordinance, that a man must hold his liquor while in public or he is subject to arrest. I also want you to put up a sign that says, if you fall asleep in here, you might just wake up in the alley," laughed Mayor Daniels, sliding a barstool closer to rest his foot on.

The barman nodded and looked towards the door when an older man came walking in. He had white hair and had whiskers down practically to his belt. His face was weathered, and he shook more than he didn't.

"Heard you were looking for me," said Willy, sitting at a table and making the mayor join him.

"I heard you are the man to talk to about minerals in these parts," he said, taking the seat across from the old prospector.

"I have been up and down most of the rivers and streams in these parts panning for gold. If that helps," said Willy, leaning back in the chair and looking around at the empty tables.

"It might. Have you ever seen any quartz like this?" asked Mayor Daniels, pulling a heavy object from a small sack and passing it to him.

Willy examined the rock and even tasted the minerals that were attached to the end of each crystal. "I believe I have," he said, not bothering to hold it for very long.

"More to the point. Where can it be found?"

"If it's the place I'm reckoning there isn't that much on the surface of the usable stone. It would be mined out quickly."

Consortium of Acquaintances

"Where can I find it?" asked Mayor Daniels, getting a little excite the prospect of finding a particular waterfall he had been looking almost three years.

"I can draw you a map," said Willy, looking over at the barman the means to convey the mayor's bidding.

"Let me get you something to write with, and let us have a shot my special stock for the gentleman. It is quite expensive," said Ma Daniels, anxious to see his elixir work.

"It's going to be hard to remember the exact location. Two sh should surely pry it from my memory," said Willy, obviously hoping had stumbled on to a rewarding situation for himself.

The mayor took a measure of the man and decided his fate. "Barm let him have three shots, but before he finishes the first, he will need take the time to draw me what I need with directions. We don't need y collapsing before you finish the map," said Mayor Daniels, laughing bit, looking over his shoulder at Darius, who was already pouring t first shot.

"It must be good stuff," said Willy, smacking his lips.

"It is. It is! I need to take my leave, now don't fret, I will return soc I need to find a man to make a pickup for me," he said, winking Darius, whose concern was showing on his face.

Willy, who believed the mayor was speaking to him, answered, "O I am not worried. Go and find your man so you can stop worrying abo your cargo."

The mayor laughed again as he walked outside, letting the ba winged doors swing.

James D FarnWorth

A special thanks

To the **people**, I met along the way.

To the **Grandview museum**
Grandview, Washington
https://grandview.wa.us/departments/parks-and-recreation/re-powell-museum/

Central Washington Agricultural Museum
Union Gap, Washington.
https://www.centralwaagmuseum.org

The city of Union Gap.
Which inspired the backdrop for this book. Small towns with rich history often go overlooked. It was once called Yakima City from 1883 until 1917. In that year, it became the town of Union Gap. Today, we drive by these small towns at 72 miles an hour, hardly registering their existence. Even though the story is a product of my imagination the locations existed.
https://www.visityakima.com/union-gap-washington.asp
https://historylink.org/File/5312

Now, last but not least, I would like to thank the
Yakama Nation.
To the **Yakama Cultural Center**, which helped me to understand some stories can not be changed and caused changes in this book to fit with the _Yakama Nations history_. I apologize if any of my character's dialog offends anyone. I did my best to hold to a respectful narration and consideration of the feelings of my readers.
http://www.yakamamuseum.com

About the Author

James Farnworth was born and raised in the Yakima Valley. He l camped and hiked the foothills of the Cascade Mountains for ma years. He was a bit of a dreamer who found himself behind gamemaster's screen at a young age. Leaving his small town for Seat was his first step to finding his writing voice. His Critical Thinki professor showed him he could write his experiences down, whi became another step to finding his voice. It wasn't until later he foun new respect for his high school English teacher. He enjoys scien fiction, history and fantasy, so don't be surprised to see cross genres n and then. These days he lives in the Yakima Valley, where he has ma his home with his family for the last 15 years. He has traveled ma times to the South Slope of Mount Rainier. Those travels inspired l first book series, The Consortium of Outlaws.

James D FarnWorth

To be continued,

**but worry not, Departure of Brigands, the next book in the
Consortium of Outlaws series will be out by February of 2022.**

Made in the USA
Columbia, SC
08 November 2021